The Anti-Social Season

Also by Adele Buck

Fake Flame

Visit the Author Profile page at Harlequin.com.

THE
ANTI-
SOCIAL
SEASON

ADELE BUCK

Recycling programs for this product may not exist in your area.

ISBN-13: 978-1-335-57484-8

The Anti-Social Season

For questions and comments about the quality of this book, please contact us at CustomerService@Harlequin.com.

TM and ® are trademarks of Harlequin Enterprises ULC.

Harlequin Enterprises ULC
22 Adelaide St. West, 41st Floor
Toronto, Ontario M5H 4E3, Canada
www.Harlequin.com

Printed in U.S.A.

To all my fellow librarians fighting the good fight
for access to information
&
In memory of Margaret Garofoli Dufresne

One

Thea's hands were sweating. They seemed like they were always sweating these days. She hated it. Especially since she'd once gotten an adrenaline rush from suiting up and fighting fires. But the adrenaline rush was now a thing of the past.

Forget fighting fires. Today she was going to set her career on fire. She fidgeted in a hard plastic chair in the waiting area. *Agita*, her *nonna* would have called it. Finally, the door swung open and Gary Landseer, the administrative officer, beckoned her inside and gestured to the chair across from his desk. She complied, taking the seat as he closed the door.

Sitting behind his desk, he glanced over the open file of paperwork in front of him, then peered at her through steel-rimmed spectacles. His brown eyes were so kind she felt like her insides had been scooped out with a giant melon baller. "Are you sure about resigning, Thea? You've been an exemplary firefighter for a decade."

She nodded. Her neck was stiff and the motion felt jerky and unnatural.

His mouth tightened and he looked at the paperwork again, humming to himself. "Do you know what you're going to do next?"

"No." Her voice was as creaky as her neck.

"That seems awfully rash."

She nearly laughed out loud at that. Her squad mates would tell him that was what she was, down to her core. Rash, brash, immature and a total goof—at least in the station house. On the job, they knew they could count on her.

Until Sean's injury.

She hadn't realized that anything was really wrong at first. Injuries happened, sometimes even catastrophic ones, and they could rattle you. She should know that better than anyone. The very reason why she'd joined the squad instead of taking a corporate job out of college was because of her favorite cousin. Luca had nearly died from smoke inhalation, and his wife had insisted that not only he get out of the job, but that they pack up and move nearer to her family in Illinois. Replacing one Martinelli with a newer model had made sense to her twenty-two-year-old brain. She'd learned the job, she'd made her mark, she'd done her part. Seen injury and loss and triumph and miracles. Seen the worst that people were capable of, and the best. She'd thought she had seen it all and could handle anything.

She'd been so wrong.

The therapist she saw after trying to power through the anxiety had said that sometimes trauma reverberated in funny ways. The echoes of Luca's accident, of him moving away, had come roaring back when Thea had seen Sean on his hospital bed. It was like watching Captain America bleeding out. Impossible. Unthinkable.

And damn. That just made her think of Luca again. His big laugh. The way he'd talk earnestly about comic books when he was a teenager and she was a kid. He'd always taken her seriously. Believed in her. Given her that first *Inferno Girl* comic, the beginning of a lifelong obsession. And here she was, unable to do the job that had meant so much to both of them.

She took a deep breath. "I…" Could she even say it? Landseer just looked at her, his eyes so damn *kind* behind those glasses. The kindness and emotion clogged her throat, choking her.

He spoke for her. "I don't need to know why you're resigning. I knew your cousin. He was a good firefighter. A good person."

"I was fine," she said in a rush. "My cousin didn't enter into it. I did the job for ten years." Why was she arguing? This was ridiculous. Get it over with, get out, figure out her next act. That was the plan.

Landseer nodded. "I know." His eyes flicked to the paperwork again. "It says here that you got an undergraduate degree in communications."

Okay… "Yeah." She hadn't known what she wanted to do when she was eighteen. It sounded creative. Fun, even. The reality was neither. What did her college major have to do with the price of beans, anyway?

Landseer rubbed his chin. "What do you know about social media?"

★ ★ ★

Mary-Pat was at it again.

Simon's jaw ached with tension as she gave an audible *harrumph* in front of the holiday display and carefully relocated a glitter-laden snowflake on the backdrop while glaring at the empty spot on the table. She didn't seem to get that the point of a library book display was to increase circulation, not discourage it. But Mary-Pat always seemed to think her displays were akin to an ice sculpture at a fancy wedding. Something to be admired and not touched. Ever.

She'd probably get even more bent out of shape when such a sculpture had the gall to actually melt.

Without saying a word—because it was pointless—Simon got up from the reference desk and fast-walked back to the children's section. He snagged a copy of *My First Kwanzaa* and returned to the display table that Mary-Pat had abandoned, presumably in a huff. For a display that was supposed to honor multiple winter holidays, Mary-Pat's selections were suspiciously Christian. Of course, this was the same woman who didn't put *How to Catch a Turkey* in the Thanksgiving display, deeming it "too silly for such a solemn holiday."

Apparently, the age two to six set were supposed to be serious about a holiday that was mostly about eating lots of food as far as they were concerned? The only thing Simon could be sure of was that Mary-Pat was probably talking about the highly fictionalized version, filled with Christian religious concepts and strangely absent of colonialism. He didn't understand Mary-Pat and didn't want to. It was bad enough that she thought she was better at everything than everyone else, forever snagging assignments like holiday displays for the events and holidays she deemed "appropriate" while ignoring events like Pride and any and all non-Christian holidays.

Simon shuddered at what she'd deem *appropriate* for those tables.

It was even worse that she had been absolutely furious when Simon snagged the role of social media manager for the library system. It was a half-time gig, but one he had hopes would turn full-time at some point.

The better to be able to avoid people like Mary-Pat. Well, people in general. When he got his masters in library science, he had been focused far too much on the information-finding portion of the job and not enough on the patron-facing part. By now, he was feeling more than a little burned-out.

He sat back down behind the reference desk just as a young girl, maybe about twelve, came up with a serious face. "Can I help you?" he asked. Her slightly skeptical expression said she was suspicious of his professional demeanor. But he always treated all patrons with professionalism. He hated it when librarians—or anyone else—talked down to kids.

"I'm supposed to write a report on ancient Egypt," she said. "My teacher said you'd have books about it."

"We do," he said. "Can you be more specific about your report topic?" He hoped for daily life on the banks of the Nile, religion, agriculture—anything other than what he both feared and knew it would be about.

"Mummies," the kid said firmly.

Yup, that.

He showed her how to search the catalog, then took her over to the children's nonfiction section, which abounded in age-appropriate books about ancient Egypt, including lots of facts about mummies. The girl's face lit up like he'd just given her a present.

Kids could be morbid little beasts, but it was fun to get that excited reaction. He asked her if she needed anything else, and she shook her head, pulling a volume off the shelf with rapt concentration. At that point, a guy about Simon's age joined them in the stacks, smiling with pride as she exclaimed, "Daddy, there's books and books and *books* about mummies here!"

"Thanks," the guy said to Simon before crouching next to his daughter to examine what was on offer. *Aw.* Simon loved it when parents had their kids come to the reference desk on their own, giving them an essential taste of early independence. The ones who talked for their kids, as if they couldn't be trusted to navigate a fairly simple reference interview on their own, were the worst.

But the kids themselves? They sure as heck weren't the problem.

"Social media?" Thea couldn't figure out why the conversation had taken this turn. "I mean, I have some accounts on some platforms." They couldn't possibly be interested in the fact that she'd blocked her racist uncle Joey in Toledo two years ago, right?

Landseer's eyes were serious. "Yeah. We've just been approved for a full-time communications and social media manager position in Emergency Services. You could be a good candidate for the job."

Thea blinked. "Seriously?"

He nodded. "Yeah. There's two schools of thought on hir-

ing for the position—take someone who already knows how
to do professional social media and teach them about emergency services, or take someone who already knows ES and
have them get up to speed on the communications part. With
you, you have the ES piece and your degree gives you a head
start on the second component. What do you think?"

"Um…" Frankly, the idea was appealing, but she couldn't
figure out if it was because the opportunity was good or if it
was because up until two minutes ago, she had no idea what
she'd do next. Her living situation was inexpensive, but her
savings weren't going to last forever.

"I'm sorry," Landseer said. "I don't mean to spring this on
you and make you make any kind of snap decision, but your
battalion chief was aware of your issues and the wheels started
rolling on this a couple of weeks ago."

"Oh." Words seemed to have entirely abandoned Thea at
this point. She didn't have any idea that people were even
aware of her, let alone having an inkling of her issues. It was
unnerving. "I mean, don't get me wrong, I'm really grateful
that I'd be considered for this, it's just…"

"Sudden?" Landseer's pale eyes twinkled. "Yeah. I get it.
But we'd like you to try it on a trial basis, especially to get
us through the winter holiday season. You know what that's
like."

Thea made a face. She did. The winter holidays: fun, family and increased fire and other hazards. Which had meant
that her family fun was only intermittent as everyone on her
squad took their turn at being in the holiday hot seat, on call
in case celebration turned to disaster. Her parents had become philosophical about it. Her sister less so, but at least this

year she could spend time with them without the specter of a callout hanging over her like the Ghost of Christmas Five Minutes from Now.

Landseer seemed to misinterpret her facial expression. "We were really hoping we could have someone hit the ground running before people turned their Thanksgiving turkeys into cinders, but we're a little too late for that. However, an awareness campaign before the winter holiday season could have all sorts of helpful effects... I mean, if you have something else lined up, we can certainly open a search."

"No!" Thea didn't know why she was suddenly so emphatic. "I mean, it sounds like an interesting opportunity. But I honestly don't know anything about social media. I mean, not as a professional thing."

"That's fine," he said. "The division chief's sister-in-law is the county library director. They've had a part-time person doing their social media for a couple of years now, and the library director has offered him up to help get you trained." This time, he looked at her over the steel rims of his spectacles, his eyes going a little stern. "But you have to know that this isn't like being on a squad. You can be personable, but keep the crude humor out of it, especially with people that high up the food chain watching you. And since it's a big change, you'll be on new-hire probation until just after the New Year."

"That sounds..." *Terrifying* was what she wanted to say. Having the pressure and focus of people that far up the county's organization chart was more attention than she wanted. But instead, she managed a weak smile and said, "Great."

"Fantastic," Landseer said, flipping the file folder with her past—and maybe her future—closed. "I'll get IT to issue you

some equipment, call the library to get a meeting set up, and
you can get started. Does Monday work for you?"

Half an hour ago, she thought she'd be unemployed by
now. She swallowed the anxiety that still clogged her throat
and said, "Monday's fine."

Released from his reference shift, Simon had ten minutes to
use the restroom and drink a glass of water before his monthly
meeting with Amy, his branch supervisor. He knocked on her
open door, and she looked up from her desk, shooting him a
distracted smile. "Come on in and have a seat," she said, waving at one of the guest chairs. He settled himself with his laptop and his phone, ready to show her the various things he'd
done over the last month as well as his plans for December.
But before he could open his computer, she raised a hand, ar-
resting him mid-motion.

"I've already reviewed your work from the last month and
it was great, as usual. Pretty sure I don't need to look over the
coming month's plans. I have something a little more urgent
I need to talk to you about."

Simon closed his half-open laptop and straightened in his
seat. "Okay. What's up?"

Amy sighed. "The higher-ups in county government are
up to their usual shenanigans, it appears. Emergency Services
is hiring a new social media manager—a former firefighter—
and they're going to need some help getting their sea legs.
The call's come from the county director. Apparently, there's
some sort of personal, family connection with the fire chief."

Something self-protective shifted in Simon. He had little
enough time to do his social media duties, what with it being

only considered half a job. But if the order was coming from that high up, maybe he'd be able to leverage this visibility into moving toward a full-time role. "I'm already pretty pressed for time with what I do as it is," he said. "Is there any way I could get some other things taken off my plate?"

Amy smiled. "I'm way ahead of you there. I couldn't swing things to full-time yet." She tilted her head in apparent sympathy. She knew how much he wanted that. "But the county came through with a grant. I can do three-quarters of your hours in social media, including the cross-training with the new ES person, at least through December. They'd come in a couple of days a week for a while to meet with you and get some mentoring."

Simon drew in a deep breath, trying to figure out what to say next. It was obvious that his agreement wasn't being called for. He was being told, not asked. But Amy seemed to want something from him. Enthusiasm, maybe? Enthusiasm wasn't generally in his wheelhouse, but he'd try. He nodded. "Okay. That sounds good. When do they start?"

Amy tapped her desk with the end of a pen. "Monday. The county's not wasting any time since the holidays are coming and they want a lot more public awareness about things like fire safety."

"That makes sense." Thanksgiving had been just one week before. The first one spent away from his family since his parents moved out to California to be closer to his sister and her family. Pro in Ashley's column: she got free babysitting. Pro in his column: his family couldn't try to meddle as actively in his life from three thousand miles away.

A win for everyone, even though Simon wasn't sure how

long his reprieve would last. Sometimes, modern communi-
cation was a curse.

Amy drew his thoughts back into the present, wincing as
if he'd reacted negatively. "I know this isn't exactly what you
signed up for when you became the library's social media
manager, but 'other duties as assigned,' right?" She followed
this up with an apologetic smile.

Simon hated it when she did this. He got that she didn't
want to be the bad guy, but he also wasn't responsible for her
happiness or comfort. Especially since she was *his* boss, not
the other way around. "Well, I guess I have a few days to get
some posts planned and scheduled, before whoever it is starts."

Amy nodded. "They're going to come here on Monday
morning at ten. I've reserved the small conference room for
you."

It was only after he'd left her office and was logging into
his social media scheduler when he realized he didn't even
know the guy's name.

Two

On Friday afternoon, Thea went back to her old station house to pick up the few remaining personal items she'd left there. The rooms felt too bright, everything a little too clear and sharp. Familiar and oddly not at the same time. Her former squad mates Sean and Felix were cleaning up the kitchen, gently bickering as usual about how to stack the dishwasher. Sean's pale Irish face was a contrast to Felix's dark-skinned Black complexion, but these two might as well have been brothers to each other and to her, closer to her than she'd ever been with her own sister. Three peas in a pod. Until now.

"Hey, guys," she said, hovering in the doorway, uncertain how to talk to them now. Sean looked up from his task, grinning broadly at her. He did that a lot now—being in love made his naturally sunny temperament even sunnier.

"Hey," Felix said, crossing the space in between them and folding her into a hug. "We're sorry you're leaving us, but you're staying part of the family, so you better not be a stranger, 'kay?"

She nodded, scrubbing her face against his shoulder, though she wasn't sure how she could face coming back here. How could she be part of the family if she wasn't in the trenches every day? She couldn't. Because she wasn't really a member of their squad anymore, and nothing Felix could say would change that.

Sean stepped up for his hug, and Thea wrapped her arms around him gingerly. "Knock that off," he said, squeezing her tightly. "I'm good as new, mostly."

"It's the *mostly* I'm concerned about," she said, trying for her usual goofy tone and failing miserably. Pulling away and reaching into her bag, she drew out a book. "I didn't get a chance to finish this, but I wanted to give it back." She held it out to him, but he waved it away.

"I don't lend books. I give them away. Either keep it or pass it along to someone else who might enjoy it."

She thought about the unknown library staffer who was going to help her in her new job. She felt like she was going to have pretty unlimited access to books in her near future, which was silly—she already had a library card. But somehow knowing that she was going to be working with this unknown person made the access to books seem even more infinite.

And it made the distance from these two guys, who were like the brothers she'd never had, widen into something more like a chasm. Felix seemed to be in tune with her mood, gripping her shoulder and saying, "You're okay, right?"

"You mean aside from washing out of the only career I've

ever known?" Wow. That was a little more real than she had planned on being, even with these two.

"C'mon." Felix grabbed her hand and towed her to the big family-style dining table on the other side of the kitchen island. "Sit."

Thea sat at the head of the table, her two friends dropping to seats on either side of her. Sean leaned back and folded his arms, a concerned look on his face, the wooden chair creaking slightly under his bulk. Felix chafed her hand in his. "You didn't wash out," Felix said.

"Sure I didn't." Thea snorted, her mood plummeting.

Sean added his soft voice to the argument. "You didn't."

Thea's gaze shifted guiltily to her big friend. She'd never told him how his injury had affected her. It felt silly, melodramatic. Making his injury, hospitalization and rehab all about her. Especially when he was back on the job and claiming to be "good as new," even if only mostly.

Felix squeezed her hand. "You did the work for a decade, Thea. If you'd washed out, you would have done it in training or in month one. You've done the work—done it well—and maybe it's just time for you to move on."

"But *you're* still here. And Sean's been here for even longer." Sean had already been in the job for years when Thea started. That was one of the things that made him seem so invincible, though obviously he wasn't.

"We're not you. Everybody's different."

She couldn't help but hear the echoes of *It's okay, you're a girl. Girls are different* in Felix's words, even if it was unfair of her. He'd never said anything like that to her, or anyone, as long as she'd known him.

Sean leaned forward and tapped her other hand with his big forefinger. "You haven't really been the same since I was in the hospital. I don't want to make this about me, but did me getting hurt have anything to do with..." He paused, not seeming to be able to find the words. "Whatever it is you're going through?"

"No. Of course not," Thea lied. "It was just time to move on, that's all." Because *move on* sounded a heck of a lot better than to admit the truth: that she was a quitter.

Simon was deep into his review of how Emergency Services had been using their social media when a tap on his shoulder made him startle. He yanked his earbuds out of his ears and whirled in his chair to find Mary-Pat standing over him, glowering.

"Does Amy know you're using library time for...whatever this is?" she asked, waving at his computer screen.

His jaw clamped tight. *Do you know you're not my boss?* he wanted to fire back. For all she knew, he could have been doing research for a patron. He coiled the wires of his buds meticulously around his fingers and placed them on his desk. The best way to annoy Mary-Pat was to not let her rattle you. Because she loved pushing people off balance.

"Not that it's any of your business, but Amy's asked me to cross-train a new social media manager coming into Emergency Services," he said, keeping his voice quiet and level. "Can I do something for you?"

Mary-Pat inhaled sharply and her face went pink. Her mouth opened slightly, but no words came out.

"I have a lot to do to get up to speed here, so if I can't help you with anything…" He looked pointedly at the doorway to his cubicle. Mary-Pat, clearly unable to come up with something else to say, snapped her mouth shut with an angry click, whirled and stomped off.

When her footsteps, muffled by the industrial carpet, faded into nothing, a soft voice sang from the next cubicle, "Ding-dong, the witch is dead…"

"Which old witch?" Simon squeaked, the mild adrenaline spike of his confrontation making him loopy.

"The wicked witch," the voice responded in artificially low tones and then dissolved into giggles. Then Chloe wheeled her chair around the corner, pointing at him and continuing to laugh.

"It's not that funny," he said, unspooling his earbud wires into a messy pile now that he had nothing to prove to Mary-Pat.

"It's *super* funny," Chloe said. "Not that I'd have the courage to freeze her out like that. You're my hero." She flattened her hands under her chin and fluttered her eyelashes.

"Knock it off," Simon said, even as he felt his lips curling into a smile. Chloe could always get him to laugh, even at the passive-aggressive bullshit that was such a feature of their workplace. She was also the only person on the planet who could get him to squeak like a munchkin on helium. He would have said she was the sister he never had, but he had a sister.

He would have traded Ashley for Chloe any day though.

"So is it true that you're training this Emergency Services social media guy?" Chloe asked, her brown eyes twinkling.

"Yeah. Apparently, he's been in the fire service for a while, looking to make a change."

She pouted. "Figures that you get to work with the firefighter hottie. Something you won't at all appreciate."

"How do you know he'll be hot?" Simon asked. "Maybe he's a bridge troll."

Chloe wrinkled her nose. "Are you kidding? Did you even see the 'hug a firefighter' booth at the county fair this past summer? Wall-to-wall hotties. Not just giant cis men, I should add."

Simon glanced at the mess that was his notes from his meeting with Amy. She hadn't given him a name. Had there been any pronouns? If Amy had said *she*, he was pretty sure he would have remembered. "I think this is a guy from what Amy told me," he said.

"Well, boo to that, unless you're suddenly bisexual," Chloe said, her usual lack of filter on display.

He turned back to his computer screen. "You do know that you're literally the only person in my life I wouldn't just get up and leave after an intrusive comment like that, right?"

The social media for the ES department was pretty basic up until now: it seemed like it was set up to just repeat headlines from the county's general communications department's press releases about the department, with links back to the full text. Probably a bot of some kind.

"I think I can actually do some good here," he murmured.

"Go you, do-gooder." Simon winced as Chloe slapped his shoulder and trailed her chair back to her cubicle.

★ ★ ★

Monday morning, Thea showed up at the library branch she'd been instructed to report to and went to the reference desk, where an older woman with perfectly coiffed hair and a sour expression was sitting. Thea'd spent most of the weekend alternately doing research on how social media professionals operated and battling nerves. At least they were different nerves from the anxiety that hounded her out of her last job.

"Can I help you?" The sour-faced woman asked the question like she doubted it.

"Um. Yeah. I'm supposed to see someone named Simon for a meeting about social media?" She wished she'd noted the guy's last name, but somehow that wasn't a thing that made it into the scanty notes she'd gotten from Landseer after she agreed to this trial run.

Sour Lady looked even more like she'd just sucked on a lemon, if that was at all possible. She picked up the receiver on the phone next to her and dialed. "Simon, you have a visitor," she said, then hung up the phone.

Okay, then. Thea tried to tell herself that this wasn't a bad omen.

"He'll be right out," the lady said and then immersed herself in the computer screen in front of her. Thea, now beyond tense, took herself off to a nearby display of new books, browsing to see if maybe she could find something she'd want to relax with later. A tall guy with auburn hair came out, glancing around as if he was looking for someone, and Thea brightened, thinking this must be the elusive Simon. But his gaze swept right over her as if she wasn't even there.

He walked over to the circulation desk and scanned the open area in front of it, then returned to the reference desk and asked Sour Lady a question. She pointed at Thea, looking even more annoyed.

Then he straightened up and turned, his eyes meeting hers. And something went *zing* inside her. She didn't usually find people attractive on first meeting them, but there was something about this guy—something almost like recognition.

His amber eyes widened, and he crossed the distance between them.

"Thea? Thea Martinelli?"

"Um, yeah. Hi. Are you Simon?" She stuck out a hand, remembering Landseer's comments about professionalism.

He blinked, and his head snapped up as if she'd smacked him. "Yes. Simon Osman. We went to high school together."

Thea froze, her hand still out. They had? She searched his face, seeking some sort of visual anchor, anything to pull her back to a memory of this man. She couldn't have forgotten him—he was too good-looking. Intimidatingly so, with his perfect bone structure and big, light brown eyes. A faint dusting of freckles across his nose seemed to tug at something. Nothing so strong as a memory, more of an impression.

She realized she was taking an embarrassingly long time to figure this out, and Sour Lady was watching with barely suppressed glee at the awkwardness that stretched between her and this man. "Yeah," she finally managed, realizing her hand was still extended and giving him a dorky little wave. "It's great to see you again. Fourteen years is a long time, you know?"

His reaction wasn't reassuring, his expression going stony in the face of her obvious lie.

Oh great. *This* was the guy who was going to help her launch her new career?

Seriously, universe? Simon raged internally. *You have to send the one girl I was utterly and completely crushing on for two years to be my trainee?*

He reminded himself to calm down. Especially since Mary-Pat was watching their stilted interchange with undisguised delight. And, as Thea had said, it'd been fourteen years. But it sure didn't seem like that many with her standing right in front of him. Her eyes still looked too big for her face, like some kind of Disney princess. Her face was leaner and her hair was cut short now, feathering over her forehead and the tops of her ears. Cute, but also practical.

He didn't know that she was a firefighter. Adult Thea Martinelli was apparently the same fearless person he'd mooned over as a teen. And she clearly had no idea who he was. Humiliation washed over him in a sickening wave. He'd received a graduate degree, achieved some professional successes, supported an institution and a mission he was passionate about, and apparently none of it mattered. He was the same dismissible dork he'd always been.

He shook himself out of his reverie and cleared his throat, which suddenly felt like he'd swallowed a handful of gravel. "Um. I have a conference room reserved. C'mon back." Without looking at Mary-Pat, he turned and went to the door behind the circ desk, hoping Thea was following him. He couldn't bear to turn around to see. His face felt like it was on fire, and given his pale skin, no doubt everyone in the library this morning could see it as easily as if it was written in words of one syllable across his forehead.

Entering the small conference room, he flicked on the lights with unnecessary force. They buzzed to noisy life overhead, and he thanked his lucky stars that this was the crappy room without windows. No more witnesses to his embarrassment, unless you counted the dingy walls in need of new paint and the faded old READ posters featuring celebrities from a decade ago in frames on every wall. "Have a seat," he said, his voice sounding gruff even to him. He waved at a chair, and Thea drew it back and sat in it slowly, as if making any sudden moves around him was a bad idea.

That just pissed him off even more. What, he was such a monster?

Check yourself. He might not be a monster, but he sure as shit wasn't being a professional right now. He sat and put his laptop on the table in front of him, carefully not looking at Thea's face as she drew out her own computer and put it down. "Um. So, you're the new social media manager for Emergency Services, huh?" What a conversationalist. Brilliant.

"Um, yeah? I was just offered the job on a probationary basis last week."

Probationary. That was interesting. "I took a look at what the account has done up until now." He flipped his laptop open and looked at the notes he'd made. "Looks to me like the communications department probably just has some sort of feed that pushes out their headlines with links to the press releases." An endless string of bad news, mostly: fires, car crashes, trees blown onto houses. Not the kind of thing that a lot of people tended to follow avidly.

She nodded and he actually looked at her. Her skin was pale, her eyes appearing even more huge than usual. "Yeah. That's been it so far. They're going to keep doing that, and I'm supposed to add updates as needed—stuff that doesn't get its own press release but keeps the community informed. But I'm also supposed to do some more public safety stuff. Be more proactive with information about preventative measures."

"That makes sense." He had to give her that. Information about accidents that had already occurred was important news, but with the exception of sharing photos from a few school visits and the like, there was a clear lack of announcements and information about avoiding disasters and other topics the average person would care about.

"I'm also supposed to make things more engaging. Give ES some personality."

He nearly scoffed. "Personality?"

Her gaze sharpened on him. "Yeah. Personality. A lot of people respond better to messages if they think you care."

Simon felt his eyebrow lift. "Sounds awfully touchy-feely for a firehouse."

Three

What was this guy's *problem*, anyway? Thea took a deep breath, trying to settle herself. Regardless of where he was coming from and what he was doing, she was the one starting a new job with a probationary period, and she could practically feel the county's eyes on her from far above. Getting along with him was important to her success.

"Are you suggesting that firefighters don't care about the people—the property, pets and, most importantly, lives—they actually, literally save?" She spoke with a measured calm that she didn't feel and usually didn't have to use outside of an actual emergency.

Simon, whose face had gone from brick red back to pale, reddened again. "No, I just… I guess I just…"

She waited. His voice seemed to fizzle out, so she said, "We care. And one of the ways we care is we do education—preventative stuff. Better to never have that accident in the first place, you know? A lot of that education is in person. A lot of it is with kids. But our reach isn't super great beyond that. We're behind the times on bigger outreach, mainly with adults, and my job is to get caught up on that. Because we actually do *care*." Damn. She hadn't put that many words together in a professional manner in a long time. She used to get tapped to do the elementary school outreach a lot when she was first on the force. Female, shorter than most of her colleagues, young, all made her more "approachable" for the kiddos. She hadn't minded it. Well, she hadn't minded the visits to the schools. She *had* minded the mentality behind her being the one assigned to them.

Anyway. She reined in her careening thoughts. He obviously knew who she was. She still couldn't remember him, though memory seemed to be tapping at her through a thick pane of glass. And not necessarily a great memory, at that. Had she pissed him off somehow when they were teenagers? Enough for the grudge to last fourteen years? That seemed a little extra, even for her.

"Sorry," he said gruffly. "I get it."

As long as she was being careful and patient, she decided to throw him an olive branch. "I think a lot of professions are caring professions. Sometimes in disguise, you know? Like, it's pretty obvious that being a librarian is one. Helping people find books they like, to spend time in worlds they will enjoy, that kind of thing."

His brows snapped together. "It's not all readers' advisory, you know."

"What's that?"

"Exactly what you were just talking about. Helping patrons find pleasure reading. A lot of the stuff we do helps people in other ways. Helping to find jobs, using the public computers, our conversation clubs for people looking to improve their language skills..." He wound down. "Sorry. Hot-button issue, you know? The whole 'oh, it must be fun to read all the time' thing. As if that is all we do."

She grabbed eagerly for this conversational life preserver. "Yeah. I got that sometimes too. Saving kittens from trees, that kind of thing. But it's not like people thought that was all we did. Just sometimes..." She trailed off, not knowing how to finish her statement. She wasn't used to talking like this. She was used to joking and deflecting.

"There are always jerks who want to minimize what you do," he finished for her.

He actually understood! This guy who'd seemed so dismissive actually *got* it. Sudden grief ripped through her. Sean and Felix had understood too. She went on, her initial excitement dampened. "Especially if you're a female firefighter. They think you must be holding the squad back. Professional kitten rescuer, but that's it."

"Or if you're a male librarian. The same people think all kinds of things about me."

"Fuck gender essentialism," she said without thinking. Her hand flew up to her mouth a split second later. "Sorry," she mumbled through her palm. "I have a lot to learn about workplaces that aren't squad rooms filled with fart jokes and pranks, you know?"

But he didn't look offended. His light brown eyes gleamed with humor. "Oh, I would give five dollars to hear you say, 'fuck gender essentialism' in front of Mary-Pat."

Thea let her hand fall away from her face. "That's the prune at the reference desk?"

He nodded, his face going somber as he pointed at his laptop. "Yeah. Anyway, we should probably get back to what we're here to do."

Two hours later, Thea looked overwhelmed. He told her that they could just start with the minimal approach that ES had taken up until that point, but she seemed determined to do it all, to learn everything all at once. Finally, he shut his computer and said, "Enough. Maybe you can go for hours without sustenance, but I need some food to keep going."

Thea picked up her phone, her eyebrows going up when she saw the time. "Wow. Sorry, I didn't mean to keep you from your lunch. Do you know a good place where I could grab something fast?"

He'd brought a sandwich. He should direct her to one of the great hole-in-the-wall places that abounded nearby and squirrel himself away in the break room to eat. The humiliation of her not recognizing him still burned. His past was sitting there like a bridge troll, just waiting to reach up a long, knobby arm to grab him by the ankle and bring him down. But somehow he didn't want to think about her wandering off all alone to eat on her first day of a new job.

"Well, within a five-minute walk, just off the top of my head, we have Asian soup dumplings, Peruvian roasted chicken, a Polish deli and an Italian place that does great pasta."

Her expression brightened. "Anything but the pasta. I almost never eat sauce out."

Sauce out? What the heck was that? "What do you mean?" The crests of her cheekbones reddened. "It's an Italian thing. When your mom or your *nonna* makes the best sauce, there's no point in eating it at a restaurant."

"Your mom or your *nonna*? What happened to 'fuck gender essentialism'?" he asked, unable to keep the grin from his face.

"Oh, Nonno—my grandfather—is gender essentialist as fuck," she deadpanned. "The only way you'd catch him in a kitchen would be passing through on his way to the dining room."

"Noted. Which of the other non-sauce options appeals to you?"

Her face went a little wistful and Simon's breath caught in his throat. Thea's face had always shown exactly what she was feeling. Which reminded him of that crush. Just as one example, the hours he'd spent working on lights and sets for the drama club when Thea was cast as Rizzo in their production of *Grease*. He'd spent hours on ladders with paintbrushes and hammers just to have a chance to watch her, to listen to her sing, to appreciate the vulnerability that underlay the toughness of the character—and imagine that maybe the performance was a reflection of her own personality? His gaze drifted to the hollow of her throat, a place he'd been obsessed with. He'd spent many afternoons imagining pressing his lips to that tender spot, of threading his fingers into her hair and making her moan. Meanwhile, she hadn't even known he existed.

Maybe he should eat his sandwich in the break room as planned.

Oblivious to his reverie or the fact that he was shifting in his seat to ease the growing tension in his pants, Thea nodded and smiled. "Peruvian chicken. But only if they have good yuca fries."

"The best." His voice had gone all creaky. "I can show you where to find it." He dug in his pocket for his phone, but was immediately arrested by the feel of her fingers on his arm.

"Come with me. My treat."

Well, hell.

Was there some sort of librarian code of etiquette she just violated? Because Simon had seemed to unwind a little out of his testy crouch while they were working. But the offer of paying for his lunch clearly put his undies in a nasty twist. His face went hard.

She reminded herself for the umpteenth time that this was the guy she needed to impress to get through the probation period, swallowed her pride and backpedaled. "Unless you don't like Peruvian chicken?" Maybe he was vegan? But honestly, she'd never met a vegan who would recommend a restaurant specializing in meat dishes.

"No. I like it fine." He pushed back from the table and stood abruptly, causing her to hustle to keep up. Dang. He could have kept up with the squad racing for the trucks when the alarm went off.

"Can we leave our stuff in here?" She waved a hand at the laptops as she picked up her bag.

"Yeah. We have the room for the whole day." He pulled a bunch of keys out of his pocket and ushered her through the door, locking it behind them, then turning on his heel and walking toward what must be a back exit, never checking to see if she was still following.

Okay, she was pretty sure that there was no violation of any sort of code of etiquette on her part. This guy was just being *rude*. Even her hellion nephews had better manners than this. She followed him out into the afternoon sun, which took the edge off the day's chill.

Thinking of her nephews, she grinned. Simon was still a couple of steps ahead of her, and she raised her voice to carry over the sound of the cars passing on the street. "Knock knock."

His steps seemed to stutter for a moment and he glanced back over his shoulder, his eyebrows drawing together. "Uh. Who's there?"

"Interrupting cow."

"Interru—"

"MOO," she bellowed, and he stopped, his eyes sliding shut and his mouth going hard. She closed the distance between them and stood in front of him.

"Is there a reason why you just told me what has to be the silliest joke ever committed to memory?" he asked, his eyes still closed.

"Silliest knock-knock joke, maybe."

"Knock-knock jokes are, by definition, the silliest jokes, so by the transitive power of silliness, it's the silliest joke." He finally cracked one eye and squinted at her.

I was hoping to remove the tree from your asshole, she didn't say. "Test audience." She grinned at him. "I figured you're a tougher sell than my nephews. They'll laugh at anything." Normally, she'd try out all the silliest jokes she could think of on Sean and Felix before springing them on the nephews, but now… Even with their insistence that she was still one of the gang, she felt adrift and lonely. And somehow, this actually seemed to be working with Simon too.

His eyes fully opened and he started walking, but slower this time. Less like a man who wanted to leave her in the dust. "You have nephews too, huh?"

"Two of them. Little monsters. You?"

He sighed and rubbed his forehead. "Just the one, at least so far. He's only three, so not sure if he's going to be a monster or not at this point."

"Oh, trust and believe. He will be. They all are, even when they're cute as fuck and you simultaneously want to snuggle them and drown them."

His eyebrows went up at the *fuck*. Damn. Second one—or was it the third?—of the day. Great. She was going to have to learn to rein it in. It used to be easy: when she was suited up, the professional, calm demeanor that every good first responder needed to cultivate would settle over her like it was just another layer to her protective gear. But outside that context? Everyone, including her, was usually about jokes and pranks, the less mature the better. It was a way to blow off steam, to decompress from the stress and tension of a difficult, often dangerous job.

But there was no duality in *this* job. She had to be a professional all the time now. She sighed as they walked to the chicken restaurant, the mouthwatering smell from the rotisserie wafting to her as Simon opened the door.

Well, if she had to be a sober, staid professional, at least she was going to have an excellent lunch.

★ ★ ★

When they got their meals and moved to a table in the corner of the restaurant, Simon reminded himself for the thirtieth time today to be *polite*, dammit. There was no reason to sulk about the fact that she'd been a princess in high school and he'd been the frog that she had no idea even existed, let alone wanted to kiss. He was an entire adult now, not ruled by teenage hormones and angst. She was already working incredibly hard to learn the job, so he might as well unclench and treat her as if she was someone he'd only just met. No history there at all. For crying out loud, it had been so long it should be as if there was no history.

She popped open one of the extra containers of hot sauce she'd ordered and dredged a yuca fry through it, shutting her eyes as her teeth closed around it with an audible crunch. "Mmm. I haven't had this in forever," she groaned after she'd swallowed the morsel.

Simon shifted on the hard plastic chair and focused on his own lunch, peeling a strip of chicken off and dipping it into his own sauce. It *was* good. Savory and juicy and falling off the bone. And now she was emulating him and her eyes were glowing with pleasure and her lips were shiny from the juices—and not to take a word out of her notebook, but *fuuuck*. Nope. There was no way to treat her like someone he'd just met. There were too many memories, too much longing wrapped up in those memories, that peeled him open all too easily.

"So what's your nephew like?" she asked. Thank god for the boner-killer that was Noah. "Is he at the 'why' stage yet?"

"What's the 'why' stage?"

She rolled her eyes. "Literally ninety-five percent of the words that come out of his mouth will suddenly be 'Why?'"

He couldn't help but laugh. "Literally? You're not one of those people who uses that word as an intensifier, are you?"

She shot him a look. "I totally am, but it's also *literally* true. It starts with a seemingly innocuous question. 'What are you doing, Uncle Simon?' You tell him you're making dinner. 'Why?' You say it's because people get hungry. 'Why?' Because people's bodies need fuel, and hunger is the way bodies tell us that the tank is low. 'Why?' And so on, and so forth, until you're ready to sign up to be a Buddhist monk and take a vow of silence because that's the only way you'll ever know peace again."

"Noah hasn't done that to me yet. Maybe he will when I go out to California to see my family at Christmas."

"It'll happen. But I thought you grew up here… We went to high school together?"

He fought a scowl at the reminder that she had no recollection of him. "Yeah. I did grow up here. But my sister and her husband moved to California and then they had Noah, and my parents moved so they could be closer to them."

Thea's lower lip jutted and her eyebrows drew together. "Wow. So you're on your own here now?"

And thank god for it, he didn't say. "Yeah. It's okay though. I'm kind of the family cuckoo."

She twirled a finger next to her ear. "Seriously?"

He sipped his soda. "Not like that. More like my family is one kind of bird, and I feel like some other bird laid its egg in their nest and I'm the result. They raised me, but we don't understand each other."

"That sounds like it sucks," Thea said, though her voice held no judgment.

"Yeah, well. I just try to stay out of the way. My sister kind of needs to be the center of attention at all times." And why was he telling her this? But there was no way to reel it back, to retract the impulsive confidence.

He braced himself for additional questions or commentary. Opening doors the way he just had usually made people walk through and make themselves all too thoroughly at home. But after a long pause, where her gaze roamed his face until he wanted to squirm, she didn't say anything else except, "So, what's on deck for this afternoon, coach?"

Four

Simon and Thea worked steadily for another few hours after they came back from their lunch, and when Simon finally noted that it was quitting time, she looked positively relieved. Whether it was about ending the workday or the fact that she didn't have to deal with his grumpy ass anymore, he couldn't say. But she was quite obviously drained, her face pale and her movements slow as she packed up her gear.

"It'll get easier," he said, surprising himself. He wasn't usually someone who said stuff like that. "When I started out, I really had no idea what I was doing and felt overwhelmed all the time." Okay, now *where* was that oversharing coming from?

She shot him a tired grin as she shouldered the strap of her bag. "Thanks. This is the first totally new job I've had in ten years, so it…it's a lot."

"At least you already know the inner workings of the fire service. That's got to give you a leg up."

She nodded. "Yeah. That was the thinking from the powers that be. Either hire someone who knows social media who can learn emergency services, or the other way around. And there I was. They seemed to think that my undergrad degree in communications was going to be valuable, but social media wasn't a big part of the curriculum when I was in school, and a lot of my class work was theoretical, anyway." She seemed less than confident about the whole situation, even though it made perfect sense to Simon. Where was this lack of confidence even coming from? She'd latched on to new concepts and ideas very readily and was learning the job at a breakneck clip even on the first day.

He opened the conference room door and said, "Well, for whatever it's worth, I think it looks like they made the right choice." When he stepped through, Chloe was in the hallway, her eyes alight with greeting. Oh great. Her teasing was about to go nuclear. She might have even been waiting for him.

Then Thea stepped out and Chloe looked like she was about to fall over from combined mirth and shock. Thea saw her and gave her a tired little smile.

"Are you the new social media person Simon's training?" Chloe asked, visibly working her face back into an expression that didn't read as utterly manic.

Thea nodded and the two women introduced themselves, Simon feeling like an utter doorknob standing there in the dingy back hallway of the library. "Anyway, I gotta run," Thea said, nodding at Simon. "I'll see you next time. Thanks for everything."

When she was gone, Chloe gave him a stinging slap on the shoulder that nearly made him drop his laptop. "Oh my *god*, Si." Dropping her voice into an artificially low register, she said, "Pretty sure this is a guy from what Amy told me." Her voice went back to its normal tone. "You got your own firehouse hottie to work with."

"Shut it," Simon said, walking toward their cubicles. "She's a work colleague, same as you."

"She is totally not the same and you know it. Her status as a colleague, if it even exists, is temporary, and she *is* a hottie."

"Keep your voice down," he whispered as he ducked into his cubicle, Chloe crowding into the small space with him. "You'll make Mary-Pat all too happy if she thinks I'm doing anything inappropriate on library property." Or at all. Ever. Anywhere.

Chloe stuck her tongue out. "To hell with that you-know-what. But seriously, Thea is exactly your type and you're *not* her supervisor. You have no authority to abuse. As if you ever would in the first place."

"Since when do I have a type?" Simon regretted the words the instant they left his mouth.

She rolled her eyes. "Oh please. I remember your heart-eyes when Anne Hathaway got a pixie cut. Thea could be her younger sister. And I'll bet you she has arms like Michelle Obama. Those firefighters work *out*. She's walking, talking Simon-bait."

"Speaking of the gym, I'm out of here," Simon muttered, jamming his stuff into his bag while Chloe snickered.

"Gotta keep up with your new lady!" she called, flexing a biceps as he headed for the employee entrance.

"Laugh it up, funny gal," he muttered. But in one way, she was all too right. He had a date with a weight rack and a treadmill at the community center. And maybe a good, hard workout would purge the restless energy from his system.

He could hope, at least.

Thea let herself into her house and let her laptop bag slip from her shoulder with a tired sigh. She forgot how exhausting brainwork could be. Normally, she'd do a bunch of physical things during her workday and wouldn't be half this weary. In fact, she'd probably be working out with her former squad mates right about now. A wave of sorrow swept through her just as a knock on her door jolted her spine upright.

She opened it to find the smiling face of her neighbor and landlady, who was holding a foil-covered plate. "Mrs. McAnally, I was just going to come over," she said, feeling guilty. That was the deal. She lived in the "mother-in-law" apartment at Mrs. M's place for ridiculously low rent and, in exchange, made sure that the elderly widow was okay, did minor maintenance around the property and generally thanked her lucky stars for the most amazing living situation in the greater DC area. "Come on in," she said, opening the door wider.

Mrs. M did, setting the plate down on the little island that separated the kitchen from the rest of the living space. She gave a little sigh like she always did coming into the converted outbuilding. "Whenever I see how cute you've made this place it almost makes me sad I didn't move into it when Kyle did the renovation." She took the foil off the plate. "Brownies to celebrate your first day on the new job."

"Aw, thanks." Thea took one. Mrs. M did make the best brownies, with just the right combination of crunch and chew.

"But you don't really mean that about this place, right?" She sent up a silent prayer. *Please don't make me give it up.* Mrs. M's property was large, private and quiet, something Thea appreciated after long shifts with a bunch of people just as rowdy and silly as she could be.

"Well, no. I still love my home, even if it is much too big for just me. But this is awfully cute," she said. Mrs. M's eldest son had started the renovation behind her back while she was hospitalized after a heart attack. Fully expecting her to be weakened by her illness and surgery, he decided that he needed to move his family into her big house and to shunt her into the smaller space under the guise of "taking care of Mom." But Mrs. M was made of sterner stuff. She recovered steadily, and when she came back home after a month in a nursing home, she informed her son that his expectation of her decrepitude or demise was premature. And when Thea's squad was called in to deal with a minor chimney fire in the main house, the older woman had immediately taken a liking to her. After Thea openly admired the apartment, Mrs. M offered her the almost-finished living space and completed the renovations.

It *was* a very nice place. Kyle had good taste, even if he was an entitled shithead.

"So, tell me all about your first day." Mrs. M bit into her own brownie while boosting herself onto one of the bar stools at the island.

"I learned a lot," Thea said. "So much so that my brain feels full. The guy they have me partnered with was kinda weird though."

"Weird how?"

"He seemed…almost mad at me? I don't know. He says we went to high school together, but I totally didn't recognize him."

Mrs. M nodded sagely. "Ah. Men don't like that."

"No, but it seemed more personal than it should have. I mean, our high school was huge. There are literally hundreds of people I wouldn't remember. I'm sure there are hundreds of people he wouldn't remember."

Mrs. M's pale eyes twinkled with humor, but she didn't say anything. "What?" Thea asked.

She shrugged. "Maybe he had a little crush on you all those years ago."

"Me?" Thea pointed at herself for good measure. "This weirdo? I was too loud, too athletic, too *much*. Nobody had crushes on me in high school. Literally nobody." She huffed a small, private laugh when she remembered that he'd asked her about how she used the word *literally*. She wasn't sure if it was an intensifier in this case or not.

Mrs. M just nodded enigmatically. "Of course, dear."

Besides, I would have remembered someone as gorgeous as Simon. But she didn't mention that detail to her landlady.

Simon was just about ready to brush his teeth and take his aching muscles to bed when his phone rang. An incoming video call from his sister. Great. She'd lived for the better part of her life on the East Coast, but she couldn't remember that she was now three hours behind to save her life. He considered just ignoring the call, putting his phone on do not disturb and going to bed.

But if he ignored her, she'd just get snippy about it when

they finally did connect. He answered the request for a video call, hoping they could keep it brief. "Hi, Ash," he said when his sister's face appeared on the screen.

His sister, never one for preliminaries, launched right in. "Okay, so you have your tickets to come out to us for Christmas, right?"

He'd never actually said he was going to go to California for Christmas. So, he hedged. "I've been keeping an eye on the prices."

She looked exasperated. "If you wait too long, you know flights'll get expensive and then Mom and Dad will have to bail you out and it'll be a whole big *thing*."

Simon bristled at the true but unfair assessment. He had chosen a lower-paying but satisfying career, but he hadn't made the decision to move his family three thousand miles away. It wasn't his fault that travel was costly. "Fine. But I can't just book when I want. I have to get the time off first and I haven't heard from my boss yet." This year it wasn't likely that he'd be able to take a lot of time, anyway. He'd taken five days last year—the first year his entire family had been out West— and Mary-Pat had pitched a fit that she wasn't able to take a week, claiming her seniority wasn't being properly respected. It wasn't likely he'd even be able to take five days this year, but he'd keep his powder dry with his sister and not give her the actual number of days until he was sure. With some people, managing their expectations meant you under promised and over delivered. With Ash, if you promised anything less than what she wanted, she'd explode. Then, if a miracle occurred and you were able to give her more, she was never grateful, just blamed you for setting her off. Best to not address it until he had some actual dates to work with.

"Well, *get* the time off," his bossy big sister demanded. "Just tell them you need it."

That's not how this works, he didn't tell his sister. Instead, he scrubbed a hand over his face and said, "I'll do my best." Arguing with Ashley was pointless. Besides, maybe that miracle would happen and he would get more than a couple of days off.

"Okay, *okay*," Ashley said, directing her words away from the screen and down. Tiny hands reached up into frame. "Noah wants to say hi to Uncle Simon." She handed the phone off to the toddler and disappeared without another word.

"Hey, buddy," Simon said, feeling, as he always did, a little out of his depth with his nephew. Part of it was being so far away, he was sure. Part of it was probably that he just never really knew what to do with kids who couldn't read yet. It was easy to talk to the kids at the library about books. Noah, though? Not so much.

"Hi, Uncle Simon. What'cha doing?"

"Well, I'm about to go brush my teeth."

"Why?"

"Because I want them to be clean before I go to bed."

"Why?"

Simon started to feel a lurking sense of foreboding. "Because if they're clean they'll stay healthy longer."

"Why?"

"Because if you don't clean them, yucky stuff grows on

your teeth and gives you cavities and your teeth will fall out and you don't want that to happen."

"Why?"

Foreboding gave way to panic. "What'd you do today at day care?" he asked, hoping to break the endless chain of one-word interrogatories.

Noah beamed and started to chatter about arts and crafts as the phone wobbled with excitement in his little hands, and Simon sighed, relieved, as he pondered the view up his nephew's nose.

But dammit all to hell, Thea really had known what she was talking about. He'd have to tell her about his successful technique that led to nipping off the endless *why?* when they saw each other again later that week.

And with that, he realized a part of him was actually looking forward to seeing her again.

His stomach twisted. *No.* History would not be repeating itself. Maybe the higher-ups would even decide that Thea could just handle the new role on her own earlier than planned. That would be nice.

Not usually superstitious, Simon crossed his fingers.

After dinner, Thea pulled down the extendable ladder that led to the storage area above her living space. Climbing up to the attic, she found the right box and rummaged through it before she unearthed what she was looking for. Back down on the sofa, she opened the stiff pages of her high school yearbook from senior year. She scanned the looping, handwritten "Stay sweet" and "Have a nice summer" messages from a lot of people she barely remembered. None of them were from Simon.

Paging through the book, a wave of weird nostalgia crashed over her. Despite a lot of admittedly good memories of friends and activities and parties, she wouldn't want to go back to being a teenager for anything, thank you very much. That confusing time, with its cascades of feelings and events that seemed so out of her control, was not something she wanted to revisit.

But guilt lurked in the recesses of her mind as she looked at group photos of clubs and teams. She wouldn't ever say she was popular. Like she'd told Mrs. M, she was just too much for most people, but she did have a small, tightly-knit group of friends back then. When was the last time she talked to any of them?

Well, she'd run into one of them at the county fair with her kids during her stint at the hug a firefighter booth over the summer. Monica had seemed happy enough to see Thea. And it wasn't as if *she'd* tried to keep in touch either. They'd drifted apart the way people did when they grew up. Obviously, they had different priorities and life paths. It was normal, right?

But the thought nagged at Thea. Glancing up, she saw the photo of her with Sean and Felix in front of their old ladder truck and her stomach did a sickening lurch. Oh. That was it.

Was she going to drift away from them too?

Forcing that thought away, she turned another page and part of a face seemed to jump out at her. Thea frowned and looked harder at the slim, youthful boy half-hidden behind someone else. Yes, it was Simon, she was pretty sure. But he'd definitely filled out in the last decade-plus. Thea looked at the caption for the photo. *Theater Tech Club.*

Ooooh. Yes, she was beginning to remember him now. Other memories tickled at the back of her brain, and she paged back through the alphabetical photographs of clubs. *Speech and Debate.* There she was, front and center, probably cracking a joke to make everyone laugh for the photographer, from the majority of expressions in the picture.

And there was Simon, one row back and three people over, staring with a sullen expression at the camera. How had she *forgotten* him? Memory, previously tapping tentatively at the glass, broke through and flooded her.

He was such a *pain in the ass.* And he'd had such coppery red hair back then. Did he dye it now? No, she decided. Sometimes people's hair got darker as they got older. That had to be what gave him that—admittedly gorgeous—auburn mop he had today.

But now that she thought of it, she could definitely see the thin-faced, skinny—yeah, kind of cute—younger Simon in this new, older, broader version. She'd kind of avoided him when they were in school. She remembered him as a stickler for rules, a very my-way-or-the-highway kind of person. The moment where she firmly distanced herself from him was in a Speech and Debate club practice, in fact. She'd made a joke as part of her argument and was still riding high on the laugh she'd gotten. He disapproved, lecturing her about how Speech and Debate was about convincing people, not making people laugh.

His disapproval hadn't just killed her buzz, it had stung her teenage pride. "Too bad we don't have a comedy club," she retorted. "I'd kill. You'd be first."

And then, if she remembered everything correctly, she went back to her friends and had a laugh. Because she'd never been too serious, could never really deal with people who were. And he seemed to have morphed from a *very* serious teen into a fully-fledged adult grump.

She wished she hadn't gone down that little cul-de-sac off memory lane. Because she still had to work with the guy through the month of December.

Slamming the book closed, she dropped it on the sofa and went to the kitchen for a beer, closing her eyes as the cool liquid slid down her throat. *Just get through the probationary period and you'll never have to deal with him again.* That was all she had to do.

Right.

Five

"Seriously, I don't see why the social media manager can't be a rotating position. I think those of us with greater experience could bring something to bear to the role." It was Wednesday morning, the library's monthly communications and marketing meeting, and Mary-Pat was mounting up on her favorite hobbyhorse: trying to unseat Simon from the position he worked so hard to keep.

Giddyap.

In the *Casablanca* casino set in his mind, Simon placed a bet with himself as to what her next angle of attack would be.

"Some of us have been making library displays very successfully for decades and know all about promoting the library's services."

Your winnings, sir. Internally pretending to be shocked, shocked that passive-aggression would go on in a library. He wondered if Thea liked classic movies, then shifted in his chair, resisting the urge to spin his pen over his thumb, his usual fidget mode. Mary-Pat would see that as showing off, and it would somehow be added to her arsenal in her ongoing attack against, well, everyone and everything that wasn't Mary-Pat. But especially Simon the Younger.

Because Mary-Pat did not see that young people had anything of value to offer. Ever. Young people meant change and change was Bad, end of story. Even *if* she could train Thea in social media, he could well imagine Mary-Pat's reaction to the former firefighter. Disaster would be an understatement, and that probationary period she was so worried about would be a real threat.

Simon swallowed. He cared about getting her through that, and not just to prove his own worth in the social media role.

Amy cleared her throat, bringing him back to the moment. "While I appreciate your zeal, the county administration has decided that the social media manager should be a professional position, to keep us more in line with other similarly-sized library systems. We fought a hard enough battle to keep it as an embedded librarian position. County Communications has continually floated the idea that library social media should be covered by a few hours a week of a junior public relations staffer's time."

Simon straightened, his pen doing an unconscious flip over his thumb. He hadn't expected this level of commitment around the job. Turf wars weren't uncommon in the various echelons of the county's government and services, so he was hardly surprised, but still.

"That seems like it would be a really bad idea, the Communications thing." Simon heard himself speak up. *Dammit.* He almost never said anything in these meetings. His lifetime of keeping his head down to keep out of conflict in his family usually worked well in this setting too. But now, Amy was looking at him and he was committed. "Someone who doesn't know what the library system is doing from the inside wouldn't be able to do anything other than reiterate a press release in fewer words on a few different platforms. And if they only had a few hours a week, they couldn't always be on the ground to cover events like drag queen story hour or author lectures." He'd personally taken photos just last week of two of these kinds of events and made posts that had gotten some good traction in the community.

Amy looked approvingly at him, and the pen made another nervous circuit of his thumb. To hell with what Mary-Pat might say about that.

"Exactly. And if we pass the role from librarian to librarian on a regular basis, not only will the work be inconsistent, we're saying we don't believe this is a professional position. That means the county will snatch it back and we won't get the community to see the richness of the programs we offer. *That* means reduced public perception of our mission and support for funding will go down. Which means, of course, funding *will* go down, and we're already like every other public library system in the country—always doing more with less. On top of that, Simon's training the new Emergency Services social media manager, further proving our leadership in this space to more senior administrators. I think what we're doing is working well, both for now and for the longer haul. Simon, I know you've only had one day with her, but how is that training going so far?"

Simon swallowed around the lump in his throat. He hadn't

quite considered how the spotlight on Thea also might have an impact on the library, and like every librarian he knew, he was all too aware of the specter of budget cuts hanging over his profession and career. "Well, like you said, it's only been one day. But she seems eager to learn, and of course, she knows a lot about emergency services."

"Good," Amy said. "Moving on, let's talk about our post-New Year displays."

And with that, Simon gladly lapsed back into silence as Mary-Pat began to hold forth.

Thea was unaccountably nervous for her second meeting with Simon.

So, okay, she was accountably nervous. She now knew who she was dealing with: Buttface McKilljoy of the Speech and Debate club, class of 2010. Trouble was, she needed Buttface McKilljoy. So she had to play nice. She was going to *literally* die trying to get through this probationary period.

Literally. He could figure out whether she meant that as an intensifier or not. Resettling her bag onto her shoulder, she trudged into the building, preparing herself for another run-in with the sour-faced woman she'd dealt with on Monday.

Only to be brought up short by the man himself, standing at the circulation desk, chatting with a woman who had her arms full of books and a lanyard with a tag that read Volunteer. Was he waiting for her? If he was, that seemed almost friendly.

Then he noticed her, looked up and gave her a terse little nod. Okay, then. That was more in character. "Hey," he said and motioned for her to follow him. As she did, a tendril of mischief began to thread its way through her.

Yeah, he might be Mr. McKilljoy, but what if she could shake him up? Make him laugh? What would that look like?

No. Bad idea. She was on probation in this job and she knew that her sense of humor was definitely of the juvenile, firehouse, toilet variety. She'd gotten away with the knock-knock joke last time, but best not to push her luck. Sighing, she followed him into the small, windowless conference room with the old READ posters and its mismatched chairs around the banged-up table.

When librarians talked about lack of funding, they weren't kidding.

"What's the sigh for?" Simon asked.

Oh crap. Had she really been that noisy? "Nothing bad," she said. "Just didn't sleep very well last night." She'd fallen down another yearbook rabbit hole again, this time looking up some of her old classmates on various social media platforms that she'd lost track of.

What? It was job research. She was putting the *social* in social media.

She settled into a chair and pulled out her laptop. Simon did the same, then shuffled his chair forward and unbuttoned his cuffs, rolling his shirt sleeves back.

After a moment, she realized she'd been focusing on his arms for a ridiculous amount of time and averted her eyes. How did a librarian get such sinewy forearms? And how was that hot? Thea's former colleagues were objectively sexy. Most of them were even featured in calendars to raise money for charity. They had sinewy forearms. They had a lot of sinew in a lot of places. But they were just…her guys. Thinking about them as hot was just weird.

Shit. Simon was hot. And her coworker, kind of. And somehow, it didn't feel weird at all.

Why was Thea looking at his arms? Simon examined himself for stains, nicks, anything that would explain this interest she apparently had in his forearms. For crying out loud, he didn't even have a tattoo. The pen in his hand made a circuit of his thumb.

Thea's huge brown eyes seemed to get even bigger. "Oh my god. You can do that?"

"What?" Shit. He was *not* supposed to be falling into her enormous eyes. But he'd felt like he was drowning for a minute.

"That pen thing. I've always wanted to be able to do that. It's on my bucket list right after learning to whistle with two fingers in my mouth."

Against his will, he was amused. "Whistling with two fingers in your mouth is on your bucket list?"

The crests of her cheeks reddened, and Simon scooted his chair closer to the table, the hard edge pressing into his abdomen. He was *not* going to pop a boner at work. But just in case, he would keep his pelvis out of her eyesight and make himself as physically uncomfortable as possible. The aging conference room chair didn't hurt in that regard, at least.

"Well, it isn't on my list anymore. One of my teammates— my former teammate—" Her face fell at that, then she visibly composed herself. "He taught me," she finished, those big brown eyes flicking up to meet his gaze, daring him. Or maybe daring herself. It was hard to tell.

Simon wanted to rush into that little breach, that moment of vulnerability. But that dare, he decided, would be unmet.

"Okay." He held out his hand, pen balanced on his middle finger. "Here's how you spin the pen." He demonstrated finding the center of gravity, pushing it slightly off, which finger flicked, which finger got out of the way then caught it as it finished its circuit. She watched with intense concentration, then tried it herself.

The pen bonked to the tabletop. She looked at him, betrayal so evident in her expression that he had to suppress a laugh. "Nobody gets it the first time. It's like anything else. You have to practice."

"Hmm." Her jaw set in determined lines and she tried again, but she wasn't offsetting the pen far enough. The pen bonked again. He picked it up and placed it, steadying her fingers with his own. Her skin was warm, and her index finger had a long, faded scar. Crap. He was *touching* her. He swallowed, his throat tight.

"Did you get this fighting a fire?" he asked, pointing at the scar. He should pull away, stop touching her. But if he did it too quickly, would she know he was affected by her? But continuing to touch her wasn't professional... His brain spun and chattered like a slipping engine belt.

She shook her head, her fingers wrapping around the pen rather than trying to spin it again. Well, she couldn't try to spin it now. Not with his hand in the way. "No. Firefighters wear gloves, remember? My cousin Luca had a cat. She was really sweet, but something startled her when I picked her up once, and her claw opened my finger right up. I was just a kid."

He winced and finally pulled his hand away from hers. Could still feel the warm texture of her skin though. "Ow. Stitches?"

"No," she said again. "Just big Band-Aids and being really awkward doing everything with my left hand while it healed. And I swear that cat was sorry. I went over to visit Luca when it was still healing and she sniffed the bandage like she was examining a kitten. Then she curled up in my lap and purred."

"Purring is supposed to have healing properties." Where had he pulled that inanity from? He nearly smacked himself in the forehead from sheer frustration.

She flicked him a startled, curious glance. "Does it?"

"Yeah. Something about the frequency of the vibrations." *Shut up, dork.* He cleared his throat, ready to move off purring and pen spinning.

"Maybe I should get a cat, then," she said.

"Are you injured?"

"No, but I do miss Luca. He was the reason I became a firefighter in the first place. He had to leave the force. He lives in the Midwest now. We don't talk very much anymore." Her eyes darted furtively up, meeting his for the barest second, then sliding away. As much as Simon had observed Thea when they were teens, he'd never seen her like this. Unguarded, vulnerable.

And dammit, he might like this side of Thea even more than the brash, bold girl he'd been half in love with at eighteen.

What the hell did she think she was doing, anyway? Baring her soul to the killjoy? But he wasn't being a killjoy just now. He was being, well, nice. Understanding. Little crinkles around his eyes seemed to indicate he was listening intently.

"It can be hard when family moves away," he said.

"That's right. Your parents followed your sister out West."

He nodded. "Yup. And we don't have any other family locally. Aunts, uncles, cousins, grandparents, they all live in other states."

She made a face. "That must suck for you for the holidays."

He shrugged. "Yeah, I'm not the most social of people, so big holiday gatherings aren't really my thing. I do like the preparation though. The decorating, the cooking, the wrapping. Everything but the big, noisy stuff."

A grin split her face. "I'll bet you're good at keeping secrets too."

He tapped his forehead with the same finger he'd used to steady her hand with the pen. "Like a vault."

His eyes, big and amber brown, were focused on her, and she felt like they were pulling her toward him. Altogether he was a tether of attraction made up of sinewy forearms, intense looks and a pointless skill that she nevertheless wanted to master for herself.

Then something in his eyes shuttered and she felt like a bucket of icy water had sluiced down her back. He straightened and opened his laptop. "So, I was thinking we'd go over the calendar of events that you prepared. A lot of the stuff we deal with day-to-day is reactive, so it's best to have as complete a calendar as possible so stuff gets auto-posted when you're scrambling."

"Okay, makes sense," she said, trying to shake the disappointed feeling from moments before.

"But another good habit to get into is to review whatever you've got auto-posting at the beginning of every week, if not more often. Because when something bad happens, a light-hearted post might make it look like you're not reading the room, you know?"

She nodded. "Probably more than most people, I'd think." She thought about one of the last times she'd answered an emergency call. A condo explosion had left a dozen people suddenly homeless and without essential clothing and other items.

Having a breezy post about a charity fundraising calendar featuring shirtless firefighters coincide with an event like that would *definitely* look like nobody was reading the room. She made a note to check her auto-posted items daily, not weekly, then looked up and caught him watching her. "What?"

He shook his head. "You just seem different, that's all."

"Different from what?"

"Different from how you were when you were seventeen."

You don't, she almost said. But that would be a lie. He was controlled now, but he'd been positively rigid as a teenager. Like the type of person who'd never so much as jaywalk, even at two in the morning with no cars in sight. There was something that seemed more nuanced about him now. "Well, I can't exactly bust out with the fart jokes in this kind of setting, right?"

Truth be told, she was still figuring out what and who she was supposed to be in this new role. Talk about reading the room. But it was just her and Simon and the goddamn READ posters in the room now. Was she supposed to take her new cues entirely from him? It wasn't like the cast of the *Twilight* movies all brandishing their favorite novels was going to be any help. There suddenly felt like too much to learn and not enough guidance or help to figure it all out.

Wait. She was in a *library* for crying out loud. "Um. Maybe you could help me out. I think I need a book."

Six

Simon blinked, feeling like the world had shifted sideways under his feet. "You need a book?" For what? Light reading? They were working. What had made her want to browse the fiction section now, of all times?

She nodded. "Yeah. Like, I've never worked an office job and I have no idea how to behave. When firefighters aren't actively fighting fires or doing things that require concentration like taking inventory of supplies, w— they're kind of a goofy bunch." Simon didn't miss the slip, the fact that she'd started to say *we*, not *they*. Not for the first time, he wondered why she'd made the career shift. With the way she apparently missed it, it was a pretty extreme change. But he shouldn't pry.

A reference interview, though? That he could do. "Okay, so you don't necessarily need a *book* for that," he said.

"Check out the librarian steering me away from books," she said, her dark eyes shining with humor.

"Not steering you away from anything. Steering you *to-*

ward a resource that's a little more responsive. More dynamic and up to date." He opened up a browser window and typed, then swiveled his laptop to face her. "This is a website that talks about workplace stuff. Answers questions, has a bunch of other resources. Its archive is organized really well too." She scooted her chair closer, and suddenly he could smell her. Inexplicably, it reminded him of a day at the beach. Her shampoo, maybe. Sunshine and clean air and maybe a little hint of coconut.

Sexy.

He swallowed hard and held himself rigidly back, not leaning in for a deeper sniff like he wanted to. She nodded, and the fragrance seemed to waft toward him. Okay, shampoo, then. She didn't seem like a cologne or perfume type of person, anyway.

Okay, now even his inner monologue was babbling.

Seeming oblivious to his turmoil, she wrote the name of the website in her notebook. Without looking up, she said, "I remember you now, you know."

He swallowed hard. "You do?"

She tried a pen spin. *Bonk.* A noise emitted from her throat.

"Did you just *growl*?" he asked, trying hard not to laugh and not quite succeeding.

She shot him a narrow-eyed look. "This is frustrating," she said, picking up the pen.

"Let's get back to you remembering me." His buoyant mood took a dip as he realized that she might not actually have the best memories of him. If he was rigid and grumpy now, he was way worse as a teen, because he'd been a smug little know-it-all then.

She balanced the pen, finding the center of gravity like he'd shown her. It seemed like a ploy so that she didn't look at him. "We butted heads pretty hard in Speech and Debate," she finally said.

His eyes widened. "We did." But just the one time. After that, it was like they were on different planets. Like she'd exiled him to the dark side of the moon. "And you ended up scoring way better than I did."

She shrugged, tried the spin again. Bonked again. "Maybe you should have tried out for Drama club, rather than doing all the behind the scenes stuff."

Oh wow. She remembered that too? "I liked being behind the scenes." He'd loved watching her act with total confidence and zero inhibition. If he tried to sing and dance, he would end up in the fetal position, but for her it was like the very air that she breathed. "But you looked like you could have gone all the way to Broadway."

She snorted, still concentrating on her pen. "Not hardly. I just had fun." Then her chin lifted and her gaze swept over his face, his hair. He felt it like a touch. "Your hair was redder then."

His skin went hot. "Yeah. Got teased a lot for it."

"That's too bad. You were cute."

Later, Thea couldn't have said how they got off high school and her embarrassing revelations and reminiscences and back to actual work stuff. They did, though, planning out a month's worth of posts ending on New Year's. After which she would be judged and either kicked to the curb or have a real job.

She sat back and stretched, feeling a crackle in her neck. "Man, I never sat still like this before. How do you do it?"

Simon chuckled. "I try to get up at regular intervals." He pointed at his smartwatch. "This thing usually tells me to get up and walk around at least once an hour, but sometimes it gets fooled."

"By what?" They'd been utterly sedentary the entire last two hours and she hadn't noticed him futzing with his watch.

His face reddened. "By typing, believe it or not."

"Seriously?" She laughed outright, then stood, stretching. It had been a week since she worked out, which also wasn't normal for her. But she'd always used the weights and other equipment at the firehouse. She could join a gym, but the idea of dealing with her new job with all its new rules and protocol *and* dealing with a new workout place with a whole other set of rules and protocol seemed overwhelming. "Can we take a walk around the building or something? I am not built to take root like this."

Simon nodded and stood, gesturing toward the door. He locked it behind them like last time, and they headed for the exit, but this time Simon didn't outpace her, walking by her side and holding the door to the sidewalk for her with steady politeness. The weather was mild, but a brisk breeze was blowing, making Thea want to move at an equally brisk pace to keep warm. Stretching her legs and swinging her arms felt really good. The sunshine on her face did too. Swags of lights that would soon twinkle when it got dark hung over the street, and the shop windows were bursting with tinsel and red and green merchandise. A children's bookshop ad-

vertised that Santa would be making an appearance on Saturday for pictures.

"You'll be happy to know that a lot of the job entails
more moving around and participating in stuff," he said after
they blew off a few of the library cobwebs. "It's kinda like
journalism—both written and photo. That's my favorite part
of it, to be honest."

She looked at him out of the corner of her eyes. "Yeah. You
don't look like you sit around all that much, to be honest."

His pale skin got gratifyingly red at that. Even the tips of
his ears went pink, and Thea suppressed the urge to tease him
about it. But she held back. He wasn't one of her buddies on
the squad. He cleared his throat and said, "Actually, we have
something going on here this afternoon if you want to see."

"What's going on?"

He shot her a sidelong grin. "Drag queen story hour with
a costume parade."

"*Shut up.* That sounds adorable."

"It is. The kids are really cute. We realized after one
Halloween that they're still raring to dress up in costumes
year-round, and this is a way to incorporate that into our pro-
gramming. It's kind of a pain in the ass in one way, because
we have to get photographic releases from the parents in order
to use any kid photos, but it's worth it because the costumes
are really creative and the kids are the most photogenic thing
you'll see all year." His eyes were bright with enthusiasm and
his hands moved enough that she could have made him an
honorary Italian. It was infectious, that passion. Also, if she
was being totally honest, really attractive.

"I could help with that," she said without thinking.

His eyebrows went up. "You really want to? I was just thinking you could observe."

"It's time for me to get some skin in the game. I feel like I've been observing for weeks."

"You've literally been observing for a day and a half."

"Oooh. You literally used literally as a non-intensifier? That's hot." Then, when she realized what had rocketed out of her mouth, her face went equally fiery.

That's hot. Thea had been joking, but the words went directly to the dirtiest part of Simon's brain. His heart kicked like a frightened rabbit and his breath froze in his lungs.

Focus, he told himself. Steer the conversation back to safe ground. "Um. Yeah. If you want to help with the release forms, making sure they get signed, that'll give me the go-ahead to take pictures of any particular kid. I usually handle all of that on my own, and that results in getting only a few photos because it's a lot to keep track of for one person."

"Makes sense," she said in a matter-of-fact way, as if she hadn't just detonated a land mine in his brain. But...was the golden-tan skin of her face a little flushed? They were moving through a patch of shade and it was hard to tell.

"I set up one of our iPads with blank copies of the release form. It's pretty simple, and the idea is to rename each signed copy with the last name of the family. Then if you can note down at the bottom of each form what the kid's costume is, that would make it easy to keep track. I won't take any pictures that aren't pre-authorized."

"You really have thought this through." Was that admiration in her voice, or was he just indulging in wishful thinking?

He shrugged. "I was trying to streamline it for one person—me—doing all of it. It will still help a whole lot if you're willing to help."

A light touch on his arm made him stop. They'd completed their circuit of the block and were now mere yards from the front entrance of the library. "Hey. Do you really want me to help? Because I offered and you keep talking as if I need convincing or as if I haven't said I'd do it. If I say I am going to do a thing, I do it. All in." Her expression was almost sad in that moment, and it felt like what she was saying wasn't just about getting photographic release forms filled out for kids in cute costumes.

He swallowed, then nodded. "Yeah. I'm sorry. I'd really appreciate the help."

"And I'll probably learn a lot from the experience," she said with a wry little twist to her mouth that made him think he should have thought about inviting her to at least shadow him on this event from the beginning. "I don't think I would have considered getting permissions for photographs, but that makes total sense, especially with kids." She sighed and scrubbed her fingertips through her short hair, making strands of it stand on end before flopping back down. Simon tried not to find this adorable. "It feels like there's so much to learn, you know?"

He nodded. "Yeah, but there's always a learning curve with a new job. It's okay."

"Is it, though? I haven't been new to a job in ten years. I feel like an old lady at the ripe age of thirty-two. And I can't afford to screw this up."

He frowned. "Why not?"

She shrugged. "No plan B. I have no idea what I'll do if I can't do this. And there are a lot of eyes on me."

That he understood, but he tried to take a page out of her book and said, "But you're so used to having eyes on you. Weren't you voted class clown?"

She grimaced. "Yeah. And I'm trying to keep a lid on that. Professionalism, remember?"

Well, so much for trying to lighten the mood. That wasn't really his strong suit, anyway. When he thought about it, he was on the absolute other end of the spectrum. Nobody ever had to worry about his professionalism because he was so cautious. Maybe she should talk to Chloe—their personalities were far more similar, and Chloe never got in trouble, so she must know where the lines were. He had no idea because he'd never gotten close enough to find out. But the idea of fobbing her off on Chloe felt like cheating, somehow. Or at least wrong. Thea was his responsibility.

"Well, I'm here to help you get everything figured out," he said. And dammit, he meant it.

Thea looked around the room full of excited kids and their parents. These freaking children were *adorable*. A toddler in a spider suit ran across the floor of the children's area, all four fake legs bouncing in a way that made her want to howl with laughter. She approached the kid and his mother and asked if Simon could photograph the child for the library social media and newsletter. The mother agreed and signed the brief release, and Thea noted the name and costume, pulling up a fresh copy for her next victim to sign as Simon snapped away on a small digital camera.

"You don't use your phone?" she'd asked when they were getting their gear organized for the event.

"Nah. I started that way, but it's a nightmare. You have to offload the pictures, segregate them from your personal stuff. There's just too much blurring of personal stuff and work. Not to mention the fact that data storage becomes an absolute nightmare."

"Oh, good point." She had that swamped feeling again, like there was just too much to learn and too much to think about, and she'd end up failing.

But now, circulating around the event, asking—and mostly getting—permission for Simon to photograph adorable moppets in creative costumes, she started to feel a little bit of confidence creeping back. Some of it had to do with Simon's declaration on the sidewalk outside the library. *I'm here to help you get everything figured out.* Were there eyes on high looking at him and judging his performance too?

She approached a little girl dressed as a robot and her dad and got another release signed. The event was starting to wind down, with Miss Lita Rarity in her sparkly dress and perfect makeup waving a final goodbye to the kids, but Thea kind of wished it would go on longer. She and Simon had gotten into a rhythm. There was an almost dance-like way they moved through the small crowd as she picked their targets and he photographed. It was sweet of him to let her take the lead, even in this small way.

Simon stepped away from photographing robot-girl and approached Thea. "I think we're pretty much done for the day," he said while he rolled his shoulders.

"You okay?"

He dug the fingers of one hand into the opposite shoulder. "Yeah. Just crouching a lot for an hour seems to make me stiffen up. Nothing a hot shower won't fix."

Sudden images of Simon in a hot, steamy shower invaded her brain. Water cascading over his skin, darkening his auburn hair, sluicing down toward—*shit*. *Shut that right down*, she told herself sternly.

No perving on the guy who was helping her embark on a new career. That had to be a rule, right? She'd never slept with anyone on the fire squad because the best way to absolutely tank her reputation as a serious first responder would be to become the target of sexualized gossip.

Well, that and most of those guys felt like brothers to her. While she could look at them and think, *Yes, from an abstract perspective, this guy is hot*, the idea of getting naked with them was a combination of hilarious and revolting. She was pretty sure that having naked thoughts about Simon should fall into the same bucket.

Her libido wasn't getting the message though. Those shower thoughts about Simon remained in their own very special, very hot bucket.

"You okay?" Great. Now he was staring at her. Fair enough—she had probably been looking at him funny.

"Yeah." She scrambled for something—anything—to say. "You were really cute with the kids," she blurted. Damn. That wasn't as risqué as telling him she'd imagined him in the shower, but it was still all too revealing of how much she was attracted to him.

His cheeks reddened in that way she was rapidly becoming addicted to. "Um. Thanks. I think the kids themselves are the cute ones though."

"It's not a zero sum game, dude. The way you got down on their level to photograph them? The way you talked to them like little humans, not puppies? Their reactions to you? All very cute."

"As cute as I allegedly was in high school?" His cheeks were pink again, but his eyes met hers boldly.

She choked. Cuter, she thought. But she could only nod.

"Okay, then. How about hitting happy hour for a drink?"

Seven

What are you doing? The control center of Simon's brain, the part that was in charge of rules and regulations and doing things the right way, was blaring like, well, like a fire truck's siren. *She'll say no*, a more prosaic, everyday voice assured. Her compliments had probably just been to assuage his wounded ego, which he didn't hide well, as cranky as he'd been this week.

But Thea was looking at him almost shyly, a little smile curving her lips. God, those lips were pretty. Full and pink and, well.

Kissable.

He swallowed hard and almost missed it when she said, "Yeah, that sounds fun."

She said yes! His inner teenager screamed. Outwardly, he managed, "Um, okay. Let me just lock up this equipment, then."

She gave him the iPad, then put her hand on his arm to

keep him from turning to go back to the staff area. His pulse hammered hard in his ears.

"Don't forget this," she said, letting the magnetic stylus snap onto the side of the device.

"Thanks." He cleared his throat. "Uh. I'll be back in a couple of minutes."

"I'll be here."

He nodded and wheeled, trying to move with enough speed to make sure she wouldn't leave without him and enough leisure to communicate that he wasn't worried about that happening. But that eighteen-year-old portion of his brain that was so excited she said yes was also absolutely sure she was going to ditch him. He locked the iPad and camera in a drawer in his cubicle and went back out into the public area of the library.

She was still there.

It felt like a small miracle, seeing her talking to one of the parents whose kid he'd photographed, a really little girl who looked younger than Noah. As he drew closer, Thea noticed him and said, "Yeah, I don't work for the library, but this guy does. I'm sure he can tell you."

Turned out, the dad wanted to know about weekly story time. Easy enough to set him up with that information and let him know where on their website the library's calendar was for all their programs.

"Ready to go?" Simon asked as the dad hoisted the toddler on his hip and wandered off to examine the children's section. He still half expected her to slap his arm and holler, "Psych! Loser!" and run off.

But she didn't. Instead, she looked at *him* as if she was surprised that he came back. She shrugged on her jacket and looped the strap of her bag over her shoulder, tucking a book she must have checked out into it. The latest collection of the *Inferno Girl* comic. "Yeah. Got any favorite places with great happy hour deals?"

The only place he'd ever gone to after work was a brewpub a few blocks down, and only when Chloe had dragged him out. "I know a place," he said as if this was something he did all the time.

Surprising him, she said, "Well then. Lead the way."

Holy crap. Had she just finagled herself a *date* with Simon?

No. Not a date. They were coworkers. Well, sort of. Could you be coworkers if you worked in entirely different divisions of an enormous county system? Did it matter when she was on probation and had to be on her best behavior? Anyway, he was way too much of a rule guy to ever want anything romantic from her.

Mrs. M's voice echoed in her head. *Maybe he had a little crush on you all those years ago.*

No, he absolutely did not. He found her annoying and frivolous. He'd made that entirely clear when they were teenagers. And even if he was less uptight as an adult, he was obviously someone who took his responsibilities seriously. Therefore, he was just being nice to someone he'd been asked to mentor.

That was just science.

He cleared his throat when they exited the building and turned to walk down the sidewalk. "Brewpub okay with you? If it isn't, there are a bunch of other options."

"Beer's fine," she said. Then silence stretched between them

as they navigated to the brewpub two blocks down, with its
shiny fermentation tanks proudly displayed in windows be-
decked with greenery and twinkling lights. Simon opened
the door and held it for her, and she nearly said, "What the
hell are you doing?" but stopped herself just in time.

She absolutely needed to learn to roll with her new reality.
And that new reality might include someone who saw her as
something other than one of the squad. Someone who held a
door for her even when her hands weren't full.

Simon led the way to a high-top table in the corner of the
dim bar. "This okay?" he asked.

"Sure." Her nerves were zinging now. This absolutely felt
like a date. She sat on one of the tall chairs and slid out of her
coat, searching for a topic of conversation. "Did you have a
good Thanksgiving?"

He shrugged his shoulders, handing her a beer menu. "I
didn't really have one. I didn't have the time to go out to
California for it. What about you?"

How incredibly sad. But he was giving those closed-off signals again, like he didn't want her to comment on him being
alone on a family holiday. But seriously, none of his colleagues
thought to ask him if he wanted to go to their place? Was
it that the library didn't have the same camaraderie that the
fire squad did, or was it his choice? "Just the usual Martinelli
chaos. We used to have a lot more family over, but my cousins have started their own families mostly. So it was my folks,
Nonna and Nonno, and my sister and her evil brood of evil."

The waitress came by and they ordered beer and a basket of
fries, the awkward silence landing over their table yet again.
Well, she'd broken the ice the last time. It was his turn now.

He seemed to know it too. He shifted in his seat, visibly uncomfortable. She wondered if he'd regretted his hasty invitation and she bit her lip, chagrined. His gaze went to her mouth then and he inhaled sharply.

"Do I have something on my face?" she asked, lifting her hand to brush at the corner of her lips.

He shook his head, laughing softly. "No. Sorry."

Her self-consciousness only increased though. The waitress returned with their beers and a promise that their food was coming out shortly. Thea took a grateful sip, glad she had something to do with her mouth that wasn't trying to think of something to say to this aggravating man. He set his beer down and looked her in the eye. "So, what do you think about the job so far?"

Good. Fairly safe conversational ground. "Well, it's definitely early to say, but I think one thing that'll be good is that it's got a creative side to it that was missing in my old career."

His eyebrows went up. "I hadn't thought of it that way. But I should have. After those plays back in high school. You seemed to really enjoy that."

She nodded, smiling to think back on that. "Yeah. It was fun while it lasted. I never really thought about it in quite that way though. I liked being a part of a group, working together to produce something. That was one of the reasons I joined the fire and rescue service."

Another awkward pause as Thea sipped more of her beer. Then Simon cleared his throat, his gaze flickering down toward the table then meeting hers again. "Don't answer if you don't want to, but why did you leave it?"

★ ★ ★

Thea's gaze snapped up to meet his, and Simon wondered if he grossly overstepped some kind of boundary. Her dark eyes seemed to bore right through him, and he welcomed the return of the waitress with their fries, pounding the bottle of ketchup to create a satisfying puddle on his plate before he risked looking at her again.

Her expression was sad. He wanted to crawl into a hole for putting that look on her face. "I'm sorry. I shouldn't have asked," he said.

"No. It's fine. It's a natural question." Her voice didn't have the same snap that it usually did. She fiddled with a fry. "It feels kind of shameful, honestly. A friend of mine on the squad got badly injured. I lost my nerve. I couldn't get it back. That's the short version, anyway."

Her confession brought him up short. He almost couldn't believe that this was the fearless Thea Martinelli. But then again, vulnerability was its own sort of fearlessness. "That doesn't sound shameful at all. It sounds really human."

She laughed, but it sounded forced. "Yeah. That's what my therapist said. I tried a few different ways to get back in the groove of things, but I just couldn't manage it. I was going to quit, but then they offered me this job."

"Was that what you wanted? To do social media for ES?"

She shrugged and stuffed a fry into her mouth, seeming to chew to buy some time before she answered. "I didn't even know it was a possibility. But now that I'm learning more of it, figuring stuff out…" Her gaze lifted from the table to his face. "With you helping, it's starting to look like something I do want."

An unfamiliar warmth bloomed in his chest. "I'm glad I could help."

Her lips quirked in a crooked smile and she looked down again. "Yeah. Me too."

Awkward silence settled over the table once more, and when Simon reached for a fry, she did too. Their hands didn't touch so much as they *collided*, their reaching fingers intertwining and sending an electrical jolt up his arm.

"Sorry," they said in unison, then Thea laughed. This time it sounded natural.

"Do you think that website you showed me will have advice for how to handle situations like this?" she asked.

"What kind of situation do we have?" Simon didn't join her in her laughter. Instead, he felt kind of loopy, like a moth that had fluttered close to a too-bright light. He didn't like this feeling. It made him feel like he was all of seventeen again and he did *not* want to go back to that stage of life for anything.

She sipped her beer, then considered him over the rim of her glass. "I don't know."

Annoyance ripped through him. She was the one who had said *situations like this*. She obviously meant something she could identify. "Oh?"

Her expression went wary at his single syllable and she shrugged defensively. "All of this is new to me. Office job, having drinks with someone who's kind of a colleague but kind of not. I don't know how to define that. If you were on my squad it would be like you were my brother. But this—" She stopped short as if she'd said too much. And maybe she had.

"So you're saying I'm not like a brother to you." He fought a smile as warmth bloomed in his chest.

She cleared her throat, shook her head. "No. Not in the slightest."

Thea'd only had half a beer. Not even that. So why did she feel so unmoored? Maybe it was because Simon had a really direct gaze. It was unnerving. His eyes pinned her to her seat, leaving her unable to think clearly or say anything.

No, he was nothing like a brother to her. People like Sean and Felix mostly made her feel comfortable, made her laugh. And she made them laugh. Getting laughs from Simon was *work.*

It was worth it though. More of a challenge. And his stern face had its own kind of rare light when he laughed. A light that she'd like to see more often, even though it sent shivers through her. Maybe that was part of it: getting Simon to laugh unlocked that free side of her personality she now felt she had to keep locked down.

She racked her brain for something to say that would unfreeze that expression on his face, something that would bring warmth to those hazel eyes.

She came up empty. Panic spiraled up through her, sickeningly familiar. *No. No, no, no.* This job was the *escape* from the anxiety. She couldn't do this now. She closed her eyes and concentrated on taking a deep breath, holding it, letting it out slowly, like her therapist had showed her. Again. Warmth slid over her skin, and she looked down to see Simon had leaned across the table to clasp her hand.

"You okay?"

She nodded jerkily as her face flooded with heat. "Yeah. I just… Like I said before. I get freaked out. I guess not just by my old job. Crap. Is this my life now?"

His brows drew together. "Were you having an anxiety attack just now?"

She shook her head. "Not quite. But I've been working at recognizing the early stages and heading them off at the pass."

"What made you anxious?"

Her empty head could only offer up the truth. "I wanted to make you laugh. That's something I'm usually good at—making people laugh. But I couldn't think of anything to say."

His expression softened. "Not everyone is a comedian."

"I know. And you're an especially tough nut in the humor department."

"Tough nut? Hard to *crack* up, you mean?" And yes, humor did dance in those earnest eyes of his. And there was a glimmer of that light, making her insides zing.

Thea groaned. "See? I was the one who should have thought up the pun. That's usually my job."

He blinked, eyes darting from hers to the table, realization dawning that he was, in essence, holding her hand. He straightened up, covering his mouth with that very hand as he coughed a little too unconvincingly. Great. It was clear that he thought touching her was a bad idea. And she wanted to crawl into a hole and pull the dirt back over her SpongeBob-style for nearly having an anxiety attack right in front of him. Over nothing. He was so together he probably thought she was the biggest hot mess he'd ever seen.

Or cancel the *hot* part. Just a mess.

"Sorry," she mumbled, stuffing fries into her mouth to keep her from having to say anything else.

"Why are you sorry?"

"For nearly losing my shit."

"Nothing to be sorry about. I had a college roommate who had anxiety. I know it can be difficult to deal with."

"Yeah, in my case it was a career ender." The thought made her feel hollow. If this was her life, would it dog her into this career as well? She took a deep breath and then a swallow of beer, seeking to head that new spiral off.

"Or..." He shot her a small, secretive smile. "You could look at it the other way. It's a career starter."

Okay. She could maybe see it that way. If she squinted and looked sideways. He still had that tiny smile on his face. "What are you thinking?" she asked.

Mistake. The question sent him spooling back inside himself, leaving only the stern exterior she'd gotten used to.

"I was thinking that Friday we'll start you making some content in earnest."

Eight

Friday morning found Simon rubbing his eyes and drinking too much coffee while he checked his email in his cubicle before Thea's arrival. Her freak-out the other night, combined with the date-like atmosphere and the way he'd practically held her hand? It all added up to make him massively uncomfortable. Yet again, it sent him straight back to high school, not a place he ever wanted to find himself again, either physically or emotionally.

At the same time, the way she'd opened up to him had his inner eighteen-year-old giving a tight little air punch and hissing, *Yessss*.

Because even his inner eighteen-year-old wasn't about to hop up and down and holler.

He could practically hear his sister telling him to loosen up. Which reminded him to email Amy since he hadn't yet heard about holiday vacation. He typed a quick note and sent it, then took another gulp of his all-too-rapidly cooling coffee and perused the checklist he'd come up with for creating social media posts that work across different platforms. So much of this job was about maximizing and reusing.

"Got a delivery for you, Simon," Chloe singsonged from over the cubicle wall. He swiveled in his chair to see her come around the corner with Thea in tow. "How's this dude treating you?"

Thea shot him a hesitant smile. "He's treating me fine. Being very patient with my inexperienced as—behind."

Chloe leaned over and cupped a hand around her mouth, saying theatrically, "You can say *ass*. Just don't say it in front of Mary-Pat. She might get the vapors." She appeared to consider this for a moment. "No, please say it in front of her. I'd love to see her get the vapors. You were a first responder. You know CPR, right?" Thea nodded and Chloe grinned her most evil grin. "Okay. So it's not like an attack of the vapors would *kill* her…"

"Thank you for bringing Thea back," Simon said, cutting her off and tabling any further discussion of Mary-Pat. She gave him a jaunty salute and retreated to her own cubicle. "We only have the conference room for a half day today," he told Thea.

She nodded. "Yeah. The other evening kind of got me thinking—like you said, it's time to start generating some of my own content. Get out into the field some."

"Sure, we could do that. What did you have in mind?"

She shrugged as they moved off to the little room that was no longer just theirs. "I was thinking pretty basic stuff. Like a video about twice annual smoke alarm testing. A lot of people suggest that you test and change batteries on New Year's and Fourth of July—makes it easier to remember, so having it ready to go for New Year's seems like a good idea. Plus it's reusable, like you told me."

He considered this as he set his laptop down on the table. "First of all, really good idea all around. The only thing is, it gets a little tricky if you're talking about an actual demonstration of household devices. Because you have to have a house that has smoke alarms. My apartment's alarms are all controlled by my landlord and centrally wired."

She shrugged. "That's not a problem. We can use my place."

"You have a house?" Maybe she lived with her folks.

"Kind of. A small one. It's not mine," she added quickly as if she didn't want him to get the wrong idea.

His eyes narrowed at her unusual caginess. "Where exactly do you *live*?"

She told him the address and Simon's mind whited out. "Christ, Thea, are you *rich*?"

Thea barked out a surprised laugh, even as she kicked herself for not expecting this response. "No. Most definitely not. My living situation is, well… It's kind of unusual."

His expression was both aghast and fascinated. Not quite as compelling as his laugh, but fun nonetheless. "Do you live on a commune on a lobbyist's estate? Are you the grandchild of a senator?"

"No! Nothing like any of that. It's a weird story, and I'll take you out there this afternoon and show it to you, but I guarantee your guesses are going to be way off."

"Huh," he grunted, then walked her through the basics of planning a video. "Even one of only a minute or two should be worked out in advance—the script, the shot plan, it all has to work together. It's easy to think you've got a shot that's lasting way too long," he told her. "Then when you have to do a voice-over over it, you realize a couple of seconds of footage isn't enough for you to say even a full sentence." He remembered learning these lessons the hard way. It was pretty cool to be able to give this knowledge to Thea so she didn't have to do the same.

"But don't you talk at the same time?"

"I try not to," he said. "It can be like walking and chewing gum at the same time—if you're walking on your hands and chewing gum with your feet. Plus, the idea of winging anything practically gives me stress hives. Better to be prepared."

"Oh-*kay*," she said, laughing a little, and she followed along as they worked to create a rudimentary shot list and script.

By the time they were done, they grabbed sandwiches at the deli he told her about before. But when they got into her car, the engine resolutely would not turn over. "Shit. I knew I was skating on thin ice with this battery," she said. "Figures I'd be planning a *literal* battery video and have this happen." She glanced at him. "This time, it's not an intensifier."

Her little inside joke gained her a tiny smile. "Let me drive," he offered. "Then when we come back, I can give you a jump and you can go get a new one."

"Good plan," she said, wondering why he was taking her ineptitude so lightly. She would have expected him to be exasperated, especially since he was made of plans and lists and checkboxes. Instead, he just rolled with it.

As they headed for her home in his compact car, prickles ran up the back of her neck. Simon was just right *there* next to her. Having his broad shoulders only inches from her made her feel like the space was filled up in a way that was unusual. She couldn't figure out if she liked that or not, that feeling of having him so close she would only have to reach out a tiny bit to touch him. There was a light scent that teased her nose too. Too light to be cologne. Maybe soap or even laundry detergent, clean and fresh.

It took them about twenty minutes to get to the driveway of Mrs. M's home, her nerves only increasing with every mile. When she pulled in, rolling down the gravel toward the big house, she could see Simon's jaw dropping as he looked at it. "You live *here*?" he asked, his voice veering toward a squeak.

"No," she said and directed him to drive around the side of the house, past the garage bays, and come to a stop in front of the converted stable. He turned off the engine and she pointed at her home. "I live there."

Thea lived on an honest-to-god *estate*. There was no other word for it. Granted, the little building that she used was compact. And the house—which he could see only part of if he glanced in the side mirror—might be a midcentury ranch-style house in whitewashed brick, but it was *enormous*, comprising two angled wings. And it was on several acres of land in a town whose zip code was synonymous with wealth.

"How on earth did you swing this living arrangement?" he asked. He already envied the quiet she must enjoy on these grounds. She probably heard owls hooting in the evening and wrens yodeling their mating songs in the springtime. She most definitely didn't hear anything like the heavy steps of his upstairs neighbor. Whom he'd never met, but had to be at least eight feet tall and normally wore steel-toed boots around the apartment if the sound of their footfalls was anything to go by.

Her cheeks were pink as she unbuckled her seat belt and reached into the back seat to grab the bag with their sandwiches. That brought them practically nose to nose, and for a long moment they stared into each other's eyes, hers looking as startled as he felt.

Kiss her, a voice hollered from what must have been the left field of his brain. Because that was a completely absurd thing to even think, let alone want to do. This must be his inner adolescent reasserting himself, even though randomly kissing girls he was interested in wasn't something teenage Simon would have done either.

And yet, he wanted to do it. He *really* wanted to do it. Her pupils, easy to see at this close range against the velvety dark brown of her irises, dilated and her breath quickened.

"Um. I guess I should show you around," Thea said. And was her voice husky or was that just his imagination?

"Okay." He cleared his own throat as they got out of the car and headed for the front door.

The exterior was painted red and looked a little like a barn with its rough wood cladding, but it was the homiest-looking barn he'd ever seen. There were large windows to either side of the front door and they had actual window boxes underneath. The boxes didn't currently have anything in them on this chilly day, but they looked like they'd been tidied up for the colder months, no dead stalks with equally dead leaves fluttering from them.

Thea unlocked the door and led him inside, and he stopped dead to gaze around at what was basically a spacious, modern apartment. It was almost a one-bedroom, but her bed at the far end of the room was only half-hidden by two ranges of tall bookcases set at right angles instead of against walls. A little galley kitchen with an island ran to the left, a living area and little dining table with four chairs to the right. The only enclosed room in the place opposite the bedroom had to be the bathroom. The decor was casual and colorful, containing a deep blue sofa with its back to the kitchen area, facing a wall with a mounted television and bright art prints in frames. A desk was tucked under one of the front windows. A perfect place to work...or to daydream.

"What... *How?*" he asked, unable to be any more articulate.

"Mrs. McAnally—the woman who lives there—" she pointed her chin at the big house, visible through the front windows "—rents it to me. In exchange, I make sure she's okay, shovel her walks, that kind of thing." She put their lunch on the island, where two tall stools sat. "Let me just go get some plates..."

Without thinking, Simon clasped her wrist before she could go past him. "It's okay. Don't go to any trouble."

For the first time since the car, their eyes met. "It's okay. I want to."

It's okay. I want to. Her own words reverberated through her skull, and a little smile hitched up one corner of his mouth.

He released the loose clasp on her wrist. "Okay. Anything I can do?"

She inhaled, realizing she'd been holding her breath. "Um. Just unpack the stuff, I guess?" Moving quickly to the cabinets, she pulled down two plates, then felt kind of silly. It wasn't like she had fancy napkins. They didn't need silverware. The deli paper that the sandwiches were wrapped in would be perfectly fine even if her kitchen island wasn't clean—which it was.

She just wanted to take care of him a little.

Shoving that thought aside, she laid the plates out and turned to get glasses for their sodas. Might as well be as fancy as she could. Rounding to the other side of the island, she sat next to him, accepting her sandwich with a shy, sideways smile.

"You aren't exactly who I thought you were when we were teenagers," he said, popping open his soda with a hiss and pouring it into his glass.

She paused, folding the tape of her half-unwrapped sandwich over on itself. "Um. Who did you think I was back then?"

"I don't know. You seemed..." He trailed off, his gaze leaving her face and roaming around her little home. "Larger than life? Always going, always doing, always in the spotlight. Invincible."

A snort escaped her and she put her sandwich on her plate, crumpling the wrapper and shoving it in the bag. "I wasn't anything like that. I was just...loud."

"You're not loud anymore?"

She blinked, her vision going a little blurry, and stuffed her sandwich into her mouth to buy time. She knew she'd felt off, weird, muted since the anxiety kicked in. Had it really changed her that much? She chewed, waiting for him to go on, to fill the silence, but he just waited until she'd swallowed her mouthful and washed it down with a sip of her drink.

"I can be," she said. "Firefighters, we're—they're like walk-ing prank factories when they're not on a call. It's a stress re-lease. I was as bad as any of them, maybe worse, for years. Making up for not being a guy, you know?"

"For one, I like that you're not a guy." From anyone else, the words would have been joking, maybe even flirtatious. But Simon looked as serious as ever.

"Well, I like that I'm not a guy too. I'm happy being who I am, mostly."

"Only mostly?"

"You're one hundred percent happy with who you are?" she asked.

He tilted his head. "Fair. I guess I'm glad you're not a walk-ing prank factory anymore too."

"But you want me to go back to being that brash, loud attention whore again? Just without the fart jokes?" Out-side of drama club, the squad was the only place where she'd been accepted for this side of her personality. Her family was constantly on her to tone it down. Even her occasional dates mostly ended up thinking she was weird.

"Who said anything about attention whore?" Those thick auburn brows drew close over his eyes, and she almost forgot what they were talking about. It was both intoxicating and difficult, being the focus of Simon's concentration.

She shrugged up one shoulder. "My sister, for one."

"That sucks. My sister is a bossy pain in the ass too."

"Oh, she doesn't mean it. Mostly. We've always given each other shit. It's practically our love language."

He just grunted at that and ate his sandwich.

* * *

After lunch, Thea pulled down the attic ladder that, handily, was positioned right next to the smoke detector. They went over the script and the shot list again, making adjustments now that they were actually in the space and he could see what they were dealing with. All the while, his brain churned with the new things he'd learned about Thea in the few short days since they'd started working together.

He'd really seen her as someone larger than life. Maybe not even really human. More of an idea than a person. He'd been very, very wrong. Vulnerability ran like an underground stream beneath that outsize personality. And maybe part of that outsize personality was a shield, protecting the vulnerability, the same way he wielded rules and careful politeness to keep people at a distance.

He was also starting to get the idea that she was attracted to him and it was doing a number on him.

"Ready to start?" she asked, and he startled out of his absentminded reverie.

"Um, yeah." He rummaged in his bag for the camera as she climbed the ladder. When he joined her and pointed the camera up, however, he realized the ceiling was tall enough that he would have to use the zoom. "Shit. I should have brought a tripod."

She glanced down at him. "How come?"

"Because zooming in on the shot like I'm going to need to is going to make the video jittery and bouncy."

She frowned at him, then glanced up at the smoke detector. "It's social media, not cinema, Steven Spielberg."

"But you want it to look good, right?" He'd told her she

didn't have to have her face in the shot, but she argued that it made it more relatable. He squashed his initial impulse to try to get her to do it his way with some difficulty, but he had to admit there wasn't just one method of getting results.

She shrugged. "I read somewhere that the lo-fi stuff actually gets people's attention more."

This was a bridge too far though. Irritation bubbled under his skin. "There's lo-fi and there's unprofessional. Besides, you're going to want people to be able to follow what you're talking about without getting motion sickness."

She sighed, looked up at the smoke detector again, then down at him. "Okay, fair. How about you get on the ladder with me?"

His brain shorted out. "How about I what?"

A teasing smile hovered around her mouth. "Get. On the ladder. With me. Seriously, if you're on it, you'll be higher. Closer to the ceiling. That way you won't have to use the zoom."

It did make sense. Of a diabolical kind. He nodded and mounted the ladder until his feet were just one rung below hers. "Okay?"

She turned to look at him and it was like being back in the car when they were so close, but even more so. Her face was just an inch or two higher than his, her soft, plush lips quirking into a little smile. The front of his body pressed lightly to the back of hers, even though he was trying to maintain some sort of space between them. "Okay by me." Her voice was raspy and she cleared her throat. "Should we run it through a few times? I do believe in rehearsal. Mr. Preparation."

"Sure. I'll just, uh, record all of it. Just in case it produces usable footage."

"Makes sense. Okay." She looked at him a moment longer, then back up at the smoke detector. "You let me know when you're ready."

"Oh. Right." He fumbled one-handed with the camera, realizing he should have set it up more completely before he was several feet off the ground.

"You can lean into me. If you want," she said. "For balance."

Balance. Right. Leaning into her would push his brain completely *off* balance. He glanced up to see if she was teasing him, but her eyes were clear and guileless. Leaning forward a little, he tried not to register how warm and wonderful her body felt against his as he quickly set the camera up. "Ready when you are," he said when he grabbed the ladder with his free hand and reestablished the distance that was so necessary to keep him from losing his mind. Then he started recording.

"Okay, so this is a standard household smoke detector," Thea said, her finger entering the frame and tapping on the plastic housing. "You should be checking it twice a year…"

Nine

Thea kept up a practiced patter honed over years of doing demonstrations for the fire department. But all the while her internal monologue was a variation on, *Holy shit, Simon is practically pressed right against my ass.* She ran through it twice, not even pausing between takes because she was so aware of his warm, solid body behind her.

When she was done, she turned to meet his gaze. "That okay?" she asked.

"Brilliant." His eyes were crinkling with a smile.

Brilliant? Dear lord. The praise positively lit her up. "Should we…get down, maybe?" She didn't want to, but she also didn't want it to get too weird. Because this was weird, right? Having sexy feelings during a smoke detector demonstration? Yeah. Definitely weird.

"Um, yeah." But he didn't move. The air thickened and time slowed.

A sudden rapping on the door startled both of them, and

Simon slipped. Thea grabbed for him, yelping, and his free arm went around her, the camera digging into her side. They swayed there on the ladder for what felt like forever, Thea clinging to his shirt with one hand and a rung of the ladder with the other.

"Thea, are you okay?" She looked to see Mrs. M standing in the open doorway, her eyes wide as she took in the scene.

Simon immediately let go of her and hustled down, his face bright red. Thea followed more slowly, breathing like she'd just run a sprint. "Yeah, we're fine. Just doing a smoke detector video. For my new job. Mrs. McAnally, this is Simon. Simon, Mrs. M. My landlady."

Mrs. M laid a hand on her chest. "Oh goodness. I am so sorry for barging in, but you're not usually home during the day now with your new job, and there's a strange car out front, and then I heard you scream when I knocked..." Her papery cheeks were white, and panic bloomed in Thea's chest.

"I'm so sorry. Your heart. Do you need to sit down?" Without waiting for an answer, she went to the kitchen and got Mrs. M a glass of water.

"I'm fine, just surprised and a little embarrassed." The older woman took the water and sipped, giving Simon a speculative once-over as he did something with the settings on his camera. Her words from the other day rang through Thea's head. *Maybe he had a little crush on you all those years ago.* Thea had no idea what he might have felt well over a decade ago. But just now? The idea thrilled her with possibility.

Mrs. M handed back the glass. "I'm sorry for barging in. I feel thoroughly ashamed of myself and won't do it again."

Thea wasn't glad that her elderly landlady had either worried enough to come over and check on her or that she'd taken the extraordinary step of coming in uninvited. But Mrs. M clearly had good intentions. "It's okay. I know change is weird. But honestly, some of this stuff is probably going to have to be filmed at home. That's where too many accidents happen so we—I will be using my space to illustrate things like cooking safety." She gestured at the gas stove in the kitchen. "This may be more of a nine-to-five, but I can also do it from a lot of places. The county isn't giving me an office."

Mrs. M patted her shoulder. "Well then, okay. I'll get used to it. And I apologize again. It was lovely meeting you, Simon."

And, nodding at his quiet response, she was gone.

When the door closed behind the old lady, Thea slumped against it. "Well, that's a new one," she said, sighing deeply and standing straight again. "I'm the person who's supposed to be looking in on her, making sure she's okay. Not the other way around."

"She seems to care about you," Simon said, almost operating on autopilot. Thea had included him in her long-term plans for her job, but just for a moment. Then she'd corrected herself, made herself stand apart from him.

And she was already making plans to do the job without him. Intellectually, he knew that was the endgame, the goal everyone was working toward.

It still stung though, that she was already making plans to fly solo so early in their partnership. Especially after that charged moment on the ladder. He gave himself a mental kick. Great place to seduce anyone—up a ladder. It was ridiculous.

The moment had been hot though. And he thought she'd felt it too. It connected in an attenuated line from the moment in the car to now, a continuum of sexual tension, not two separate incidents.

He cleared his throat. "Um, we should probably get this footage onto your laptop. Do you know anything about video editing?"

Seeming to sense his mood, she nodded silently, her big, dark eyes fixed on his face. "Everything okay? I'm sorry about Mrs. M. She's never done that before and—"

He cut her off before she could finish. "No, I'm fine. None of my business, anyway." He rummaged in his bag and found the cable, holding it and the camera out to Thea.

"Oh. Okay." She took the equipment from him and set it on the island, then went to fetch her laptop. She plugged it in to start the transfer then looked at him again. "Yeah. I've taken a lot of video of my nephews over the years. I think I can edit it up just fine."

"That's great. I can send you some resources I've collected too." He thought about leaving then, getting away from all this awkwardness and going back to the library...until he remembered that he'd driven them both. And a rideshare for Thea to get back to her car would probably be ridiculously expensive out here. Not to mention being a jerk move for him to make, stranding her, even if it was in her own home.

"Can I get you something while this transfers? A glass of water or something?" Her face was starting to look anxious again, and the grumpy vines that wound themselves defensively around his heart frayed a bit. He was so used to thinking of her as someone who had everything figured out, but he was learning that she was just as human as anyone else.

"Yeah. Thanks. That'd be nice."

She went to the cupboard, taking the glass she'd given to Mrs. M with her and putting it in the sink before she filled up a clean one with fresh water and handed it to him. "Here. Again, sorry."

"Thanks. She seems to care an awful lot about you," he said, grasping for a new topic. Any topic.

Thea nodded and checked the progress of the video transfer. The library's camera wasn't new by any stretch of the imagination, and the progress bar was doing its usual gradual inching forward. "She's a really nice lady. I didn't mention it before, but she's kind of got me here as a buffer against her son. He's had his eye on her house for a while and started renovating this building as an accessory apartment for her when she was in the hospital a while back."

Simon felt his eyes bug out. "What the hell?" He knew something about being used and taken for granted by family, but this was next-level.

Her eyes narrowed. "Yeah. I'm not a fan. And not just because I get to live here. Bossing around the elderly isn't a good look. And she's not even that old—only in her midsixties. She might not even be retired now if she'd been in the workforce. But everything worked out for the best. I have a cool place to live, Mrs. M has someone to check on her, and Kyle still lives in a huge house that anyone else would think was ridiculously luxurious. Everyone wins, even if he doesn't see it that way."

★ ★ ★

Simon's eyes had stopped doing that guarded thing again. Not for the first time, she wondered what had made him the way he was. Or maybe he was just born wary. He handed her the glass, now empty, and she was so preoccupied it nearly slipped from her fingers. They both gasped and gripped the smooth sides of the tumbler, fingers touching. Electricity sizzled up her arm.

How was it that keeping a glass from crashing to the floor had her heart racing and her breath coming fast? But Simon was breathing hard too, and his pupils had spread across his eyes until there was just a tiny ring of golden brown around the edge.

Without thinking, Thea went up on her toes and kissed him. There was a shocked moment where they both stood, lips touching, unmoving. Then Simon angled his head and slid his free hand around her waist. She looped hers around his neck and deepened the kiss with him. They were still holding the glass as if they were in the middle of some sort of weird ballroom routine that included an empty tumbler. Their lips sipped and teased, testing and questioning. Thea almost brought her tongue into play, then froze. "I'm sorry," she mumbled against his lips, still clamped to his body by his arm.

"Why?"

Under her hand, she could feel the frantic beat of his pulse. "I... Are you okay with this?" she asked.

An incredulous laugh gusted over his lips. "How would you think I wouldn't be okay with this?"

"Well. I kissed you. I didn't ask."

He finally loosened his hold on her and leaned back, pull-

ing the glass from her hand and setting it on the kitchen island with quiet deliberation. "I kissed you back. Are you
sorry you kissed me?"

She shook her head. "I just don't know what I was thinking."

"Did you want to do it?"

"Yes."

"Do you want to do it again?"

Electricity zinged through her body again and her breath
went shallow. "Yes."

"Well, let's do that, then." He raised a hand, began to slide
it behind her neck.

"Okay." But suddenly, all her frantic urgency had morphed
into shyness and uncertainty.

Simon's brows drew together, his hand stopping, heating
her shoulder but somehow unsatisfying. "Or we could not if
you changed your mind."

She shook her head, anxiety twisting her gut. "I haven't. I
just… The whole professional thing. I don't know how this
works, remember? And there's so much on the line."

He traced her cheek with one gentle fingertip, his eyes
following his touch. "We don't really work together. I'm not
your manager. I'm temporarily helping you get your feet under
you." Something shifted in his expression, tightening, for a
bare moment. "But you're getting your feet under you so fast
I don't even know what you need me for. There's no professional issue here."

"You've thought about this, haven't you?" He nodded, and
energy fizzed from her belly out to her extremities. She hadn't

been wrong. The attraction between them, the connection, it was *real*. "So there's nothing stopping us?"

"Well, we probably shouldn't make out in the library stacks, but…" Those eyes drifted up to meet hers, and his lips tipped up in that rare way that she was learning to crave.

She covered his shy grin with her mouth, and they both opened for each other at the same time. Their tongues did meet, brushing and tasting sweetly at first, and then more urgently. Time went away until she pulled back, dazed, breathing fast and realizing she had his thigh clamped between hers, her hips grinding slowly to try to ease the increasingly urgent ache pulsing from her clit. She froze.

"Oh god. Zero to sixty there. I'm sorry. Again."

Simon needed to clear his head. Thea was saying something. What, he couldn't have said. Her lips, the lips that were moving, were even more full and plush than usual, redder from kissing. His gaze moved up to her eyes, huge and dark.

His jeans were uncomfortably tight around his cock, which desperately needed adjusting, and the way she was riding his thigh was criminal.

He blinked. "I'm sorry. What did you say?"

Thea's lips quivered, almost a smile. "I didn't mean us to get that carried away."

"But you meant us to get a little carried away?" He hadn't had that hot of a make-out session in…when? Ever?

"I don't know what I meant. I just know I wanted to kiss you."

I've wanted to kiss you for longer than you know. He kept the thought inside. There was something too raw, too vulnerable, about exposing his teenage self like that. "Well, I think you know how much I wanted to kiss you too. I think it's kinda obvious, actually."

Her hips slid forward and met his, and he had to stop himself from groaning aloud. "Oh. Yeah. Almost as obvious as me humping your leg." She smiled gleefully as he adjusted himself, and then he did groan with relief. Or, a bit of relief. His erection was now upright, at least. "I could've helped with that, you know."

With a huge effort, he set her back a few inches. "You could've. And we could've ended up over there on your bed." He felt at once confident and daring saying this. It'd been a long time since he'd been this free with anyone, but the evidence of their mutual interest and lust was established enough that he found himself unusually assured.

"Yeah. We could be there right now. But we're not. Why?" Thea's eyes had gone all clouded with worry.

He cupped her jaw in both hands and kissed her softly. "Because I think we should do things in the right order."

"What do we need to do first?" she asked, pouting slightly as he drew back.

He laid a finger on her lips and drew it back when she went to nip at it. "We need to get to know each other first. Not as colleagues, not as me helping you learn a job, but as people."

"You're saying...?"

"I'm saying we should go on a date."

Ten

It took a week for them to be able to schedule that date. Daytime meetings were fraught, the sexual tension between them always simmering, regardless of whether they were doing a training session, an event where Thea shadowed Simon, or the two events where Thea took the lead and Simon acted as her camera operator and advisor.

Despite the distraction, Thea found the library and its operations fascinating. She was well aware of the kinds of political machinations that occurred behind the scenes with county services and funding, but it seemed like the library was operating with five times the issues that Emergency Services did. Simon, for his part, seemed intrigued by the safety services and lessons that she found to be second nature, asking cogent questions that helped her translate her message to an adult audience who wasn't so well-versed in all things fire safety. Their back-and-forth as they discussed different ways of delivering emergency services messages to adults was energizing, and learning new techniques for creating and editing videos and graphics was fun. Simon wasn't just a sexy distraction, he was a great collaborator.

For the next week, she arranged for an equipment demonstration, scheduling it at a different firehouse than the one she used to work at. It was still too soon to go back.

Maybe it would always be too soon.

The thought was a sickening wrench. She hadn't been back since that day she picked up her stuff. Nobody on the squad had reached out either. After work one night, she went to the local community recreation center and signed up, touring the facilities and discovering a nicely laid out gym with newer equipment than she was used to at the firehouse.

She didn't need anyone else to work out, after all. She could do that on her own too. She pumped iron, her muscles complaining after her period of relative inactivity, then set herself on a punishing run on the treadmill with plenty of incline intervals. It wasn't like she *needed* that strength for her job now. But she wanted it. It was a part of her, even if her old squad and her old life wasn't anymore.

Finally, Saturday night loomed. She'd checked on Mrs. M and made sure the hoses and outdoor faucets were empty and ready for a cold snap. Maybe it was premature, but she needed to feel busy, and the weather had been trending colder than usual this December. In advance of the decorators who would make the big house ready for the holiday, a grounds crew had strung lights on the trees lining the driveway.

For her part, Thea cleaned her own little house and even considered her own holiday decorating for the first time and dithered over her clothes. She even messed around with makeup, putting some on, taking it off, then reapplying in a way that felt less clownish to her. Simon hadn't told her what they were doing, just maddeningly informed her that whatever she wore wouldn't matter.

"What do I wear if he says clothes don't matter?" she'd asked her sister on a panicked video call.

Giada rolled her eyes. "Whatever you want, goof. Do I have to come over there and dress you?"

"At least you asked first," Thea said, pointedly looking at the screen. Her sister had a habit of just showing up whenever she felt like it, even though she knew Thea hated it.

"Whatever," Gia said. Then her attention sharpened to something beyond her screen and a crash resonated through Thea's speakers. "Matt, you stop knocking over Nic's blocks or so help me, I'll take all the blocks away." A howl from the two boys was cut off almost magically by her sister's raised finger and a sharp *ssst!*

"You're a wizard, I swear," Thea said. "I can never get them to settle down that fast."

"They know I'm not kidding about the blocks. This isn't baseball. They only get two strikes."

"Tough, but fair," Thea commented. "But back to me. What the hell do I wear?"

"Easy. If you can't decide, just wear black," her sister said.

So now, here she was, minutes from Simon's arrival at her house. Examining her outfit, her hair, her clothes in a full-length mirror in a way she hadn't for years. She'd dated when she was on the squad, but mostly guys she met from various charity events the team had taken part in. Those guys saw her as a firefighter first and foremost. A novelty, usually, which was why they never lasted long.

She didn't know what Simon saw her as.

A knock at her front door startled her out of her musings. Well, she guessed this was what she was wearing, right or wrong.

Simon fidgeted on Thea's doormat, wondering for the twentieth time if he should have brought her something. Flowers, maybe. Except that seemed too conventional. But what did you bring as a gift for a date who was unconventional the way Thea was? Maybe, given her background, she'd *enjoy* a bouquet of...what, roses? No, too much pressure on both of them. Daisies? Maybe that was too ordinary.

Before he could think of another type of flower he hadn't brought, the door swung open and there she was. Her eyes looked bigger, deeper. Silvery jewelry dangled from her ears and her mouth...

Oh man. Her bare mouth was usually a pretty, pale pink, but she'd put something on her lips to deepen the color and they were shiny like they had been during that first lunch.

He tore his gaze away from her mouth, realizing he'd fixated on her lips for a little—or a lot—too long. Her eyes were dancing with humor.

"So, you going to finally tell me where we're going?" she asked.

He shook his head. "Nope. You willing to take this expedition on trust?"

"Sure," she said, grabbing a coat from a hook beside the door. "Do I need anything besides this?"

"Nope. Just yourself."

She nodded, then stepped out, closing and locking the door behind her. "Let's get to it, then."

They walked to his car, Simon wishing he'd at least kissed her cheek instead of staring at her like a poleaxed goon. He realized a beat too late that he could have opened the car door for her, but was already halfway around his front bumper on the way to the driver's side. Getting in, he let a little frustrated growl escape his throat.

"You okay over there?" Thea asked.

He chuckled. "Yeah. I guess there's no point in trying to be suave or cool or anything like that, is there?"

She leaned into his space and nudged his shoulder with hers. "Spoiler alert. I don't like suave or cool. I like you."

He shot her a smile which felt tight. "Spoiler alert, I like you too." *I always have* hovered in the air between them. But somehow that felt like too much to admit when he was already feeling so off balance and raw. He started up the car. "I can tell you that we're taking the Metro to our destination. That okay?"

She clutched her chest in exaggerated horror. "What, and leave the suburbs?" Dropping her hands to her lap, she laughed. "Sounds cool. I'm intrigued."

He should have felt relieved at that, but somehow he only felt more anxious. Thea might not be the fearless woman he'd taken her for before, but she was still his iconic crush. Could he even begin to measure up?

Good grief, but Simon was wound up tight. Thea clocked his nerves ratcheting tighter and tighter as he drove them to the Metro station, then as they rode the train, then as they ascended the absurdly long escalator at Dupont Circle. On an impulse, she grasped his hand as they stepped off into the glow of the evening streetlights. He glanced at her, startled, and she squeezed, hoping she wasn't fucking everything up and overstepping.

His expression softened and he adjusted his grip, lacing his fingers through hers, and she felt tension in her own shoulders she hadn't been aware of easing. She shook their clasped hands gently and said, "This is going to be fun."

"You think so?"

"I know so."

"How are you so sure?" His face looked like he was trying for teasing, but it still came off as unsure.

She stopped them in the middle of the sidewalk and faced Simon, ignoring the annoyed grunt of a man who had to detour around them. "Because I'm with you."

He sighed. "I'm not fun."

"Who says?"

His expression was resigned. "Everyone."

"Good thing I'm not everyone. Where are we going?"

His gaze shifted to the left. "I saw you checked out the latest compilation of *Inferno Girl*?"

Excitement started to rise in her, though she tried to keep her cool. "Yeah?"

He must have seen her reaction, because while his lips didn't curve, the impish glint that was a prelude to the smile she loved so much sparked in his eyes. "Okay, then." He stepped out, pulling her along with him through the tourists, the office workers heading home, past a busker with a guitar belting out an unfortunate homage to Springsteen's version of "Santa Claus is Comin' to Town." Their destination was a comic shop on the second floor of a converted row house just outside the circle. "Go ahead and browse. I have something to do," he said. She lifted her eyebrows, but didn't question him otherwise, just went to the shelves to look at the titles while he conferred quietly with the woman behind the counter. Thea was just tugging out something that looked interesting to her when he came back to her side, a slim paper bag in his hand. "Here."

"What's this?" she asked, taking it from him.

He rolled his eyes. "It's for you."

She slid a book out, the latest edition of the comic book series she'd checked out from the library the week before. "Thanks. That's so sweet." He'd noticed what she liked to read. How incredibly darling and on-brand.

"But wait. There's more." He gently opened the cover and pointed at a black Sharpie squiggle on the title page. The squiggle resolved itself into text: *Thea—glow brightly!* Then another squiggle she couldn't make out.

Then she gaped as realization hit her. "Oh my god. Did Suzanne St. Pierre *sign* this? For me?" The comic that she and Luca had first bonded over.

Suddenly, she missed Luca and the squad so hard, her chest felt like it was going to collapse in on itself. But conversely, her heart was swelling with bubbly, fluttering, giddy joy. Somehow, Simon had known. He'd *known* what this book meant to her and he'd gone above and beyond by getting a copy for her signed by the creator. She felt seen in a way she never had before.

He nodded. "She was in town earlier this week. They had an in-store event, so I ordered it for you."

Warmth swelled in Thea's middle and her eyes prickled. *Do not cry*, she told herself sternly. "This might be the most thoughtful gift anyone has ever given me." Dammit, her voice was wobbly.

Simon looked stricken. "Are you okay?"

She nodded, blinking. "Yeah. I just didn't expect anything like this. You caught me off guard. People don't get me gifts very often." She traced her finger over the signature. The artist had also included a little doodle of the eponymous heroine next to her signature—rougher than the way she was usually rendered, but all the more precious because it had been drawn specifically for her. "Thank you," she finally said, closing the cover and sliding it back into the paper bag to keep it safe.

"Come on. Unless you want to get something else while we're here?"

She shook her head, and this time, he took her hand in his, lacing their fingers together as he led her out of the store.

"I have to admit I really have only one trick for this date and I'm basically repeating it," Simon admitted as they waited to cross the street.

"You taking me to see my favorite singer and getting some signed merch?" she asked. "Wait, you're not, are you? Because I'm not sure my poor little heart could take that."

"Nah. But I'll bear it in mind for the future if you let me know who your favorite artist is."

She shot him an impish, sideways look. "I'm not sure I

should tell you. I feel like you're way too good at this whole gifting thing."

In reality, it had just been luck. He happened to get the email from the comic shop about the signing the day after they'd decided to go on a date, and a quick phone call had been enough to reserve a signed copy for her even though he couldn't be at the event in person.

But honestly, nothing had prepared him for the way her face went all soft and full of wonder as she realized what he'd done. Like many librarians, he didn't have much use for books as objects. He was far too used to weeding copies from the collection if they were outdated, damaged or just worn-out. What books contained—their knowledge, their entertainment, their wisdom—was what really interested him about them.

But he also made an exception for books that were unique in some way: signed or specially bound or otherwise exceptional. So, it was easy for him to imagine that such a book would also be nice for Thea. "What did you mean when you said people don't usually get you gifts?" he asked as they crossed the street.

She shrugged, the paper bag that contained her book crinkling audibly under her arm. "My family says I'm hard to buy for."

Hard to buy for? She was literally the easiest person he'd ever bought a gift for. Granted, the opportunity fell in his lap, but even without the artist's signature to make the present meaningful, he could imagine all kinds of things she might like. Music from her favorite artist—he'd have to figure that one out—a day trip to a special place, a small luxury that she wouldn't usually buy for herself. Thea definitely seemed like the kind of person who didn't buy herself a lot of little luxuries. Her home was cozy, but spartan. She didn't wear jewelry very often from what he could tell. He liked the idea of figuring out what might be precious to her, what she might treasure.

"Here we are. Like I said, one-trick pony over here." He waved at the door of the bookstore/café, wondering if he should have taken her to the annual Christmas market in Penn Quarter instead. "This time, if you want to buy a book, I don't have any surprises planned."

Eleven

No surprises? This entire trip into the city had been a surprise for Thea. She'd gotten a tiny taste of what might be a passionate side to Simon the other day, but she hadn't known he was capable of the kind of tenderness that would make him observe something that she liked and make a present of it for her. Her family's idea of gift giving was giving her something that *they* liked. Her mother and sister—who did all the gift purchases for her father and brother-in-law as if it was some sort of wifely duty—were two peas in a pod: they liked what they considered to be cute, collectible things. Stuff that sat on shelves and needed to be dusted. Thea never saw the point in such things for herself, and most of the items she'd been gifted of that nature were not gathering dust in her house. Instead, they were wrapped in newspaper and stored in boxes in her attic. She kept a handful of the newest ones out for when her family visited so they didn't ask where their presents had gone.

It would never occur to her sister or her mother to gift a

comic that she and Luca had bonded over. Instead, they just said she was "hard to buy for" and got her knickknacks or occasionally and more usefully, gift cards. She'd never really seen the point in giving gifts until tonight. Turned out, a gift could be just that: a gift, and not an obligation to gush over something she'd never in her life want to own.

She went into the bookstore café, buzzing with quiet conversation and instrumental Christmas music, with Simon, accompanying him through the rows of shelves to the restaurant in the back. Their reservation was noted and they were shown to a cozy table with a window view where they could people watch. People scurrying home with laptop bags and the occasional bouquet of flowers. People obviously on vacation, strolling slowly and looking around, to the annoyance of the scurrying locals. People on the bicycles and scooters for hire that were dotted about the city, threading their way sometimes perilously through pedestrians and automobile traffic.

A busy, hustling scene completely at odds with her tucked-away little home, and even at odds with the suburban town square where Simon's library branch sat.

"Did you ever want to live in a real city?" she asked after watching the shifting groups of people for a few minutes.

Simon looked up from his menu, then glanced at the street scene she'd been observing. "I don't know that I ever wanted to live in a city," he said finally. "I thought about visiting a lot of them. I had this idea when I was a teenager that maybe I wanted to be a pilot."

"Really?" A startled laugh burst out of her. "A dashing debonair kind of guy? Literal jet-set?"

He snorted, his pale cheeks reddening. "No. I liked the

idea of seeing new places all the time. But that was all it was. When I realized that I'd have to somehow learn to fly, that kind of sent the idea out the window. My parents didn't have the money for flight school, and I didn't really like the notion of throwing myself into the military without the guarantee of actually becoming a pilot."

"Huh. I don't think I can see you as military in any capacity." She'd worked with a few people who'd gone from military service to fire and rescue, and Simon, while he could be rigid, didn't seem to have the same kind of personality that those people did. "What made you go into libraries?"

His gaze drifted out the window as he formulated his answer. She wished he'd look into her eyes instead, to give her the tiniest window into his thoughts. But then he surprised her with his honesty. "Like many people, I gravitated to it first because of reading. I was crazy about fantasy as a kid, especially those books where someone is magically chosen, seemingly ordinary, then marked out as special. Like King Arthur. But when I got into the program, I realized it was about more than that, and kind of similar to the reasons why I wanted to be a pilot. To seek out new things, new experiences. But instead of new places, it was knowledge."

Had Simon ever opened up like this to anyone? If so, he couldn't remember it. He'd been a librarian for nine years now, and the reasons for taking on that career seemed a long way in his rearview mirror.

"Do you still like that aspect of the job? Because the whole social media thing seems like it's a left turn from that."

Damn, but she was perceptive. He dragged his gaze from

the street scene outside and met her eyes, dark and questioning. "Well, surprisingly enough, I often don't love dealing with people."

She put her hand to her chest, feigning surprise. "You don't say."

He felt his face crack into a reluctant smile. "I know, I know. I'm such a social butterfly. It must be a shock."

She turned her water glass between her thumb and forefinger, apparently thinking. Then she looked up at him. "That's just it though. You've got to be the least social social media manager the world ever created. Or are social media managers born, not made?" There was just the tiniest corner of the insouciant brashness in her speech now, the fearlessness he'd found so compelling and so intimidating when they were teenagers.

He nodded, acknowledging her point. "Funny thing about being a social media manager—it's more about the media than the social. Especially working in a library setting. It's not like there's a ton of interaction. There's a couple of weekly events where we do a 'what are you reading' or 'ask for book recommendations' features, but my colleagues who do more readers' advisory help a lot with that part, which is the most social of all of it. For me, mostly it's planning and creating." That was him. Creating something and putting it between himself and the world. Hiding. It had always worked for him, but with Thea he wanted to be seen a way that excited and scared him in equal measure.

"That makes sense. You said you liked the planning and wrapping part about the holidays the best."

She'd remembered that? His face felt like someone had

taken a blowtorch to it. "Um. Yeah. I do," he mumbled at his menu.

A long pause stretched between them, punctuated by the sounds of the café's other customers talking, silverware and china clinking. Then, finally she asked, "I'm sorry. Did I say something wrong?"

His chin shot up. "No. No, I'm sorry. I'm just…not used to being noticed, I guess. Not used to people remembering what I say."

Her eyebrows drew together. "Seriously? Why not?"

He shrugged, embarrassment spidering up his spine. "I don't love attention. I prefer to fade into the background." He knew he'd blast right into the family spotlight when they got the email about his holiday travel. His prediction had come true: Amy had only been able to give him a few days, with nearly two of them eaten up by travel. Ash was going to have one of her tantrums. The knowledge created a constant low-level hum of dread in the back of his mind.

"There's fading into the background and there's completely disappearing. I mean…" A blush crawled up her cheeks, but she took a deep breath and continued. "We're on a date. You don't want me to pay attention to you?"

"No—I mean, yes. I just… I don't know what I mean." God, he hated how he sounded, all confused and lost.

She gazed at him for another long, sort of uncomfortable, sort of warm moment. Then she reached her hand across the table, palm up. "Not to prove that I remember the stuff that you've said to me, but is this more about feeling like you're a cuckoo in the nest?"

A tightness he hadn't previously been aware of released

from around his chest and he took a deep breath, covering her palm with his. "Yeah. Maybe."

"I think maybe we might have more in common than you think."

Simon's hand against hers felt deliciously warm, somehow private and intimate in this public space. His light brown eyes seemed to anchor her in place.

"How so?" he asked, his voice soft, a caress she felt along her neck.

"I don't always feel like I fit with my family either," she said. Too impulsive. Too confusing. They loved her, but they did it in that way where they threw up their hands and said things like, "Oh well—that's Thea for you."

He blinked, looking confused. "You seem like you fit in anywhere."

Her lips tightened and she shook her head. "Nope. I really do not."

"I'm sorry." His hand convulsed around hers. "That really sucks. Especially when it seems like everyone all around you understands everyone else and you're the only one left out."

"Right?" she asked, a gush of relief running through her at being understood. "My mom and my sister are on the same planet. I'm in another galaxy."

"And your dad?"

"He's just kind of checked out. Into his own thing. Work and golf and that's pretty much it."

Simon chuckled, but there was no humor in it. "Yeah. My dad's kind of the same. He retired early, so it's pretty much all golf all the time. My sister creates her own whirlwind of drama wherever she goes and Mom backs her up one hundred percent. Nobody understands what I do at all."

That feeling of being seen, of being *understood*, blossomed in Thea's chest, fierce and hot. "Oh my god. Nobody understands what I do either. Everyone thought firefighting was a phase." That blossoming feeling collapsed almost as quickly as it came. "Maybe it was."

Simon's grip on her hand tightened and he leaned across the table toward her. "You did it for ten *years*, Thea. That's a decade, not a phase."

"No. I guess it's not." But doubts still nibbled at her like mice. Voracious, tiny bites eating away at her.

A waitress seemed to appear at their table at that moment, breaking the soap bubble of their connection. Their hands unclasped and they leaned back as she recited the specials and asked if they wanted to order drinks. Thea, flustered, looked at the beer options and asked for the first one that looked good. Simon, seeming similarly discombobulated, ordered the same.

"I'll just put those in and give you another minute so you can decide on dinner, okay?" the waitress said brightly before she strode off to the next table. Thea glanced over the top of her menu at Simon, wondering if they could re-achieve that fragile intimacy that they had experienced for a couple of moments again.

"Anything look good to you?" Simon asked without looking up. His cheeks still looked a little pink.

"Um." Thea focused her attention on the menu again. "Crab cakes," she said decisively. "What about you?"

His gaze slid up to meet hers. "Will you think less of me

if I get the pasta? I don't have any prohibitions about—what was the phrase you used?"

"Sauce out," she answered, shaking her head. "Nah. I don't hold it against people that they're not lucky enough to be Italian. You have my blessing to eat the ravioli. Besides, it's pesto. That's not sauce." It gave her a little glow to know that he'd obviously been listening and paying attention to her as well.

"Pesto isn't sauce?" His eyes now were twinkling with amusement. "What is it, then? A condiment?"

She huffed. "You know what I mean. Mama's sauce is *sauce*. Marinara. Gravy."

"Gravy?" He started laughing. "I haven't heard that one. In my world, gravy is the thing you make with turkey drippings and flour."

She rolled her eyes. "You have so much to learn."

He placed his menu on the table, meeting her eyes directly, and her breath caught. That look was almost as potent as his rare smiles, but it did something different to her. Her thighs clenched together and her belly fluttered. "I look forward to it."

Thea blinked. Then a little smile curved her lips, her dark eyes lighting in a way that made him wish they weren't in a restaurant—or any public place, for that matter. If he could, he would wish them back to her cozy little house on that quiet estate.

The return of their waitress with their drinks broke their eye lock and they ordered quickly, Simon glad to not have the menus between them anymore. When she was gone, Thea traced a finger down the condensation on the side of her glass. "You pay attention to the things I say too, apparently."

"What?" His shoulders tensed. What did she mean?

"The *I don't eat sauce out* thing. You remembered." Her gaze flickered up to meet his, then she took a sip of her drink, seeming to concentrate very hard on the glass's path traveling from the table to her lips.

Relief flooded through him. "Of course I do."

She snorted. "There's no *of course* about it."

He leaned forward, seeking to catch her gaze again, but she kept her eyes fixed on the table. Anxiety bubbled up in his chest, but he pushed through it. "Of course there's an *of course*. I've always paid attention to you."

She laughed softly. "Always. What, is always two weeks? While you're training me in my new job?"

"No."

"No?" Now she looked anxious, and he scrubbed his face with his hands, the urge to confess his teenage desire warring with his pride. He extended one hand until she clasped it, her expression worried. "Thea, it might be corny, but I had the *hugest* crush on you in high school." He swallowed hard. The truth was out there now. He braced himself for laughter. For rejection. For…something else he knew to dread but didn't know what it would be.

A stricken look flooded her face. He released her hand, waving it between them. "Sorry. Forget I said it." God, if he could only erase the last minute of his life from existence. To start over.

"Stop." Her huge brown eyes were shiny.

"I'm sorry," he said again. His hand dropped into his lap. God, he'd made a mess of everything.

"No." Her eyelids fluttered, blinking furiously, then she focused on him hard, making him want to squirm in his chair. God, did she think he was a stalker or something? "No, that's not what I mean. You had a *crush* on me?" Her voice squeaked.

His chin came up then down, a slow confirmation. It was out there and he couldn't take it back. "You don't have to… I don't know. I didn't say it because I wanted anything from you—a reaction or whatever. I just. Well. It's true. That's all." His rapid babble finally trailing off, he sat there and wished the ground would open up and swallow him.

She shook her head, swallowing as if her throat hurt. "I didn't take it that way. Like you wanted something from me."

"So why do you look so distressed?"

Her eyes, which had been wandering around the restaurant, looking at anything but him, suddenly focused on his face again. Yeah, they had a definite sheen to them. Christ, if he'd made her cry…

"It's just that I was such a *jerk* to you back then," she blurted. "And then I didn't even remember you. No wonder you were pissed off. And to have you apologize to *me*? It's just. Well. It's a lot."

"You weren't a jerk." She just hadn't seen him the way he saw her. Or *thought* he'd seen her. Because the Thea in front of him now was so much more than he'd ever imagined.

"I was." Distress was stamped on her face.

"Well, if you were, then I was one too. We were adolescents. We were probably legally required to be jerks. Hormones alone would make that guaranteed."

Her lips wobbled into a faint smile at that. "Yeah, I guess that's factual."

"I know it is. Besides, we got a new start, right?"

"Yeah. I guess we did." And her fragile smile felt like a lifeline.

Twelve

It was fully dark and the restaurant had become packed and noisy as they ate. They shared samples of their entrées, and Simon expressed joking gratitude that his ravioli met with Thea's approval.

To her relief, dinner passed without any more big emotions. As they were eating their last few bites, Simon told her his nephew had reached the "why" stage. "You pegged the conversation precisely," he said, shaking his head. "It was like the seagulls in *Finding Nemo*, but instead of 'mine,' it was 'why?'"

"Oh man, yeah. And you only have the one nibling so far, right?" she asked. He nodded. "Matt and Nic are just eighteen months apart, so it felt like just when Matt had finished with it, Nico started."

His eyes bugged out a bit at that. "Wow. Not sure I could handle that much *why* in my life."

She shrugged. "Toddlers. The original existentialist monsters."

He'd been taking a sip of his drink when she said that, and his shoulders convulsed as he barely succeeded in swallowing, his eyes blinking and watering. "Jesus. Warn me when you're going to be funny next time."

"I thought you said it was hard to make you laugh," she teased.

He took a deep breath and let it out in a whoosh. "Normally, yes. But that struck me just right. And true. And funny."

"Comedy frequently comes from truth," she noted as she set her silverware down on her plate.

"How were your crab cakes?" he asked, his hazel eyes warm with laughter.

"Delicious. I'm stuffed."

"No dessert, then?"

"Well. Not of the food variety," she blurted. He froze, and she wondered if she'd gone too far. Damn her lack of filter. Then his lips twitched, a tiny movement that she would have missed if she wasn't watching him so closely. He swallowed, his Adam's apple bobbing, and he picked up his napkin and wiped his mouth with care.

Clearing his throat, he said, "I want to be very clear. Are you expressing…interest? In me? Physically?"

There was something about his serious demeanor, his careful question, that made her giddy. How was it that precision could be so *hot*? "Yes. Is that a problem?"

"Not at all." Their waitress approached the table, and he politely declined dessert for both of them. "Just the check, please."

The trip back to Thea's house was interminable. Simon had to suppress his desire to fidget on the subway, to zoom down the nighttime roads in the car. He'd intended a low-key date where they could discuss books over dinner and maybe browse the bookshop afterward as a no-pressure end to the evening.

Well, that had gone completely out the window.

Thea seemed to sense his agitation, humming quietly along to the song playing in the car, a secretive little smile curving her generous lips. Finally, he pulled up in front of her house, his headlights illuminating her front door and the wintery window boxes to either side.

"You wanna come in?" Her tone was teasing, but when he turned to look at her, her eyes seemed a little anxious.

He gusted out a sigh and turned the car off. "Yes. Very much so."

"Good." There was mischief in that single syllable, and god, the crush he had on her back when they were teens was absolutely nothing to the rush of desire that flooded through him now. They got out of the car, and Thea fumbled with her keys at the door. Her hands were shaking. For him. His knees felt weak. Finally, she had the door open and he followed her inside as she flicked on a light and turned to face him. He just stared at her for a long moment, his hungry gaze taking in her huge eyes, the way she bit a corner of her bottom lip, her rapid breathing. Then he stepped forward, cupped her jaw in both hands and bent to kiss her.

Her lips were so unbelievably pliant and responsive. She stepped forward and his hands slid around to the back of her head, spearing into the soft hair there as she wrapped her arms around him, aligning their bodies. He moaned into her mouth at the feel of her pressed against him, strong and warm and *Thea*.

"Tell me what you want," he murmured against her mouth. "I don't want to get this wrong."

"More kissing, for now," she said, her voice throaty. They stumbled toward the big blue sofa and Thea collapsed onto it, pulling him down with her. His skin felt tight and hot as they kissed again. This time, her fingers were wound in his hair and the little tugs she gave him made electric shocks shiver down his spine. Their tongues tangled as Simon pushed one thigh between her legs, an echo of their last kiss. She groaned and rocked her hips against it as he flicked open the top button of her blouse. A memory made him stop and glance at the front door.

"Your landlady isn't going to burst in again, is she?"

Thea shook her head, laughing. "She won't do that again. She knows your car now, anyway."

He laughed, then grunted as her hips ground against his leg again. "Man, this feels a little too much like high school." He kissed the skin exposed by the open button, then curled his tongue into the hollow of her throat, gratified by the noise she made. "Making out on the couch, worried if someone's going to burst in on us..."

He lifted his head and saw humor glinting in her eyes. "It's kinda hot," she said. "Were you this hot in high school?"

A surprised laugh barked out of him. "Whatever I am now is, well, not what I was when I was eighteen."

"Well, I like now-Simon. Kiss me again."

"So bossy," he said, but his tone was approving. The warm haven of her mouth, the friction of her body, the slightly illicit feeling—all of it was conspiring to make him come in his pants if he wasn't careful. He opened another button, his eyes checking her expression, gratified when she smiled and pulled him down for another kiss, encouraging him.

Thea was going to *explode*. Simon's thigh was clamped so hard between her legs, she felt like he must be losing blood flow. But he felt so good, so right, so wonderfully *there* on top of her. And yeah, it did kind of feel like an echo of teenage make-out sessions, but the sweetness of it combined with that illicit thrill—well, it really did it for her.

He tugged another button open and now the lacy edges of her bra were visible. She'd picked a nice, matching set in a deep navy blue in the hopes that something like this might happen. He sucked in a breath, his eyes flicking up to meet hers. "Very pretty," he said, tracing a fingertip over the scalloped cup.

"Glad you like it." *Glad you're* seeing *it*, she thought. His light touch was giving her goose bumps, shivers racing down her spine. She squirmed, her clit throbbing where it was pressed against his leg. "Stop teasing me."

"Is it teasing or is it foreplay?" he asked, making another light pass over her pebbled skin.

Her only reply was a frustrated groan and another grind of her hips.

"Shh." He opened the rest of her buttons and kissed her neck then, and oh *man*, but it lit her up. His hand spread across her belly as if he needed to hold her down, to keep her from floating right up to the ceiling like an enthusiastic helium balloon.

"Should we move this to the bedroom?" she asked, needing more room, more Simon, just *more*.

His serious gaze roamed her face. "You sure?"

"Very sure." She was nearly panting in her eagerness. Surely he could see that? Was he fucking with her when he could be fucking her?

"Okay, then." He levered himself up, then held out a hand to pull her to her feet. Her knees wobbled for the first few steps toward her bed and she almost felt lightheaded. But Simon continued to hold her hand, leading her steadily toward that lovely expanse of mattress. When they got there, she let her shirt slide to the floor, his gaze wandering over the bare skin of her torso and arms. That erection that she'd felt before pushed ambitiously against the fly of his pants, and she reached with eager fingers for his belt. He didn't stop her or try to slow her in any overt way, but when he reached forward and cupped her head again for another kiss, the languid, drugging slide of his tongue made her fingers stall and still on the buckle.

"You're way too good at that," she said, her voice hoarse and her fingers tugging at the leather again.

"What?" His gaze scanned her eyes as his thumbs stroked her cheeks.

"Kissing. Getting me wound up."

"Good," he said, then groaned as she got his fly open and pulled out his cock, solid and hot and just right in her hand. She squeezed gently, then stroked, watching his face to see what he liked. His eyes closed and he let out a tiny sigh. But when she sank to her knees, he stiffened. "Thea…"

She nuzzled her cheek along his length, inhaling the scent of clean man and desire. "Do you not like oral?"

A fractured chuckle fell from his lips. "Oh, it's not that I don't like it. It's just that I'm so keyed up I'd last about twenty seconds. And I don't want that to be our first time."

"Okay." She licked him then from root to tip, enjoying the quiver that went through him. "But you've teased me already. Only seems fair I get to return the favor." Then she circled his crown with her tongue, cradling his balls and grinning up at him when he groaned again.

He tugged her to her feet, shuddering as the moisture from her mouth cooled his cock. Well, that was one way to slow his raging libido. Threading his fingers with hers, he pulled her close and kissed her, tasting himself on her lips, then resting his forehead against hers. "We haven't even had the 'are we safe here?' conversation."

"You mean testing? It's been ages since I was with anyone, but I've been tested since."

"Good. Same."

She looked at him speculatively, tracing her lower lip with the tip of her tongue. "So, what are you up for, if not a blow job?"

Her blunt question made a surprised laugh gust out of him. "Oh, I'd be up for that, it's just I feel like I want more…parity for our first time."

"Hmm. Okay. I like that you're already considering a second time."

He blinked. It was true. But where had this confidence come from? He hadn't felt like this since he'd been in his master's program. Maybe it was just that she was clearly very into, well, everything. Him. Their make-out session on the sofa. Her own partial nudity and his. Everything.

"I think I want to learn what gets you off. And have you learn the same about me."

She gave him a quizzical look. "I'm a pretty simple gal."

"Hmm. Let's see." Disentangling their fingers, he ran his hands up her back until he got to the clasp of her bra. Unhooking it, he threaded the straps off her shoulders and let it fall to the floor. He cupped her breasts, two overflowing handfuls of smooth skin tipped with brownish-pink nipples. "Are your breasts sensitive?"

She tilted her head, looking at him. "Not particularly."

"Okay, so this doesn't really do it for you." He pinched her nipples lightly. She shook her head. "Okay, how about this?" He tried it again, but harder this time, tugging a little. Her eyes widened. "A simple gal, huh?" Dipping his head, he brought his mouth to her, using suction to get the same tug he'd given her before.

"Oh!"

He chuckled and bit her hardened nipple lightly, giving the other one another teasing tug with his fingers. This time, the noise she made was a kind of gulping "Unf."

"Let's see if we can figure out some more things about each other," he mumbled against her skin.

Thirteen

The top of Thea's head was going to pop right off and he hadn't even touched her clit yet. Nobody had ever gone so far as to nearly manhandle her nipples, bringing them right to the edge of pain, but not quite. She hadn't even thought of that when she touched herself.

He might be learning things about her body, but it was apparent that she was going to be learning some things about herself as well.

Grabbing his shoulders, she pulled him backward until they both sank to the bed, his erection sandwiched snugly between them.

"One second. Have to be more naked," he muttered, pushing himself back to standing, unbuttoning the top button of his shirt, then grabbing the back of his collar and pulling it off over his head with his undershirt. Then he pushed down his pants and underwear, pausing to toe off his shoes before he could get them all the way off.

"Now you," he said as he kneeled. She raised herself up on her elbows to watch as he unzipped her short boots and then stripped her out of the rest of her clothes. He seemed a little more frantic, moving a little faster. But when he finally stood, he did it slowly, as if he knew she wanted to look her fill, to see all of him in the low light filtering from the one lit lamp in the main part of the house. He made her mouth water, with his broad shoulders narrowing to a trim waist, and that lovely cock standing up with a slight curve, making it point back toward his belly button. When her gaze traveled back up to his face, she noticed one of his eyebrows was arched. "Yes?" he asked.

"Yes. Very much yes." She nodded her head with an eagerness that made him laugh, low and sexy. "Come here and yes me up."

"Whatever the lady wants." He wrapped his fingers around her ankles, warm and sure, making her shiver. Urging her legs apart, he kneeled between them, running those lovely hands up the outside of her legs, then down the inside. She bit her lip as he repeated the slow slide of skin over skin, getting closer to where she really wanted to be touched, stroked, pleasured. The next time his hands swept up, they traveled from the top of her thighs, across her belly, then back down again. Her nerves were humming, zinging, crackling, and she was wound up with desire.

The next pass up led his hands to the sides of her breasts, then he rested his hands on the bed to either side of her body. She nearly growled with frustration, and he smiled, a slow, knowing thing that made her wonder what the hell happened to stern, rules-driven Simon.

"You're good at this, aren't you?" she asked.

"I hope you think so."

"But when did you—oh." She nearly levitated off the bed when he repeated that trick with her nipples, this time with his mouth, sucking hard. The not-quite-pain shot straight to her clit and she couldn't quite suppress a moan.

"When did I learn to map out a woman's body?" His eyes seemed dark in the low light as he looked at her. She must be a mess. Not that she cared.

"So, did you take a class in cartography or something?" She tried to sit up, to reach for his cock, but he held her wrist in a firm clasp.

"Not yet. I've still got some things to learn about what makes *you* excited. And no, smart-ass, no class. But being one of the few straight guys in a graduate program that's at least ninety percent women meant I had a lot of female interest. I like learning. I like giving people pleasure."

"That simple, huh?" She'd been in a career with about 90 percent men but didn't have the same latitude to date or experiment. The indignation that started to rise up in her was quickly headed off when he slid down on top of her, that glorious erection pressing into her belly as he found that sensitive spot on her neck *and* tweaked one of her nipples just right.

She couldn't be indignant when she felt this good.

Simon hadn't been lying when he said it had been a while since he'd been with anyone. But apparently, sex was like riding a bike. And Thea wasn't shy about letting him know what she liked.

And he liked that she liked it.

"Are you going to fuck me anytime soon?"

He lifted his head and shook it, enjoying the way her eyes went wide.

"Please?"

"I like the sound of you begging," he murmured into her neck, enjoying her squirming pleasure under him.

"Please, please, pleasepleaseplease? Simon Says fuck me?"

"Just for that, I'm going to draw it out even longer." He bit the juncture of her neck and shoulder. God, the friction created by her squirming underneath him was getting him closer than he wanted to be. He raised up on his elbows, kissing her long and deep. That quieted the squirms, but didn't exactly take the heat off his arousal.

"What's your game?" she asked when he raised his head again.

Game. Yes. Brain back in the game. He took a deep breath to center himself. "Like I told you. Mapping out your body. Finding at least some of the places that make you go wild."

"What about you?"

"The game works both ways if you want it to."

That brought a gratifying gleam to her eyes, even in the low light of her bedroom. God, this woman. She made him feel scattered and whole all at the same time.

"I want." With those two low-voiced words, she went still under him. Softening, seemingly expectant.

"Were you so keyed up because you thought I wasn't getting anything out of this?" he asked softly.

"Maybe. Partly. You said you wanted it to be equal."

"Equal doesn't need to be simultaneous."

"Noted." She stretched her arms over her head. "Do your worst. Or your best. Or both."

"Hmm." He shifted off her, lying on his side and tracing his fingertips between her breasts, down her belly, and then finally, lightly touching her clit. She hummed and her eyes slid closed. "Do you want to tell me what you like, or would you like me to figure it out?"

One eye slit open, looking at him. "I have no problem asking for what I want, but I've liked the part where you figure it out so far."

"Okay. But also tell me if there's something you don't want. Or if I'm doing something wrong."

"You got it." Her voice sounded almost dreamy now, as if she was sinking into sensation, trusting him.

The sound made his cock twitch. He pressed on the tight bud, watching her expression closely. She sighed and a tiny smile lifted the corners of her lips. Then he slid his middle finger into her, using his palm to create friction as he pumped into her gently. He added another finger, watching all the while to get the feedback that told him he was on the right track. But when he pulled his fingers out, slick with her moisture, and touched under her hood, her brows drew together and her breath hitched.

"Too sensitive?" he asked.

"Yes."

"Good to know. Sorry." He filed that for later, wondering if a wet tongue was soft enough to engage her clit directly. For now, he slid his fingers back inside, gratified as her hips circled a little, helping him create the friction he knew she was craving. He leaned forward and gently bit her earlobe, gratified by an additional squirm. "Do you feel good?"

"Mmm-hmm."

"Good. Do you feel sexy?"

She murmured another affirmative.

"Good." He nuzzled her neck, kissing her in that spot he'd found before. "Are you going to come for me?" Her eyebrows had drawn together again, but this time in fierce concentration, like she was chasing her pleasure. Remembering how hard she'd gripped his thigh between her legs, he added some pressure, and she let out a low moan. "You're close, aren't you?" Her inner walls were clamping down on his fingers and her hips were grinding against his hand in earnest. If she'd heard him, she didn't respond, just kept moving with him as he finger-fucked her. Finally, he bent down and sucked one nipple into his mouth, biting gently and tugging. She shouted, her head thrashing as her orgasm rippled around his fingers. He kept steady pressure on her clit until she shivered and went still.

Thea inhaled a huge, shuddering breath. That was definitely in the top five of the best orgasms she'd ever had in her life. She opened her eyes as Simon drew his fingers out of her, leaving her feeling a little empty and bereft. When he put those fingers in his mouth and sucked them clean, she felt her eyebrows shoot up.

"Why, Mr. Osman. You're like Clark Kent but with sexy times. Your glasses come off and you become NastyMan. Like Superman, but better."

His head ducked. "Sorry."

She twisted, grabbing his head and kissing him. "What? No! I like it. I just never knew you had it in you. And now I have something to look forward to having in me…"

He gave a little chuckle at her joke, and she let go of his face, resting her cheek on her hand. "You know what this means, now, don't you?" she asked.

His gaze, which had been down since she'd called him NastyMan, lifted to meet hers. "What?"

"It's time for me to figure out what you like. Unless you want to tell me."

He rolled to his back, his cock standing erect from its nest of auburn hair. "Oh, I'd love for you to find out."

"Maybe I'll even surprise you." He'd surprised her, after all.

"Maybe you will." His voice was like hot caramel drizzled over ice cream, warm and languid and slow.

"Hmm. Where to begin…" She considered his body, long and lean and absolutely mouthwatering. He folded his arms behind his head, a sly smile playing at the corners of his lips. She moved to the foot of the bed and grasped one of his feet, running the ball of her thumb firmly up his sole. He hummed with pleasure, but it was a *that's nice* sound, not an *oh god, I'm going to come* sound. She clasped his ankles, spreading them a little, then ran her hands from his ankles up to his inner thighs. This time, the pleasurable hum was more intense and she could feel goose bumps rising on his skin. "I feel like I'm getting warmer," she said as her fingers crept higher.

"Something's getting warmer," he agreed.

She didn't answer, just brought one hand up to the apex of his thighs, stroking from his ass to his balls. He swore softly. *Bingo.* "Interesting."

"You're evil," he said, but his eyelids stayed closed, apparently trusting her to continue. She continued to stroke upward, testing the depth of his belly button with one finger. That made him startle and twitch, face contorting.

"Okay, not that, then," she said, heat crawling up her cheeks. But there were no recriminations. He just settled himself back into his supine pose, somehow vulnerable and confident at the same time. She moved upward, tested her tongue against his nipple, nuzzled his neck, tugged his hair. All of these achieved positive responses, but nothing like the electric surge of her "evil" touch between his legs. Returning to kneel between his legs, she grasped the base of his cock with one hand, stroking upward with a light, teasing touch, then gradually increasing the pressure until she found what made his breath hitch and his thighs tense. She tongued the crown while steadily stroking, watching his face contort and his chest heave. Then she touched his ass again, stroking up as his butt clenched and he groaned. She lifted her head, eagerly watching as his eyes squeezed shut.

"Oh *god.*" The strangled cry was accompanied by a hot spurt that splashed onto his belly as he came. She stroked him through the rest of his pulsating orgasm until his body shuddered to a stop. He groaned faintly and then cracked one eye, looking at her. "Okay, then."

Thea laughed delightedly while he raised himself up on his elbows. "Kiss me," he said. She immediately crawled up his body and lowered herself onto him, her kiss all openmouthed carnality, her body pressing his back to the bed.

"Now we're both all sticky," he murmured against her mouth.

"Shh. That's what showers are for," she said, tangling her fingers in his hair and deepening the kiss until they were both panting. "Come on," she said, pushing herself up off him and standing by the bed, her hand extended. He took it, feeling sheepish at the mess he'd made of both of them. It was always like this—an odd sort of comedown after the bubble of sex. Reentering the real world. He followed her into the bathroom, a gorgeous expanse of white tile and glass that made him blink in the sudden glare.

"Sorry. I wish I had a dimmer in here," she said as she went to the big glass-walled shower and started the water.

"This is… Wow," he said as his eyes adjusted to the brightness and he was able to take in the big room, the shower with its multiple heads and the meticulous details. Like the rest of her home, this room was no contractor's special.

Thea tested the water temperature, then beckoned him over. "Nope. Mrs. M's son built this out because he thought she'd move in here in her waning years—which he also thought were imminent. She finished the build without the grab bars that he'd planned, but it's still roomy and easy to get around."

He moved to the shower stall, where she was testing the water temperature with one hand, his gaze roaming over her body. She was strong, the muscles in her shoulders defined, flowing into sculpted biceps. He trailed a fingertip over the swells and dips of those muscles, watching her face as the corners of her lips tipped up.

"Like what you see?" she asked, straightening her spine.

"Yes."

"Well then." She tugged him into the shower enclosure and stepped under the spray, letting it run over her hair and cascade down her body. He soaped his hands and ran them over her shoulders and down her arms, enjoying the slick, nearly frictionless feeling of his skin sliding against hers. She pushed her wet hair out of her eyes and squinted at him, grabbing the soap in her own turn and smoothing her hands over his chest, cleaning off the semen. "Someone was more than a little dirty," she said.

"Someone was inspired." He kissed her, stepping closer, their slick torsos meeting under the rushing water.

They continued to kiss and wash each other until Simon noticed his fingers resembled prunes.

Finally, wrapped in towels and with their hair still damp, Thea said, "Do you want to stay the night?"

Her question made his heart flutter and thump like a frightened bird. He knew what he wanted, but he had to know if she was just being polite. He knew better than most how sex could feel incredibly intimate, but could also be an illusion of intimacy. The fantasy of his adolescence was dissolving into a reality that might be even better than what he'd imagined all those years ago. But could he trust it?

"Do you want me to stay?" he asked.

"Yes."

To hell with it, then. "Okay, I will."

Fourteen

After she found him a spare toothbrush and they finished getting cleaned up, he followed her to her bedroom. The cool sheets felt wonderful against his clean, bare skin. His arousal still simmered beneath the surface, but fatigue nibbled at his limbs and made reality feel a little hazy. It had been a long time since he'd gone to bed with anyone, and it surprised him how much it had taken out of him.

Thea turned out the light, then he could hear rustling as she turned. "So you were a Casanova in library school, huh?"

The question, seemingly floating out of nowhere in the darkness, made him laugh. "Heck no. I was just going to do what I did in college—maybe date a little and mostly keep my head down, do the work, get my degree. But I was a lot more visible in graduate school than I was in college."

"Visible how?" He could almost hear the crease between her brows as she tried to puzzle out what he meant.

He turned to his back, folding his hands behind his head,

and took in a deep breath. Let it go. "I was kind of rare in that environment. Straight, cisgender men aren't exactly common in library programs, you know?"

More rustling and a finger poking him in the sternum. "Sure. That was the only reason. Nothing to do with you being a hottie or anything." He poked her back for her sarcasm and she laughed. "The women came to you, huh?"

Simon's face went hot. That was exactly what had happened, and at first, he'd been bewildered. He'd later found out that it had all begun because he'd gone on a single date with a classmate he'd met at orientation. Apparently, the news that he was attracted to women had spread like wildfire through the graduate program. Since he was set on completing his degree in one year, he had a heavy course load and developing a social life hadn't been a priority.

But one had found him all the same.

"Um. Yeah. I'd had one serious girlfriend in college. She was…very direct, I guess you could say. I learned a lot from her. And when a library classmate offered me a no-strings fling, it seemed like a good way to blow off steam just as I was finally getting the hang of being in graduate school." He'd learned a lot more from her—like how he couldn't take for granted that her body wanted the same things as his ex's had. How to pay attention to subtle signals, to learn when things worked and when they didn't. He'd always liked learning and experimentation and getting gold stars for doing a good job.

"And a lot of women can really *talk*, so I'm guessing word got around," Thea said, her voice soft.

She was perceptive as hell. It should have been almost disturbing. But for once, feeling seen wasn't scary. He *wanted*

Thea to see him. All of him. "Yeah. When we stopped seeing each other, it was like they were operating off one of those number machines at the deli. It was kind of frightening, honestly. The attention was too much. I kind of shut everything down and went into that first exam period feeling like I was wearing armor the whole time. But when we came back from winter break, there was this woman I sat with in a couple of classes. We became friends and then more. For a while." It had gone on like that to the end of his jam-packed year of classes. Little micro-relationships that didn't last, where neither of them even expected it to last. Until it was the last one and she'd thought they were going to continue after they graduated and went on the job market.

And then, Simon had realized he'd been assuming, taking things for granted all over again.

He wasn't proud of how that had ended. But he didn't regret that it had. What he had now was far more than what he'd imagined with Thea when they were younger. It was better. And he wasn't going to screw it up by not paying attention.

Thea listened intently to this stop-and-start story. The faint light of the moon made Simon's outline barely visible now that her eyes had adjusted to the dimness. "So there were more people you had 'more for a while' relationships with?"

He shifted, the sheets sliding against his skin, and she wished she felt confident enough to wrap herself around him as he talked. But she'd long ago learned that intense physical intimacy and intense emotional intimacy could be very different things and confusing the two could lead to explosive problems.

His voice rasped out of the dimness. "Yeah. It was only a year, and trust me, I wasn't a Casanova at all. It wasn't messy or anything. The both of us would get really busy working on more than one project or paper at the same time or getting into exams and the connection would just kind of dissolve. Or in one instance, she graduated before I did and moved on. No hard feelings or anything like that."

"Sounds like there's a 'but' lurking somewhere there."

He sighed. Shifted. The covers moved down and she tugged them up against the chill. "Yeah. The last woman I dated. I'd gotten used to thinking that nothing was going to come of any of it, you know? We were graduating at the same time and that's when I learned we had opposite assumptions. She thought we'd look around, find an area of the country that might have good prospects for the both of us and move. I never had any intention of leaving this area."

She did some mental math. "Plus, you were young."

"Yeah. Twenty-three. In hindsight I wasn't in any position to be playing house with anyone. I had so much learning and growing to do." He paused and she could almost hear him thinking. "But at the time, it was just confusing. She'd been so sure that I wanted what she wanted."

Thea considered his personality: the stern, almost dour side. The playful side. But even in both of those extremes and in between, he'd told her a few things. He wasn't entirely shut off. And presumably he'd known that other woman longer. "Had you talked about it?"

There was a bit of silence, then he said, "She said we had. But we hadn't said, 'Let's make plans.' It was more she said things like, 'Have you ever thought about living somewhere else?' and I'd say that sure I had, because who hasn't considered such a thing? But she never continued the conversation, so I thought it was just filling dead air." Another silence. "I learned later that there's a strong passive-aggressive streak in the librarian community."

"Huh." Passive-aggressive could get you injured or dead in an emergency services squad, but those kinds of stakes weren't as high in most other jobs. Still, Thea found herself judging this unknown woman a little even as she empathized with her. "Do you know where she ended up?"

"Last I knew, she moved to Arizona. We're not in touch."

"Sounds like she might have gotten what she wanted."

"Hope so. She wasn't a bad person, just, well—like I said, we were both young. I didn't necessarily know what I wanted, but I knew I didn't want to settle down just yet."

"Do you know what you want now?"

More sounds of him shifting and she felt him coming closer. Then a light touch on her arm, as if he wasn't sure where she was in the dark, moving to slide up and around the back of her neck. "Not completely, but a heck of a lot more than I did at twenty-three. What about you?"

It was nice, that warm hand cradling her neck. More than nice. This guarded man, this human *vault* had opened himself up to her.

She took a deep breath, settling herself. "I think I'm kind of the same. Especially with the whole career change and all that. It's unsettling, you know? But this is really nice."

He moved his hand down her back, tugging her closer, and she rolled so she was spooned up against his front, body heat radiating into her back. "Yeah. It really is."

* * *

When Simon woke up, it took him a few moments to get oriented. The ceiling was too high, the morning light came from the wrong side. The view outside the window wasn't of another building and three floors up. It was ground level and looked out on a dormant winter garden with trees in the distance.

Memories of last night flooded through him. *Thea.* Rolling over, he found her curled up facing him, her face looking impossibly young and relaxed in sleep. He resisted the urge to trace a fingertip over one rounded cheekbone or brush aside the hair falling across her closed eyes. Carefully, he eased himself out of bed, finding yesterday's clothes and slipping them on. The air in her little house was chilly, but not unpleasant once he was dressed.

Not to mention he had no desire to wander around her place naked if Mrs. M was going to show up unannounced again.

Padding in socks to her little kitchen, he located her coffee and filters and made a pot, finding cups in the cabinet above. While he waited for it to brew, he wandered over to the shelves that made up the walls to her bedroom. Not quite reaching the ceiling, they were nonetheless built-ins, not afterthoughts. Closer to the kitchen, they mostly contained a few cookbooks and larger items that he guessed didn't fit into the little kitchen's cupboards. There was one hand-thrown bowl that looked like it might be a piece of art or might be useful. Maybe both.

The rest of the shelves making up the longer side of her bedroom were almost entirely taken up with books. Fiction in a variety of genres. Biographies and a few histories. At the far end of the bottom shelf was a set of training manuals for emergency first responders. Scattered among all this literature were a few framed photographs, mostly older shots of Thea and what had to be her older sister and her parents. There were a few newer photos of her with two little boys: the monster nephews, he guessed.

And then there was a single photo in a simple frame of Thea that had to have been taken within the last couple of years. She was standing in front of a gleaming red fire truck in bright sunlight, grinning maniacally and dressed in what looked like a firefighter's uniform: navy shirt and trousers, a logo over her breast. To one side of her was a Black man a few inches taller than her, and on the other side was an enormous guy who looked like a model from a Brawny paper towel ad. Both of them were dressed identically to her, and they all had that indefinable ease of close colleagues or even found family. Friends.

Some of her old firefighting squad.

A pang went through his chest when he realized he hadn't really heard her talk about them. She'd talked a bit about the job, but if these two men were the only nonfamily members sitting on her shelves in the same pride of place as her family, they must mean something to her.

Not that he'd been super forthcoming about any of his own stuff. But he wondered if the fact that she didn't talk about them had anything to do with her anxiety.

The coffeepot burbled to an end at that point, so he wandered back into the kitchen to pour himself a cup. Taking it over to the sofa, he pulled out his phone, intending to check his email, but his attention was arrested by a half-familiar book cover on the coffee table. He leaned forward, putting the cup down and picking up her copy of their high school senior yearbook.

"Yeah. I went down memory lane." Thea stood on the threshold of her bedroom in a short bathrobe, scratching the back of one calf with the toes of her other foot, a blush flooding her cheeks. "I don't usually keep that out. It lives in the storage space up there." She pointed at the ceiling.

Simon patted the sofa cushion next to him. "Well, let's come have a walk down memory lane together, then."

She'd been lured out by the smell of coffee, so she detoured to the kitchen to pour herself a cup before she walked to the living space. Curling up next to Simon, she grabbed the supremely ugly afghan of crocheted granny squares her *nonna* had made for her when she went to college. It was hideous, but it was also warm. She tucked half around her lap and feet and offered the other side to Simon, who smiled and draped it over his knees.

"Do you want me to turn the heat up?" she asked.

He turned a tiny, wicked smile her way. "Not if keeping it chilly will make you cuddle with me."

Well. She didn't need any more encouragement. She liked this side of Simon, unexpected as it was. Scooting closer, she rested her head on his shoulder, and he wrapped an arm around hers, heat flowing from his body. "Where should we start? Which end of memory lane? The end with the flowers or the weeds?"

He flipped the cover open, revealing all the handwritten

notes expanding out from corners, etched in sturdy blocks in the middle of the page, or in one case, spiraling out from a center letter and making the reader turn the book around and around to read the message. "My adolescence was pretty much all weeds, but it looks like you had a few more flowers," he said.

"Oh, mine had plenty of weeds. I just had some creative friends. I guess they were flowers, now that you mention it."

His finger traced the spiral of well wishes that someone he didn't know had inscribed and he nodded. "Yeah. That might've helped. If I'd let it."

She captured his finger, then wrapped her hand around his. "Adolescence isn't fun for anyone. It wasn't fun for me, though I had some moments of joy. I think maybe you're mourning something that wasn't really possible. Except maybe for the truly popular kids. And it seems to me that if someone truly enjoys adolescence and it isn't an illusion or an act, they usually end up peaking young. I wouldn't trade."

He turned his hand in hers, squeezing. "I just guess I never let myself be young when I was young. I mean, I was never good at it—letting go, being spontaneous, any of it. I didn't try anything creative when I could just… I don't know. *Do* stuff. Try stuff."

She thought about what she knew about him. And what she didn't. "Your job now has a certain amount of creativity. Does that help?"

He nodded, shifting a little as he closed the yearbook and put it on the coffee table. "Yeah. It does. I just wish things had been different back in the day. Maybe I'd be better at my job now."

She sat up a little, indignant. "You're awesome at your job. I wouldn't have thought of half the things you do to make everything run smoothly that you've taught me."

He tugged her close again, tucking her head under his chin. "You're talking about admin stuff, process stuff. I'm talking about creativity. Reaching people. Because process helps grease the wheels, but it isn't what really connects with people. I worry sometimes that I'm too cut off, too rules based."

She cringed internally, remembering that had been exactly her impression of him. "But there's another side of you," she almost whispered. "I saw it last night, but I've seen it before too. Your focus is so strong, you pay such attention. You're so good with kids."

He barked a laugh. "You should have seen me panic when Noah busted out all the *why* questions and I realized you were right."

She poked him in the ribs just enough to make him squirm a little. "Yeah, but everyone panics when they get that fire hose of *why?* I saw you with those kids at the library. You see them as people. That matters."

"They are people though." He seemed puzzled.

She sipped her coffee, suppressing a smile. "You'd be surprised at how many adults don't seem to remember that though."

Fifteen

Simon leaned forward slowly, not wanting to disturb Thea while he grabbed his coffee. "Speaking of kids, I was looking at your shelves while you were sleeping."

She turned her head to look at him, a crooked grin on her face. "Really?"

He leaned back, cradling the warm mug. "Yeah. Your nephews are cute."

"Still monsters though." But there was affection and pride in her voice.

There was a long silence while they sipped their coffee. "I saw the photo of you and your former colleagues too."

She didn't stiffen, but she did go still, like a small animal wanting to be overlooked by a predator. He went on, gentling his voice. "But the only other photos you have out are of your family. Obviously those guys—from your old squad— are important to you."

"Sean and Felix."

"You don't talk about them," he said, not sure why he kept going. Usually, he was comfortable with cues that people wanted silence. But her silence about them felt wrong, somehow, a discordant note in her usually harmonious personality. It nagged at him, worried him in a way he couldn't quite articulate.

"No. I don't." The words should have sounded like a closed door, but her voice was soft. Sad.

Alarm twisted through him. "Did they do something to you?"

She turned in his arm, anguish in her big brown eyes. "No!" It was his turn to freeze. He hated that he'd pushed her to this corner. Why couldn't he have just kept his mouth shut? He was usually so good at that. But around Thea, his usual filters seemed gone. Obliterated. His worry for her had overridden his usual caution.

She swallowed, her throat convulsing, her eyes closing. "They're like brothers to me. Sean—the big guy—he got really badly injured in a callout in the spring. I thought he might die. And…" She ran a hand through her hair, shaggy with bedhead, strands sticking straight up in a way that in any other context he would find endearing, but now he found distressing. Her gaze lifted to meet his again, glassy with unshed tears that ripped his heart open. "And that was when I started to lose my nerve. I went into emergency services when my favorite cousin had to leave it. I felt young, invincible. But Sean really *was* the most invincible guy I'd ever met. And there he was—alive, but completely reliant on his girlfriend for just about everything. Pale. Sick. Injured. It rattled me in a way I didn't know was possible." Her face crumpled, her mouth going square with grief.

Simon took her cup from her hands and put it down on the table with his, then folded her in his arms. "Is he okay?"

She nodded, her hair rubbing against his shoulder.

"Good." He hated to see her like this, but maybe she needed to get that grief out. It didn't seem right that she should wall off such a traumatic event and never talk about it. "I'm sorry," he said as tears began to soak through his shirt. "But you know what? In some ways you're my Sean."

"What do you mean?" She sniffed, and he grasped her shoulders, pulling her away from him a little so he could look her in the eye.

"I thought you were fearless. I thought you were invincible. Turns out, you were more than that. You were brave."

Her eyebrows crimped together and she sniffed again. "What's the difference?"

"Fearless means you either don't feel anything or you ignore what you feel. All too often, it's foolishness. But bravery means you know what fear looks like and you work through it. Bravery also knows when you've had enough and says so. You did both of those things."

She sniffed and her eyes slid sideways.

"How is Sean now?" He didn't feel great that the question came easier now that he'd learned the big man had a girlfriend. But there was always Felix. How she might've felt about him now that they weren't colleagues anymore. *Shut it down*, he thought. *She said those guys were her brothers*. Plus, she was here with him. She'd chosen him. She'd opened up to him. Accepted his comfort when he offered it.

Another sniff. "Sean's all better. Or he says he is. He's back on the job."

"Do you miss it? The job?"

She seemed to seriously consider the question. "Sometimes? I like learning new things, so the new job has been really fun in a way I haven't had much of for a long time. But mostly I just miss the squad."

There was the truth he'd suspected all along. "And I bet they miss you too."

"Yeah?" Her voice, so small, so cracked, nearly broke his heart.

"Yeah. And I'll bet they'll be ready for you whenever you're ready for them."

Wrung out from the unexpected emotion, Thea stretched, shrugging off Simon's arm. He was being so sweet, but sweetness was going to crack her open and she wasn't ready for that. "Breakfast?" she asked with a sort of unnatural chirpiness that sounded harsh in her own ears. "I'm glad you figured the coffee machine out. It's an unexpected luxury, waking up with caffeine already made."

Okay, now she was just babbling.

She slid forward, ready to get up, but looked back. It was a mistake. Never look back. His face was a little sad, a little understanding. A lot heartbreaking. She took a deep breath and extended a hand. "How do you like your eggs?"

"Doesn't matter. What would you say to going back to bed?"

A grin stretched her face. "Oh, are you tired?"

He skimmed the shell of her ear with a fingertip, making

her shivery and ticklish. "Exhausted. I'm not sure how I am still upright." How did he make his face so serious but still show laughter in his eyes?

"Well." She linked her hand with his, tugging him back toward the bedroom. "Let's get you off your feet. I'd hate to have you collapse."

"You did spend a decade in emergency services. I assume you have the skills to keep me alive."

She turned in the doorway, lifting her fingertips to feel the pulse in his neck. His heartbeat was strong and sure. Maybe a little fast. "I think you need mouth-to-mouth." She cracked up then, not able to maintain a poker face while making a joke that corny.

He cupped her cheeks, stilling her laughter. "Yeah. I think I do." The kiss that followed started with a nip of his teeth on her lower lip, then progressed to a confident press of his mouth on hers, their faces slanting, tongues tangling until she was breathless. The backs of her legs hit the edge of her bed, and she realized he'd walked her backward without her even being aware of it. He pulled back a little, reached into his back pocket and pulled out his wallet. Finding a condom, he tossed it on her bedside table.

"Now..." he murmured, tugging gently at the tie that belted her robe closed. "Last night, I came up with some theories I want to test this morning."

"Theories?" she asked as he pushed the robe off her shoulders. It puddled at her feet and she straightened her spine. He'd made it clear last night that he liked her body. She liked it too—it was strong and capable—but his appreciation was next-level and it gave her an additional boost.

"Yeah. Theories." He kissed her again. "Lie down in the middle of the bed."

"Okay…" She complied, watching him as he took his shirt off, then climbed onto the mattress at her feet. "Just the shirt?"

"For now," he said, grasping her ankles and pulling them apart. Then he slid his palms up the inside of her legs, making goose bumps break out on her skin. Finally, he lowered himself, draped her knees over his shoulders, and his mouth covered her pussy.

Holy shit.

Ah, yes. Thea's clit was exquisitely sensitive and she *definitely* liked his tongue. He tickled it lightly, the barest touch with the tip, and she groaned. He gave her another lick, tracing the edge of one labia, then giving her clit another one of those delicate touches that had pleased her before. Her taste, her smell intoxicated him, and he ground his hips into the mattress, his own arousal competing with his desire to make her wild with pleasure.

He lifted his head and looked up her body as he slid one finger into her, curling it upward, pulling a shuddering sigh from her. "What do you want?" he asked, letting his finger pulse and curl inside her, seeking to stimulate her as much as he possibly could.

"More." The single syllable was another ragged groan. He grinned and dipped his head, increasing the pressure of his tongue on that swelling, stiffening bud as he added another finger. Her head thrashed on the pillow and her thighs trembled on his shoulders. God, she was so close already. But he knew her orgasm would be more powerful if he drew it out.

He lessened the touch of his tongue but kept up the insistent pulse and curl of his fingers. She shuddered again. "Bastard."

He chuckled and nuzzled into the soft flesh of her inner thigh with the dusting of whiskers that had bristled into being overnight, eliciting another groan, this one almost a wail. He gave her skin a gentle nip with his teeth and returned his mouth to her pussy, teasing and licking until he could hear her panting, her chest heaving.

"Simon." Her voice was ragged, pleading. Almost a whine.

"Mmm." He gave her a more muscular lick, and her hips shifted restlessly. He debated keeping her there on that knife-edge for as long as he could, savoring her reactions: breath sawing, legs trembling, hands curling into the coverlet as if she could rip an orgasm out of the cotton.

"Please." Now she was barely whispering. "Now. Please. Now," she chanted.

He took pity on her, flicking her clit with his tongue until her whole body shuddered and she sobbed out her release, her inner walls squeezing his fingers.

Drawing his soaked hand away, he licked away the remains of her arousal, amused at the way she peered at him with narrowed eyes.

"You're *evil*."

"Were you satisfied?" he asked, army crawling up her body until he could kiss her.

"You know I was." Another tremor went through her body, then she softened underneath him. She drew in a long breath, let it out. Then, seeming to regain her energy, she slid her hands between them and fumbled with the button of his jeans, getting it open and barely able to slide the zipper down since he was practically lying flush on top of her. His throbbing cock protested as he reduced the pressure by lifting his hips, and she shoved his clothes down, his erection springing free like it was escaping jail. She twisted and stretched an arm out to try to get the condom he'd so casually tossed on the bedside table. It was just beyond her reach and she gave an adorable, furious little grunt of frustration.

"Patience," he soothed, rising to his feet and pushing his jeans and underwear off. Free now to roll over, she did, snagging the packet. But before she could get on her back again, he got back on the bed, smoothing his hands over the tight curve of her ass. "Mmm. I didn't get a good look at this before."

"Look your fill." She pulled her knees underneath her and rose to her hands, pushing her butt against his erection.

"Oh, you are really going to kill me, aren't you?" he asked.

She swayed back and forth, brushing him with her ass, then lifted the condom, wafting it in time with her hips.

"You say *I'm* evil," he muttered, snatching the packet from her fingers.

"Payback's a bitch and so am I," she said as he dealt with the wrapper and rolled it on, then rubbed the head of his cock up and down, paying special attention to her clit until she collapsed to her elbows and whimpered.

"There we go." He grinned and slid home.

Oh, she'd suspected that Simon would feel good when he finally got inside her, but he felt *good*. He smoothed his hands down the slope of her back as he drove inside. There was something tender and oddly intimate about such a nonsexual touch combined with his unrestrained carnality. He drew out again, dragging himself ever so slowly until she was almost empty, then filling her up again with the same agonizing, gradual motion.

Bracing herself on her elbows as he pressed himself just a bit tighter to her body, she looked back over her shoulder. "You are king of the long buildup," she growled.

He gripped her hips and gave her another long, slow thrust. "What makes you think I don't like drawing out my own pleasure the same way I like to draw yours out?"

She grunted as he slid home again, her sensitized, swollen flesh magnifying every sensation. "Fair. I guess."

"C'mere," he said, wrapping his arms around her waist, lifting her and leaning back until she was resting on his thighs, his cock still inside her and her back pressed to his chest.

"What are you doing?" she asked, her own voice hazy in her ears. He couldn't exactly thrust in this position, but she did feel lovely and full.

Sliding his hands up her torso, he cupped her breasts and began to tease the back of her neck with his lips and teeth and tongue. Thea knew her neck was sensitive, but impaled on him like this, her knees wide, she felt exposed and helpless and very, very turned on. Each nip, lick and kiss seemed to send signals to her clit and he hadn't even touched her there since he entered her.

Then he started to play with her nipples, pinching and tugging in the way he'd done the night before, stopping just shy of pain, sending more sensations shooting through her.

"That's it. Take it. Take me," he murmured against her neck, nipping one earlobe. She began to rock, to undulate, seeking more sensation as she ground on his cock, almost finding what she was seeking—incredibly—with no external stimulation of her clit.

She groaned, a ragged, frustrated sound, and he chuckled, hot breath puffing against her skin. Then a particular twist of her hips and a well-timed tug on her nipples sent her unexpectedly spiraling, shuddering, *soaring*. Simon cursed, and she dropped back to her hands and knees as he began to pump into her in earnest, a final quick snap of his hips punctuated by a soft moan of satisfaction.

Thea's eyes slid closed as she collapsed onto the bed, Simon following, covering her like a living blanket. Both of them breathed hard, as if they'd been running.

"I need to deal with the condom," he mumbled almost unintelligibly against her neck.

"Ngh." She wasn't capable of more at the moment. She didn't want him to move, but she did know he was right.

He pushed himself up as if gravity had doubled, and she heard him go to the bathroom, the toilet flush, the water run. Then he was back, rolling her to one side and the other so he could get the covers over her and slide in beside her as if he was just as at home here as she was. She realized, as he tucked her hair behind one ear and gave her a slightly loopy smile, that she didn't feel put out or that he was being presumptuous. She liked that he felt at home here, in her place.

"I didn't know my body could do that," she said when the power of speech returned to her.

"Do what?"

"Come without direct contact on my clit. How did you know?"

He shrugged one shoulder. "I didn't. I just experimented with what I knew turned you on."

"Man of science," she mumbled right before she slid back into sleep.

Sixteen

Something in Simon's chest seemed to turn over on itself as he watched Thea drift off. It felt strange: protective and almost tender. This tough, brave woman had been vulnerable enough to cry in his arms, give him pleasure and let him draw pleasure out of her body. That vulnerability felt like an impossibly precious gift.

His musings were interrupted by a buzzing from his pile of clothes on the floor. He swore softly and slid out of bed, his eyes on Thea, but she was apparently a sound sleeper. He found his phone and sent the call to voicemail before he even saw who it was. Then he checked his call log and groaned silently. *Ashley.* His family had apparently read his email letting them know about his short dash there and back over Christmas.

Scrambling into his clothes, he grabbed his shoes and his phone and padded quickly to Thea's front door. He shoved his feet into his shoes and slipped outside, closing the door silently behind him. Damn. It was cold. He should have grabbed his coat. Well, he couldn't now. His phone was already buzzing again.

"Hey, Ash."

"I got your *email*," she said as if the words *you coward* were appended to her statement.

"Yeah, I figured you would. That's what it's for." Simon shoved his free hand into his pocket and paced, aware of the flapping of his shoelaces he hadn't had a chance to tie.

"What the fuck, Si? You're only coming for two whole days? And you're arriving at midday on *Christmas Day*?"

Simon's teeth ground together. He hated when she used that nickname and she knew it. "Yeah. I told you I didn't think I was going to be able to get a lot of time, what with last year and all." Clammy sweat coated his forehead and he shivered in the cold.

"Last year you weren't even with us for a week. Can't you tell them you need more time?"

"No, I can't. I already told you I can't. At least I was able to find a good deal on flights. No need to bother Mom and Dad."

"Whatever. We have family *traditions*, Simon. And you won't be pulling your weight."

What she meant was he usually happily did a lot—if not most—of the prep work because he liked that behind-the-scenes planning kind of gig. But it would never occur to Ashley that she could do some of these things. Or, God forbid, ask her husband to pitch in. Once everything was just how she liked it, it couldn't possibly change. "Yeah, we had family traditions when everybody lived within a half hour's drive from one another. But obviously, traditions change. I can't be there. Use this as an opportunity to show Noah what goes into an Osman Christmas."

"You know I can't do half the stuff you do, Simon. The family needs you to do all the stuff you always do." Oh great. The whining had started. And he heard the not-so-hidden message: it wasn't his presence that she wanted. It was the work he put into the holidays. The distance from the rest of his family, both geographic and psychological, was making some things that had previously been easy to ignore painfully clear.

"Well, then simplify. The family will do just fine with fewer traditions, and I'll see you on Christmas Day. That's the best I can do. I am not losing my job because you can't make sugar cookies."

"It's not just the cookies, and you know it." Ashley's voice had taken on that dangerous, silky note that the entire family watched out for.

"Fine. Just do what you can. Noah won't care. He's a little kid. Christmas will be magical for him no matter what."

"What about the rest of us?" she snapped. But Simon heard the real message. *What about me?*

"Again, I'm not losing my job because of this. You guys were the ones who moved. Maybe you need to make some new traditions."

At this point, Simon could hear his brother-in-law's deep voice in the background, and Ash said briskly, "Okay, fine. Whatever. I'll talk to you later," and hung up.

"Well, that went better than I would have expected," Simon muttered to himself. A hard shiver racked his whole body. The cold had sunk its claws deep in him as he stood there having this pointless argument. Turning to Thea's front door, he tried to twist the knob. It was locked.

Shit.

"You might want to come inside and warm up over here, young man," said a familiar voice. Turning away from Thea's door, he saw her landlady standing at the back of her house, her expression stern.

Busted. He didn't know quite what for, but he knew trouble when he saw it.

Simon followed Mrs. M in through a set of French doors that led into a spacious, comfortable living room with a lovely view of Thea's little house and the gardens that stretched to the side of it. There was a real fire crackling away on a brick hearth, and a newspaper lay folded on one of the chairs to one side of the fireplace—she must have seen him as he slipped outside and had his call with Ashley.

"Sit," she said sternly, pointing to an armchair on the opposite side of the fireplace before settling into what was obviously her favorite chair. He sat. If he was going to get the third degree, at least he'd enjoy a radiant heat source.

"Well, young man. Do you often slip out of bed to have a clandestine phone call with another woman?"

It took Simon a second to process what she'd said. "Wait—you think that was a clandestine phone call?" He'd braced himself for the possibility of a moral judgment about him staying the night at Thea's. This he didn't expect.

"You went out in the cold to take it. I assume Thea's home, otherwise you would have stayed inside." Mrs. M was giving him what probably passed for a steely gaze with her kids, but

Simon just felt kind of warm and fuzzy that she was so protective of Thea. He guessed not a lot of people felt the need to protect her.

"Yeah. She's asleep," he admitted. "I didn't want to have an argument with my *sister* and wake her up."

The older woman blinked. "Your sister?" Then her disconcertingly pale eyes went hard again. "You're not just giving me the runaround?"

"I wouldn't." Simon unlocked his phone and scrolled through his photos, finding one that his mother sent him a few weeks ago. Ashley and Ray on the sofa, with Noah between them. They'd all been looking at a picture book. Noah was probably asking *why?* He turned the device to Mrs. M and she peered at it. "That's my sister and her husband and my nephew. She's upset that I can't come out to California any earlier for the holidays, and she keeps winding me up about it."

Her gaze transferred from the screen to his face. "Sounds like there's more of a story there."

He sighed and shifted in his seat, lifting his hips so he could stuff the phone into his back pocket. He gave her the barest outline of his situation: the family's move west, his remaining here, the holiday situation between last year and this. Ash's insistence that he bend reality and the library's scheduling needs to her will because they conflicted with her demands. As his story unfurled, Mrs. M relaxed into her wing chair, a sad little smile on her face.

"So when I saw Ash had called, I knew it was going to be drama and Thea was asleep and—" Belatedly, he realized he was essentially talking about Thea's sex life to her landlady. Not cool.

"And you had your very unpleasant conversation with your sister in the cold and then ended up locked out. Then you had the additional unpleasantness of being interrogated by an old lady." Those pale eyes were twinkling with humor now, and Simon felt a surge of affection for this woman who had Thea's back.

"No," he said carefully, his eyes not leaving hers, "I was escorted into a very comfortable, well-appointed room with a lovely fire to burn away the chill by someone who is clearly protective of someone I admire a great deal."

Mrs. M raised one long finger and pointed it at him like a fencer leveling an épée. "Nicely played, young man."

Thea woke up in slow stages, floating lazily into full consciousness. She stretched, feeling twinges from muscles she rarely used and a dull, satisfying ache between her legs. Cracking her eyes open, she looked at the pillow next to her.

Simon was gone.

Bewilderment and hurt flooded through her together with adrenaline. She sat up suddenly, looking around her bedroom. His clothes were gone. But his wallet was still on the nightstand. *Weird.* She got out of bed and tugged on a pair of sweatpants and a T-shirt. Shivering, she added a hoodie and a thick pair of wool socks to her oh-so-sexy getup. Padding out into the living area, she saw his coat still on the row of hooks by the door and his keys were on the kitchen counter. But no Simon. *Even weirder.* His car still sat out in front of the house.

She cracked the door open. Again, no Simon. *Where the hell did he go?* Then she spied the curl of smoke coming from Mrs. M's chimney. Grabbing her own keys and stuffing her feet into boots, she fast walked to the patio at the back of the big house and the French doors. Peering through the glass, she could see Simon deep in conversation with Mrs. M.

Well, that answered the *where* question, but the *why* question was still wide-open. She tapped on the glass and Mrs. M looked up, then waved her in.

"What is it you two have against coats?" the older woman asked with mock crossness as Thea shut the door behind her.

"What are *you* two up to?" Thea asked, taking a seat on the love seat that faced the fireplace, flanked by the two armchairs Simon and Mrs. M sat in. She felt weirdly like she was at a job interview.

"Simon went outside to take a call and got locked out. He didn't want to disturb you, and I saw him out there in the cold, so I invited him in." She turned a twinkling, mischievous gaze on him, and he gave her an arch look in return.

Okay, these two were totally up to something.

"What's the real story?" she asked Simon.

"Well, Mrs. M thought I was sneaking out of your house to talk to a girlfriend."

Ice shot through her belly. "Girlfriend?"

Simon held up a hand. "Which I was not. I was taking a call from my bossy sister. I knew it would be an argument, so I didn't want to risk waking you up. I had thought Mrs. M was worried about your virtue when she called me in on the carpet."

Thea's landlady waved a dismissive hand, the huge diamond she still wore on her left ring finger winking in the firelight. "Virtue schmirtue. Thea's an adult woman and I am not her mother. I don't worry about her making her own decisions, but I do worry about her tender heart sometimes."

"Tender heart? Me?" Thea pointed at her own chest.

Simon nodded solemnly. "Mrs. M has a definite point there."

"I'm not so sure I like that you two have decided to gang up on me," Thea said, but she couldn't keep her mouth from curving into a smile. Their obvious care for her was as warming as the fire on the hearth.

"It's for your own good, dear," Mrs. M said with a satisfied smile. "I like this young man." Her expression went thoughtful as her gaze ping-ponged from his face to Thea's. "How about I make you two some breakfast? Unless you're eager to get back to your romantic idyll."

There was something that Thea didn't usually see in her landlady's face. It looked like loneliness. Without looking to Simon for confirmation, she nodded briskly. "We'd love it."

"Have breakfast catered by a wealthy widow" hadn't been on Simon's list of things to expect today, but he found himself settled happily in a bright, sunny kitchen. While he wasn't an expert on interior design, it occurred to him that the pale green cabinets were old enough that they had gone past "dated" and slid toward "funky and vintage." Mrs. M refused all offers of help and bustled around, getting coffee brewing and pulling out an enormous cast-iron skillet that looked exceedingly well cared for.

"How does everyone like their eggs?" she asked as she settled the pan onto the stovetop. Simon expressed a preference for scrambled and Thea agreed. She shot him a quick look that

seemed half happiness and half gratitude, and when Mrs. M
went to turn on the stove, she mouthed *thanks* at him. As if she
wasn't sure he'd be on board with hanging out with Mrs. M.

Of course, he mouthed back at her and, impossibly, her expression got even sunnier.

"How long have you lived here, Mrs. M?" he asked his
hostess.

She paused, a carton of eggs in her hands. "Well, Mr. Mc-
Anally and I bought the house over forty years ago just before
we had our first child—that would be Kyle." She directed the
last bit to Thea with a theatrical eye roll.

"Ah. He's the one who started the renovation that ended
up being Thea's house?" Simon asked.

She nodded, briskly cracking eggs into a bowl. "Yes. He's
a busybody, but he's my busybody and I can handle him."

Simon privately figured there was very little this redoubt-
able lady couldn't handle. "How many children do you have?"

She seasoned the eggs and fetched a fork from a drawer,
beating them soundly until they were frothy. "After Kyle
there's Kara and Katrina—don't ask. Mr. M had a thing for
names beginning with *K*, lord rest his soul."

"Do they all still live in the area?" His interest in Mrs. M's
life earned him another approving look from Thea, though
he didn't feel he deserved it. The woman was interesting in
her own right; it wasn't like he was buttering her up.

Speaking of butter, the cast-iron skillet sizzled with it, and
Mrs. M tipped the eggs into the hot pan. His mouth watered
as the aroma hit his nose. Mrs. M stirred the eggs and then
popped bread into the toaster. "Kara is in Atlanta, but Katrina
stuck around and now works with her brother. Though I use

the term *with* with some reservations. She and Kyle have always butted heads."

"Where do they work?" Simon asked.

She shot him a startled look, as if he should have known. "The company their grandfather founded. McAnally Construction."

Oh. Now the big house on the huge lot in one of the most expensive zip codes in the area made sense. Simon felt like he should have realized it before. The huge block letters of McAnally Construction signs were all over projects in downtown DC. And if the late Mr. McAnally's father had been the one to found the company...

Yeah. The family's wealth made perfect sense now.

Mrs. M twinkled at him. "Putting two and two together, young man?"

He raised a hand in surrender. "Yeah. You got me. My dad worked in commercial real estate before he retired, so I feel like I should have figured it out before."

She shrugged, stirring the eggs with a spatula. "Boring stuff, real estate and construction. You should tell me more about your work. Thea tells me you're a librarian. What is that like?"

Seventeen

Thea wanted to crow with glee. She hadn't been at all sure how Mrs. M would feel about Simon being here. After all, this property was the older woman's home, and even though Thea lived in the little accessory house, she was always aware of that fact.

She hadn't even had time to consider how Simon would feel about Mrs. M. At least, not consciously. Some people, her sister included, found her friendship with the older woman odd. As soon as she'd said yes to Mrs. M's breakfast invitation, she was flooded with the worry that he wouldn't value her landlady and friend the way she did. But she should have known better. The tension that seized her gut when she'd accepted the offer was now leaching away.

He clearly valued the older woman and her perspective. And that gave her a warm glow, watching them chat about libraries, his job, social media and the training he'd been giving Thea. It turned out that Mrs. M had been on a school library advisory board when her kids were young. "Not one of those horrible book-banning ones either," she said, pointing a spatula at Simon.

"Kindred spirits, then," he replied.

"You bet." She got out napkins and cutlery and handed them off for him to set the table while she dished up breakfast. Then they were sitting and eating and laughing over some of Simon's stories about kids' reference questions, which managed to be utterly astonishing and awfully cute.

"Ah, yes," Mrs. M said. "Raising three children taught me that they were always going to surprise me. I never did get used to the way just any old thing would fly out of their mouths. I kind of miss it sometimes. Though we all say that Katrina never did have a filter installed between her brain and her mouth. Especially as regards her brother."

"Is he her boss as well as her brother?" Simon asked in evident horror, and Thea was reminded that he'd had to sneak out of her house because his sister was so bossy.

Mrs. M shook her head. "No, thank goodness. At least, not yet. They're both vice presidents. The current CEO was the chief financial officer when my husband was alive. But whenever he decides to retire, that succession battle is going to be bloody. Kyle is already entitled enough, much as I hate to say it. I often wonder where I went wrong with him."

Thea scooped up a forkful of eggs. Mrs. M had a knack with them—they were fluffy and delicious.

"It didn't even have to be anything you did," Simon said.

"What do you mean, dear?" The older woman looked at him with keen interest.

He shrugged. "The world tells men we are automatically in charge."

Thea nodded agreement. "It takes some powerful conditioning and for the man in question to really consciously reject those messages for it to stick."

Mrs. M sighed. "I suppose that's true. It's certainly true of Kyle and some of the members of the board. Truly tedious men. Not like our Simon here." At that, her eyes glittered with humor and mischief again. Simon's cheeks went pink at her words.

"Oh, are we sharing him now?" Thea asked, gratified to see his face flame even hotter at that. "Sorry, I'll stop," she said, regretting the teasing immediately. It definitely wasn't his type of thing.

"Thanks," Simon said softly, stacking their empty plates and cutlery and getting to his feet, shaking his head at Mrs. M's objection. "No, I can at least put some things in the dishwasher since you cooked. Want another cup of coffee?"

"*Such* a nice young man," Mrs. M said, winking conspiratorially at Thea. "For what it's worth, I approve."

Simon didn't usually love being talked about like he wasn't there, but there was a kind of warm theatricality to Mrs. M. Even before she voiced her approval, he could tell he was being tested. He didn't mind. He was glad Thea had someone looking out for her. He refilled her cup, then loaded the dishwasher in the sunny kitchen.

"What do you young people have on tap for today?" Mrs. M asked.

Thea's gaze met his as he straightened up, closing the machine. "I don't know that we have any plans. What about you?" she asked.

Mrs. M sighed. "I have the decorators in today to get the old place trimmed up for the holidays."

"Decorators?" Simon asked.

She chuckled, a small self-deprecating sound. "Yes, I have decorators in to swag greenery and lights, hang wreaths, set up my little tree in the den, and set up a truly grand tree in the formal parlor. We didn't used to do it that way when Mr. McAnally was alive and the kids were still living here, but I'm not up to doing all of that by myself. And the house needs to look nice for the annual Boxing Day party I host." Her face lit with a sunny smile. "You should come, Simon. Thea will be there."

"I honestly wish I could, but I'll be in California." His gut felt hollow at the thought.

She nodded, her face shuttering to a mask of correct politeness. "That's right. With your family. Where you should be, of course."

But Simon wasn't really sure that was true anymore. While last year's trip had felt mandatory, he hadn't thought much beyond it. Was that really going to be his life? Traveling to the West Coast *every* Christmas to make sure everything was just so for Ash? When his family had lived here, it was easy to shove aside the thought that maybe he was only valued for what he contributed, not who he was. This year was making that thought inescapable. As horrible as the realization was, he also felt a trickle of something—relief, maybe—that he'd identified the real reason why he didn't want to travel.

"I have a few last-minute presents to pick up for my family," Thea said. "Nothing big, just stocking stuffers, but my family likes those almost more than the big presents. Well, the adults do," she amended with a grin. "For the nephews, the bigger the better as far as they're concerned."

"I need some more wrapping paper," Simon said.

"Sounds like you and Thea have a date with a big-box store," Mrs. M said. She was back to being all twinkly and unsubtle about the fact that she liked them as a couple. But Simon wasn't even sure if Thea was up for another date, let alone being a couple. He needed to pump the brakes on this.

"Thea might have other plans," he said.

"Thea is definitely headed to the big-box store for small toys, socks and everything in the tiny travel section aisle," she said, getting to her feet. "If you want, we can go together."

Well, okay, then. Maybe Thea didn't have other plans. That didn't mean she was on board with the couple-y stuff Mrs. M seemed to be pushing.

He'd have to make sure he didn't come on too strong.

Thea led the way back to her house, Simon trailing behind. But before they could open the front door, the sound of a car coming down the long driveway made her turn. "Oh good grief," she muttered when her sister's minivan pulled into view.

"What's the matter?" he asked.

"My big sister. Incoming." Apparently, she hadn't taken the umpteenth clue-by-four to the head yesterday about showing up unannounced.

The minivan came to a stop and Gia jumped out. "So, you are alive," she said, lifting one eyebrow as she took in

Simon in yesterday's clothes. Not that Gia knew that, but it felt like she did.

"Simon, this is my sister, Gia. Gia, this is Simon Osman."

Gia coolly took Simon's hand and shook it. "You were her date."

He nodded.

"From last night."

"Yes."

"Interesting."

The crests of Simon's cheekbones went red, and Thea wanted to snap at her sister. But decades of dealing with her sibling meant she knew that snapping would only fuel Gia's judgment. Instead, she folded her arms casually and drawled, "What'cha doing here all of a sudden?"

Her sister shifted the strap of her handbag on her shoulder. "We'd talked about going shopping this weekend."

Thea felt her eyes narrowing. "Yeah, we'd mentioned it was a possibility, but we didn't talk any further about it. You certainly didn't say anything when we talked yesterday."

Gia shrugged and her gaze slid away from Thea. "Well, you weren't answering your phone this morning, Henry has the boys, and I was in the neighborhood..."

Giada Lucia Martinelli-Jaszek, you fucking liar. She kept those words inside since she couldn't call her sister out in front of Simon. Not when she'd already embarrassed him. But there was no possible way her sister just "ended up" in this neck of the almost-literal woods.

Simon stirred then, muttering something about getting his stuff from inside her house. Considering how much of his stuff was still in her bedroom, that was probably a good idea.

When the door closed behind him, Thea gave her sister her best face-melting glare. "*In the neighborhood?* Where exactly were you headed? It's not exactly like I'm between you and Costco. Or literally anything else."

Her sister didn't say anything, her eyes flicking to the side and her mouth twisting in annoyance.

"Just what I thought. What the actual hell is wrong with you showing up like this out of the blue?"

Her sister's eyes snapped up to meet hers. "What the actual hell is wrong with *you*, sleeping with someone on the first date?"

Thea's rage expanded in her chest until she felt she might explode. "The actual hell that it is none of your business, *big sister.*"

Giada's finger stabbed at her, accusing. "That's right. I'm your big sister and I always will be *and* I was worried about you. A one-night stand out here in the goddamn wilderness? What were you thinking?"

Thea rolled her eyes and flailed her arms, ending the gesture with pointing at Mrs. M's massive home. "I don't live in the wilderness. I was thinking that I know Simon, he's a really good guy and we'd have a nice time together. And I was right. *And* you may always be my big sister, but I'm a grown-ass woman now and you don't have to pretend like I'm your child. Don't Nic and Matty keep you busy enough?"

Gia's hands landed on her hips. "Yeah, they do, but you're so goddamn impulsive and always have been, that when I didn't get any responses to my texts or phone calls until it was practically the goddamn afternoon, I got worried." But there was something shifty in her sister's eyes as she said it.

Thea's jaw tightened. The argument was old and she knew it was no longer relevant, but it still stung. She pointed back at her sister. "You didn't get worried. You got curious. No, not curious. You got *nosy*. What, are you trying to live vicariously through me or something?" She flung up a hand, dismissing her sister. "Never mind. You have your own life. Make your own choices."

Gia's spine snapped straight. "Yes, I have my own life, but I'm also worried about *your* choices, Thea. What the hell are you thinking? I'd figured you had settled down after ten years as a firefighter. But now? New job, new man, what's next?"

Thea shook her head, feeling like flies were buzzing around her face. "Why do you care?"

"Because I don't want to see you becoming the drama queen all over again."

Thea rolled her eyes at the accusation, trying to ignore the gut punch her sister landed on her, but Gia went on, relentless. "No. Listen. You sleep with a guy right away, you're going to get attached, and next thing you know he's going to be calling you a stage-five clinger and running for the hills. For all you know, this guy's just using you for easy sex."

Thea reared back like her sister had slapped her. At that moment, she didn't care what her sister thought of her. Gia didn't know Simon at all. A fierce, protective feeling swelled up in her. "I think you need to go now," she said, her low voice shaking.

Gia's face went stricken. When Thea went quiet in an argument, shit had gotten real. "Thea, I'm sor—"

Thea held up a hand and, in a similarly low tone, said,

The Anti-Social Season   183

"No. I don't want to hear it now. Just get back in your car
and go home."

She turned her back on her sister and walked into her house,
careful not to slam the door.

Simon froze inside Thea's front door. He'd intended
to get his things—especially the things he'd left in Thea's
bedroom—and slide away quietly, but the sisters' argument
was all too audible through the wood. Gia especially had a
carrying voice and she used it to stunning effect.

He thought over the last day. He'd had such a good time,
been carried along so easily on the wave of, well, everything
he and Thea had shared, that he hadn't thought much outside their little bubble. Even hanging out with Mrs. M was
fine. She was, weirdly, a part of the bubble. She didn't judge,
at any rate.

Gia was judging.

She was, apparently, judge, jury and executioner.

Simon winced as Gia called her sister a "stage-five clinger."
Yikes. That definitely hadn't been his experience. And now
he was some predator using her for sex? Outrage flooded his
body. He couldn't hear Thea's response, but he moved away
from the door when the knob began to turn, making it as far
as the bedside table, where he picked up his wallet.

She didn't seem to notice him though when he left the
bedroom. She closed the door carefully, as if she was afraid it
might shatter, and then leaned back against it. Her face was
pale and she took in a deep, shuddering breath. Forgetting
his outrage for a moment, Simon pocketed his wallet and
strode over to her, stopping just shy of where she stood, his

hand hovering beside her cheek. He'd moved without think-ing—to comfort or protect or he didn't even know what—but something in Thea's posture stopped him from touching her.

Her big eyes lifted to scan his face. "Did you hear all that?" Even her normally confident voice sounded wobbly.

"Not all of it." Not her reaction to her sister calling him a predator, basically. What had she said in reply? Had she de-fended him, or did she think his history in grad school meant he really was some sort of serial womanizer?

Thea's eyes seemed to lose focus and she blinked, then straightened her spine, moving away from the door. Simon dropped his hand and took a step back, giving her space. Her jaw clenched and she gave a little nod. "I guess you have things you probably need to do," she said.

It took a moment for her words to sink in. But yeah, it was unmistakably a dismissal. Pride snapped his spine straight and outrage made the edges of his vision flicker. "Oh. Yeah. I guess I do." He walked back to her countertop and scooped up his keys. When he turned, she was still standing in front of the door, her expression unreadable. "Um. I guess I'll see you next week for work, then."

She gave another little nod. She didn't look at him, but somewhere past his shoulder. "Yeah."

"We don't have the library conference room—did you have a place where we could meet up?"

She seemed to shake herself, almost as if she'd been in a trance. "Um. I'll figure something out. I'll text you Monday."

"Okay, then." Shrugging on his coat, he moved toward her to say goodbye in some fashion. Thea moved away from him almost abruptly, as if she'd been stung.

Chest hollow, Simon opened the door. He paused, turning to say—what? He didn't know, and Thea was glaring at him like she wanted him to leave.

So he left.

Eighteen

"Fine. Just everybody fucking leave me. That's just great," Thea muttered to herself as she heard Simon's car start up and the pop of gravel under his tires as he turned and pulled out of the driveway. "Just do whatever you want, say whatever you want and get the fuck out of here." On one level, she knew the only person she was really mad at was her sister. How *dare* she judge Thea for, well, anything? And how mortifying for Simon to be collateral damage from her sister's attack.

But Simon had also hurt her with his rapid departure. She should check the driveway for skid marks, he'd left so fast. She rubbed her forehead and walked over to get a glass of water, but filling it and bringing it to her lips reminded her of their first kiss. *Dammit*. She gulped defiantly. Nothing was going to ruin hydration for her. Not her sister, not her...whatever Simon was. Whatever their relationship was. If there still was a relationship.

She drained the glass and put it in the sink, groaning.

Whatever Simon was, she was going to have to see him next week. Normally, she'd take out her frustrations on a weight bench or heavy bag. But for now, her new job would have to do. Which meant she was going to need some social media campaign ideas and a place to work and maybe film. Rubbing her temples to try to batter back an incipient headache, she went over to her desk and flipped open her laptop. She pulled up a holiday calendar and blinked at the myriad of choices she had. Grabbing a sticky note, she recorded the dates for Kwanzaa, Diwali and Hanukkah for the year. Damn, her late entry into this job was doing her no favors. For one, Diwali was already over. Mentally, she kicked herself.

Okay. Next year. If she got a next year. But she had time to create some Hanukkah safety messages. Kwanzaa too. She tapped her pen against the pad and then looked at it. Positioning it on her thumb, she tried a spin.

Bonk.

Okay, fine. Bucket list item canceled. Picking up the traitor pen again, she bit the end, thinking. Ray from her station was Jewish, but she also knew several Jewish firefighters at other stations she could tap to see if they were willing to do a safety video about the festival of lights. She wasn't ready to go back to her station just yet.

She smacked her forehead with the heel of her hand. Her *old* station. Not her station. She didn't have a station.

Quickly, she wrote their names on another sticky note, starting with the most gregarious guy she'd met at various charity events.

Yeah. Larry Cohen was her top pick for this job.

★ ★ ★

Simon got home without remembering a minute of his drive. How had things gone so wrong so completely? Just as he was pulling into his parking spot, his phone rang, his sister's name on the screen.

He practically chucked the phone through the windshield. The last thing he needed now was Ashley's petulant demands. He let it roll to voicemail.

Predictably, as he was unlocking his apartment door, it rang again. This time it was his mother. Again, he sent the call to voicemail as he turned on the lights on his little table-top Christmas tree and tossed the infernal device on his coffee table, then headed for his bathroom for a shower. As he scrubbed his body, his brain frantically scrambled for something to do, somewhere to go where he could just ignore the world and escape his thoughts.

He'd had the girl of his dreams.

Literally.

But then it had all gone to shit.

He sighed and shut off the water, pushing the shower curtain out of the way with unnecessary force. Wrapping a towel around his waist, he cleared the fog away from the mirror and considered his face. Somehow, he didn't look even a fraction as exhausted as he felt.

God, things had been going so well. From his living room, his phone shrilled again. Well, given his situation, he shouldn't be surprised that Thea's sister—that *anyone's* sister—could ruin something. His was well on her way to ruining the entire Christmas holiday season with her endless, ramping expectations. He finished drying off and pulled on sweatpants and a faded old T-shirt from grad school that read Fear the Turtle across the chest. Dragging himself back to the living room, he picked up his phone. Three more calls from his sister and one from his mother. One voicemail from Ashley. With a sinking feeling in the pit of his stomach, he tapped to listen.

His sister's terse voice poured out. "Simon, stop ignoring my calls. I can't find the recipe for Grandma's sugar cookies, and it will absolutely not be Christmas unless we have them." That was it. No actual request for assistance, no please or thank you, no acknowledgment that he had his own life to live and wasn't just an accessory for his sister and her holiday ambitions.

Plus, those cookies were fiddly and tricky. There was no way his sister was going to get through even rolling out a batch of the dough without a meltdown he was going to be able to hear from three thousand miles away.

Instead of calling Ashley back, he tapped his mother's contact entry. Maybe it was cowardice, but he was fine with that just now. "Thank god you called," she said as soon as she picked up the phone.

"Nice to talk to you too, Mom."

He could practically hear her waving away his comment. "Why can't you answer your phone when we call you?"

"Because I'm doing other things. Living my own life."

"Well, you need to help your sister. You know how she gets."

He did. And dealing with her demands was difficult enough when she lived twenty minutes away. But he'd grown up knowing that dealing with her demands was also easier than triggering one of her raving meltdowns. The last year had given him some more perspective on how the family's constant stance of appeasement wasn't the best strategy. Now that he could see things more clearly, he wished he'd started drawing boundaries earlier.

"I can't bake with her from the East Coast, Mom."

"I know. But you can send her the recipe, right? And maybe walk her through it on a video call."

A month ago, he might have. "No," he said, his gut churning.

"What?" His mother legitimately sounded as if she didn't understand the syllable.

"No. I'm not going to hold her hand. I'm not going to turn myself inside out just because she might have a tantrum."

"But Simon, you know how she gets!"

He did. And he knew his Mom would probably end up coping with the fallout. But he'd just endured his own emotional roller coaster and he didn't have the energy to cope with any of it. "I do. And I'm sorry. But there are limits to what I can do from here. She's just going to have to either come to grips with the fact that our traditions will have to change or she's going to have to learn how to do a whole lot of new stuff. I've gotta go now, Mom. Love to you and Dad."

And with that, he hung up.

On Wednesday, after fielding an excruciating call from her sister that contained a very serious, clearly very rehearsed apology for her nosiness and judgment, Thea fidgeted in the dayroom of the firehouse. Larry Cohen had just given her a cup of coffee. The building where he worked was a beautiful older brick structure, very different from the modern building she'd called home for a decade. It had great, deep sills in the tall windows. Perfect for a menorah.

In fact, there was a beautiful example of one sitting on one of the sills now, an asymmetrical work of silversmith's art. Two candles were seated in it, both of them unlit.

Thea gestured with her coffee cup. "Did you put those out just for me?"

Larry shook his head. "Nah. First night isn't until tomorrow. But that's good for your project, right?"

Thea stiffened. "That won't be a problem, right? Lighting a candle before you're supposed to?" She couldn't imagine lighting an Advent candle before its time. God might not smite her, but her mother sure would.

Larry gave her a broad smile, his eyes twinkling. "No. Especially not for a safety video. Don't worry about it. I just wish it was darker. The flames won't really show."

Thea peered at the setup. At least it was an overcast day, but she took his point. Night would have been better. "Next year," she said, hoping it was true. "I'm learning how to do a lot of the kind of planning that this job requires. Different from making sure there's a full inventory on a ladder truck, you know?"

"Guess so. Where's that guy who's supposed to be helping you, anyway?" Larry got to his feet and tossed the dregs of his coffee in the sink before putting his cup in the dishwasher.

Thea checked the time. It wasn't like Simon to be late. He had acknowledged her text instructing him where to meet her yesterday, so she knew he'd read it. "I'm sure he's on his way."

"Should you call him?" Larry asked.

"If he's driving, I doubt he'll answer," she said.

"Good point. And good for him. Would hate to be called out to a vehicle crash caused by one of our own."

"Aww, you still think of me as one of your own?" Thea couldn't help the ridiculous surge of warmth in her chest at the thought.

Larry winked broadly and pointed cheesy finger guns at her, making her laugh. At that moment, Simon was escorted in by one of the station's younger crew.

"Here they are," the kid said before leaving. Simon's expression was grim as he took in Larry, and Thea's laugh died in her throat.

"You okay?" she said, her shoulders going stiff.

He cleared his throat. "Yeah. Some traffic I wasn't expecting. Sorry I'm late."

"No worries," Larry said, approaching Simon with his hand out. "Larry Cohen. Welcome."

"Simon Osman," he said, shaking the firefighter's hand, his face set in its old, sternly forbidding expression.

Leaving Thea wondering what the hell was wrong now.

Jealousy was an ugly emotion, so Simon wasn't exactly proud of himself when he found Thea laughing merrily with a very handsome former colleague. Larry Cohen seemed to be one of those effortlessly charming guys, with curling dark hair and a broad, easy smile that only made Simon feel even more stiff and awkward than usual.

The fact that he'd apparently been flirting with Thea—and that Thea enjoyed it, if her laugh was any kind of indication—only made Simon feel worse. The way their extended date ended on top of his family's drama had corroded his weekend. Then Mary-Pat had been up to her usual shenanigans, hijacking yesterday's readers' advisory social media event by trying to override his and Chloe's suggestions with what she considered "classic" literature.

Chloe finally put an end to her meddling by pointing out that the readers' advisory lunchtime social media feature was something Mary-Pat never wanted in the first place, and telling her that "long-dead white men aren't the answer to everything."

Mary-Pat then marched into Amy's office to complain about "new librarians who don't know their place and are completely ignorant about the literary canon." Thanks to a door that wasn't quite closed all the way, the entire library staff now knew that Amy had told Mary-Pat that she needed to stop overstepping her nonexistent authority, do her job and stop causing drama for the entire library.

While this had, admittedly, been a glorious moment for the rest of the staff, Mary-Pat's subsequent iciness meant that patrons had been made uncomfortable and created a lot more work for everyone else. So, despite the way his weekend crumbled, Simon had been looking forward to getting out of the library and into the field with Thea.

Only to arrive to this cozy scene.

She looked up just then and said, "What do you think?" to Simon, and he realized she'd been conferring with Larry about something. He just didn't know what.

He cleared his throat. "Uh, I'm sorry. I didn't get that. What were you saying?"

She gave him a funny look. "I was wondering if we should

have me sort of interviewing Larry or if he should just talk about menorah fire safety on his own."

His rusty brain rumbled to life. On the one hand, Larry was the guy who was being cast as the expert for this specific video. On the other, Thea's ideas and the fact that she wasn't camera shy would make her the face of Emergency Services' social media. Plus, she was worried—irrational as it probably was—about her probationary period. Putting her in front of the camera might help to cement her role there. "I think you should both be in it."

"Great!" they both said in unison, and Simon's stomach sank. Super. He was now going to video them both being super chummy and full of chemistry. Just what his week needed. Sighing, he set up the tripod and camera, softly explaining to Thea how she would do this on her own, paying special attention to where the edges of the frame were so she didn't end up with half her content not filmed. Larry looked on, apparently intrigued.

"Do I get a script?" he asked.

"Nah," Thea responded. "I have my intro kind of planned out, but it's not like we're doing a scene in a play or anything. The idea is to have it be more of a conversation."

"Well, if there's anything I can do, it's talk," he said. "Let's see if you're as good at this as you were in a ladder truck." Another wink made Simon's stomach loop itself into knots.

He didn't even want to think about what Thea and Larry might have done in a ladder truck.

But he had a job to do. "Okay. Let's do a few takes and see what happens."

Nineteen

Something was definitely wrong with Simon. Thea tried to banter with Larry like she always did with her firefighter colleagues, but Simon's mood was putting her off. They did a few takes and Larry was great: witty, friendly and informative. But Simon was distracting her, and she felt like she was just a stiff sidekick.

Maybe that was okay though. This was supposed to be more Larry's show than hers. After all, while she'd certainly seen plenty of menorahs, she wasn't Jewish, and aside from the basic fire safety principles, she had nothing specific to bring to this particular party. The best she could do was to be a reliable sidekick.

But she wasn't even doing that properly.

They finished another go and Simon frowned. "Can we try it one more time? It's fine, but usually you're more animated, Thea."

"Yeah, what's up with you?" Larry playfully grabbed her

shoulders and gave her a gentle shake. "Man, you're tight as a board." He followed up with kneading her muscles, and she couldn't help but let out a tiny groan. "That's better. Loosen up, girl! Make love to the camera!"

He said that last thing with such an exaggerated impression of a fashion photographer from a bad movie that she finally laughed, but it felt weak. They launched one more time into their now-familiar routine and that felt a bit better. Just as they'd finished and were taking deep breaths, Simon fiddling with the camera, an alarm ripped through the old brick building.

"That's me. Sorry, gotta go!" Larry hollered as he raced out of the room. Thea fought the impulse to hustle, to suit up, to slide into her familiar place in the driver's seat of her old ladder truck. To slot back into her old life and the comfort of familiarity. She could hear the familiar sounds of people moving, gear clanking and trucks starting under the blaring alarm. The desire to respond was even more hardwired into her than she'd thought, and the loss of it felt so final, like a vault door slamming shut.

Suddenly, everything seemed too much. Her eyes stung and her mouth trembled. She looked to see if Simon had noticed her moment of weakness, willing him to not glance up from the camera he'd been studiously focused on.

His eyes lifted from the tripod and met hers squarely, his hard expression melting as the trembling of her mouth infected her jaw and her eyes filled with tears. She barely registered the way he rushed across the room to cradle her jaw in his palms, his touch so light, so gentle, so *warm* that the tears spilled, flooding her cheeks, her nose running despite her desperate sniffling.

"Thea. Sweetheart. What's the matter?" His worried eyes scanned her face—including the snot fountain of her nose. Her eyes closed without her consent, and she let him gather her into his chest, her lungs heaving with the sobs that had hijacked her body.

"I... I just..." The sobs were too big, her grief was too huge to contain. And too *sudden*. Why, after all the therapy and everything else, why was this happening now?

"Shh." One of Simon's hands wrapped around her waist, drawing her close. The other cupped the back of her head. She felt impossibly sheltered, cherished.

Loved.

Oh god. This wasn't love. She really was Gia's stage-five clinger. She sniffed and reared her head back, Simon's fingers spearing into her hair. "I'm okay," she gurgled.

Okay, that wasn't convincing.

His worried eyes said the same. "You're not okay. And it's okay to not be okay."

The tears that she'd thought she'd wrangled into submission surged back into her eyes. "Is it? What do I have to cry about? I have a cushy job now—if I can keep it. I'm not running into burning buildings anymore like Larry."

Simon's restless hand settled on her neck, warm and comforting. "Do you want to run into those burning buildings again? Or is your real worry that you're still on probation?"

She heaved a huge, shuddering breath. "Yes?"

Thea's body was so warm, so lovely, so *present* that Simon wrapped his hand around the back of her head and pulled it back to his chest, feeling a little like a heel for enjoying her closeness as she heaved a shuddering sigh and looked up at him. The anger, the defensiveness he'd felt about her rejection had melted away the instant he saw her trembling chin and watery eyes.

Smoothing a thumb over her cheekbone and catching a tear, he brought it to his mouth, licking the salt of her sadness away the way he wished he could make all her troubles disappear.

Her pupils dilated as he pulled his thumb away with a soft pop.

"I'm a mess," she said, her eyes filling again.

"Shh." He covered her mouth with his, thankful for the empty room. "You're okay," he mumbled against her lips, and the intimacy of it nearly undid him.

"I'm not okay though. If I was okay, I could watch someone run off to a callout and feel nothing." Her voice was still clogged with tears and she sniffled hard.

"Hang on," he said, letting her go and rummaging in his messenger bag. Pulling out a travel pack of tissues, he handed her one and watched as she wiped her eyes and gustily blew her nose. He handed her another, and she gave him a watery smile, then blew her nose a second time. When he tried to hand her a third, she held up a hand.

"I'm okay. Thanks." Her voice was raspy, but it wasn't so congested anymore. He tucked the tissues away, then pulled her over to a nearby sofa. The silence after the insistent alarm felt deafening. Pulling her down beside him, he wrapped his arms around her and held her against his chest.

"Tell me, what's wrong?" He rubbed her back, hoping to soothe her somehow. He thought he knew why she was so upset, but assumptions were pitfalls. She might not answer, but he had to ask.

She sighed, her back rising and falling under his sweeping hand. "I guess I just wasn't ready to be in a firehouse when the alarm rang and not be, well, not be a part of it." The last words came in a rush, and he squeezed her close to him, as if sheer proximity could make everything better. "I thought I was more okay," she went on. "I thought that the time and the therapy and the new job... I was doing so well, I thought..."

He waited to see if she was going to finish. When she didn't, he stroked her hair and murmured, "That's not how people recover from stuff though. It's rarely fast and it's never linear. And a new, very different job is its own kind of stress. It's okay if you have big emotions."

She twisted in his arms, looking up at him with red-rimmed eyes. "Big emotions? You sound like you've been studying up to talk to your nephew."

Okay, so yeah. Maybe he had. "Having big emotions isn't just a little person thing though. It's an every person thing. And our society is really bad about letting people know it's okay. But it is."

"Are you looking forward to seeing your family next week?" Then she paused, her brow furrowing. "No, it's *this* weekend. You leave on Sunday, don't you?"

Exhaustion flooded through him at the thought of flying to the West Coast on Sunday—Christmas day. "Yeah. And almost as soon as I get there, I have to turn around and come back."

She straightened, and while he didn't love the loss of her warm body tucked against him, he did love the indignation that sparkled in her eyes. "You're going to the other side of the country for just a couple of *days*? How is that okay?"

He took a deep breath and held it for a few beats of his heart, then let it go. "Well, my family is demanding and my job didn't give me a lot of holiday leave this year. It's a combination of history and seniority. So I made the best of it."

"By spending as much time traveling as you will seeing your family?"

Reflexively, he said, "It's not quite *that* bad."

She rolled her eyes. "Okay, how bad is it?"

Simon's face flooded with several emotions in quick succession. Exasperation, contemplation, then he gave her a keen-eyed glare. "Fine. It's annoying as hell. It's a waste of time and money. But what else was I supposed to do?"

She blinked. "Um. Maybe *not* do Christmas with your family this year? Just throwing that out there."

"I wish," he said, scrubbing his hands over his face. "But my sister will lose her shit so entirely you will be able to hear it from space."

"Your sister, who moved her family thousands of miles away, will lose it if *you* don't relocate your own carcass to where she is?" Thea willed all of the disbelief she felt into her question.

"I know," he groaned. "But I don't know what else to do."

Say no? But she didn't voice the thought. She didn't exactly have much of a leg to stand on with unreasonable family demands. Having your sister show up at your house because she was being nosy about your sex life was pretty much the definition of an unreasonable family demand, after all.

He sighed. "My sister is… How do I put this? She's difficult. She's demanding. And she almost always gets her way.
Frequently, she does this by being incredibly difficult."

"Ah." Thea was reminded of her cousin Joe. His tantrums
were legendary when they were all kids, and her aunt and
uncle's family had basically rewired their entire lives around
his demands. Looking back, she guessed that in the short run
it had seemed to make life easier.

In the long run, it had been disastrous.

"So basically she runs roughshod all over everyone else,
doesn't respect boundaries, and as far as she's concerned everyone else is completely unreasonable and nothing is ever
her fault, huh?"

He blinked in obvious surprise. "Yeah. Pretty much. How
did you know?"

Textbook narcissist, she thought but didn't say. It wasn't her
place to diagnose anyone, let alone someone she'd never met.
"I had a cousin who was similar."

"You make it sound like a syndrome or something."

Shit. Busted. "Yeah, well. It's a type," she said, hoping she
didn't sound too evasive. "Speaking of sisters, I want to apologize for the way mine showed up and…" *Ruined everything?*
She took a deep breath, regrouping. "I'm sorry she showed
up like that. I had been really enjoying our time together."

His expression, which had been keenly focused on her, softened. "Yeah. I had too." He looked around the empty dayroom as if he suddenly remembered where they were. "Do
you need to get any additional footage or anything while
we're here?"

Dammit, she'd hoped for more than *I had too* from him.

For a second she dithered, wondering if she could think of additional footage that she did want. Maybe a close-up of lighting the menorah? But no. Larry had done that during their demonstration, and fiddling with religious objects that weren't hers felt wrong. "No," she said.

This might be it for them. He was leaving Sunday, and their training time was up.

He checked his watch. "Okay then. I guess we should get packed up and go."

Heart heavy, she pulled out her laptop and opened it up for him to transfer the video files. They stared at the progress bar in silence for what felt like hours and when he pulled the cable out and started to pack up his gear, Thea wanted to sink right through the floor. Then he took a deep breath and his shoulders set as if he was about to say something difficult.

"Can we start over?"

Simon felt like he'd jumped out of a plane with no parachute. Thea just looked at him as if he'd lost his damn mind.

"What…what would that entail?" she asked.

Okay, fair question. Terrifying, but fair. "Um, since this is the last time we have together as sort-of colleagues, I was kind of wondering if we might actually date. Just date. Not worry about nosy or bossy sisters, not worry about social media campaigns. Just spend time. You and me."

"You mean like a relationship?" Her voice came out on a funny sort of squeak.

He gathered himself. He'd thought he was jumping out of a plane before? That was a toddler's jump into a puddle. This was the real thing. "Yeah. I mean like a relationship.

You make me crazy, Thea, but I just like you so damn much and I can't imagine not having you in my life." He watched her face closely, looking for a shift, a softening, anything that could let him relax, to let go of the tension of waiting for her answer, a lessening of the horrible vulnerability that he couldn't seem to run away from.

He'd told her once that she was brave. He'd thought he knew what that meant. He hadn't had a clue.

"You left," she said. "After Gia came by and said all those horrible things, you just walked out."

He blinked, confused…and, yeah, hurt. "You didn't seem to want me to stay. You seemed embarrassed that I was there, that your life was so out in the open in front of her."

Her mouth tightened. "My sex life, you mean."

He angled his head to acknowledge the truth of her statement.

She took a breath, let it out. Then she said in a rush, "Did it ever occur to you that having you walk out like that made me feel that *you* were embarrassed by *me*? And after I'd told my sister to leave because she was being a total bitch to you and about you."

Shock and denial blazed through him, followed rapidly by shame. Caught up in the moment, he'd only considered that she hadn't seemed to push back against her sister's characterization of him as a user, maybe even a predator. But he hadn't heard Thea's side of the argument at all. Her voice, in contrast to her sister's, had been barely audible. "You did?"

"I thought you heard everything."

"I heard everything your *sister* said. You weren't as loud."

She chuckled, a low, almost mirthless sound. "Yeah. My

sister's loud. Did you think I wouldn't stand up for you when she said something that awful about you?"

Confusion roiled his gut. "I didn't know what you said."

"So you assumed I didn't?" Her dark eyes blazed with challenge.

How had he gone from trying to get her back to defending himself from her? "I didn't *know*. You were miserable and seemed to want me gone. I went."

She sagged as if some cosmic marionettist had suddenly cut her strings. "I *was* miserable. I'd had a wonderful night and a great morning and I was looking forward to spending more time with you. Instead, I got Gia being a nosy, bossy big sister. And you left."

Twenty

God, he knew all about the nosy, bossy big sisters. But it wasn't just about that. "You *told* me to leave."

"I didn't." Her eyes, impossibly huge, lifted to meet his, suddenly unsure. "Did I?"

He nodded, the stinging, sinking feeling he'd had in that moment echoing through him. "You did."

"I am so sorry." She closed her eyes, sighing and scrubbing her eyes with the heels of her hands. "I was just so mad at Gia, and embarrassed, and—"

"Stop," he said, tugging at her wrists. "Your eyes are already red. You'll just make it worse."

She snorted at that. "What an attractive picture."

His heart gave a savage twist at that. "You are. Attractive. To me. If that matters." He felt like his entire soul was laid out for her perusal but he didn't care. Between his sister and his job, he felt like he spent all his time staking out boundaries, policing them, and all too often capitulating to the demands of others that he bend.

He didn't need to guard his perimeter with Thea. He knew that now. She wasn't a conquering army. She wasn't even demanding. The personality traits that had scared him before were shaved into perspective now. She wasn't brash, she was expansive. She wasn't scary, she was brave. She hadn't rejected him, she'd just been embarrassed by her sister.

And she was the person he wanted to explore new things with. To expand his boundaries instead of defending them.

"Do you have anything else you need to do today?" he asked.

"Well, work. I have to edit this video, upload it, plan and schedule some other posts for later in the week…"

"You're going to go back home to do that?"

"Yeah."

"Would it be okay if I came back with you?"

"Don't you have to go back to the library?"

"No. I'm at your disposal for the rest of the day." He hoped she got the not-so-subliminal message that he was trying to send her way.

"Ah." Her chin lifted. "Are you suggesting that we play hooky?"

"Certainly not." He infused his tone with all the shock he could. "I'm thinking you need some assistance with the tasks you've got on your plate for the rest of the day, and since I'm still your mentor, I'm going to make sure you complete them to the highest level of quality."

Her dark eyes sparkled with mischief, and joy surged through his veins. "And *then* we play hooky?" God, the fact that she wanted to spend time with him soaked in like a healing balm.

Cradling her chin in one hand, he kissed her lips softly, a promise and an admonition. "Yes. If you're a good girl and do all your chores first, then we play hooky."

Driving back to her little house, Thea felt like her blood had been carbonated. She knew that her ping-ponging emotions were going to leave her wrung out and exhausted by the end of the day, but at least she was going home on a high, not a low. She kept glancing in her rearview mirror to make sure Simon was behind her, even though he knew the way to her home well enough. When they pulled up in front of her house, Simon got out of his car and looked over Mrs. M's place. His eyes lit with appreciation of the greenery and the twinkling tree that could be seen from the French doors in the back.

"Very nice," he murmured.

"Says the connoisseur of holiday preparation," she teased.

"That's a beautiful tree," he said.

"Oh, that's just the 'family' tree. The big one in the formal living room is *really* grand. It's entirely covered in hand-blown glass ornaments."

He turned wide eyes to her. "Seriously? That must have cost a fortune."

She snorted. "Is it lost on you that my landlady is a seriously wealthy woman?"

He exhaled, the breath puffing out his cheeks. "No, but she's so down-to-earth it's easy to forget."

"Come on, let's get our work done. The faster we conquer

Mount To-Do List, the faster we get to the playing hooky part of the plan."

His eyes narrowed with amusement at that, and he followed her into the house. When they were inside, he looked around. "Mrs. M doesn't decorate your place as well?"

Thea's eyes roamed her space as if she was seeing it for the first time. "No. Her house is hers and, well, this house is hers too, but it's *my* home. I never really saw the point of decorating just for me."

"You don't have your family over here during the holiday?" he asked.

She set her bag on the little desk and started to pull equipment out. "Nah. We all go to my parents' house on Christmas day for a big feast. And presents, of course."

"Of course." His lips twitched.

"Are you, the guy who's literally going all the way across the country to see his family for Christmas, going to judge me for going to my parents' place one town over for the same holiday?"

"Nope, not even if they don't know how to give you gifts." But his eyes still twinkled with mischief.

"Oh, don't tell me. You have a tree and fake candles in every window of your apartment and I don't even know what else. I'll bet your place looks like Santa's freakin' workshop." Thea blew a raspberry at him, feeling suddenly more like herself than she had in a long time. She used to joke with her squad the way she was doing now. Something inside her was unlocked by her time at the firehouse with Larry today. She still missed Sean and Felix and the rest of the guys, but it wasn't a closed ache anymore. It was an open one, one that held the promise of seeing them again instead of the constant denial she'd somehow decided was necessary.

"You're partly right. I have a little tabletop tree. And I will cop to devoting my kitchen table—which is also my dining table—to create a gift-wrapping station. I eat at my coffee table for the entire run-up to Christmas."

Thea's heart felt like it flipped a full one hundred and eighty degrees at that. She hadn't even seen his apartment yet, but she could imagine how he'd made it cozy with his own brand of holiday preparation. It was so special, so *Simon*, she almost couldn't take it.

After eating a quick take-out meal, Simon set up his laptop at her dining table while Thea sat at her desk. They worked quietly in tandem for a couple of hours until Thea finally stretched, yawned and shut her computer with a gentle click.

"And that, she said, is all she wrote. And posted. And scheduled. Are you done?" she asked.

"Just one finishing touch on this program notification," he said. Graphics weren't his strong suit, but he worked hard to make them clear and readable and, hopefully, attractive. Uploading it with the text and alt text for the image, he checked it carefully, then set it to post and repeat several times a day until the event itself. He still felt weird about repeating posts, but he also knew that was the key to actually getting the information in front of their patrons. Attendance at most library events was good, and had apparently been on the uptick since he'd taken over social media duties. He knew that part of that was due to this kind of diligence. "Okay." Closing his laptop, he swiveled on his chair and beckoned Thea over. When she got closer, he scanned her face, looking for traces of the emotional storm she'd endured earlier. She looked a little peaked, but far from upset. He cupped her face in his hand and ran a thumb over her rounded cheekbone. "How are you doing?"

She leaned a little into his touch, smiling wanly. "Good. A little tired, maybe, but good."

"Excellent." Heart thumping, he leaned in. When she smiled a little, he closed the distance between their mouths and kissed her gently. She hummed softly and his heart beat harder, the kiss heating up as their heads angled and tongues twined.

She tugged him off the stool and pulled him toward the bedroom. "Are you sure?" he asked. She nodded, tugging harder at his hands. "Wait," he said, halting their progress. When she turned toward him, eyes wide and questioning, he smoothed his hands over her cheeks. "What is it you're looking for from me?"

"What do you mean?" Her brows drew together.

He took a deep breath. "I know we have great sexual chemistry. But I want to make sure we're on the same page."

"Do you think you'll hurt me?" she asked, her voice tiny.

"I hope I won't. But I also hope you won't hurt me. I was very casual about sex when I was younger. I'm not anymore. And it seemed like we were well on our way to being something more to each other before…"

"Before Gia came along and blew everything up?"

"Well, yeah. But also before we didn't really communicate as well as I think we should. So talk to me, Thea. What is it that you want from me? Is it just sex?" He searched her face before he admitted, "Because I'm not sure I can do that with you."

She stepped closer to him, and this time her hand came up to cup his cheek, her gesture an echo of his own only minutes before. "I want you, Simon. Your body, your generous spirit, your weird prickliness, your adorable way with little kids, all of you."

His heart felt like it was swelling hard enough to crack his sternum. "Seriously?"

She nodded and went up on her toes to kiss him again. "So if you want to make love or cuddle or just watch a movie, I'm up for it. Because I just want to be with you."

Thea watched his eyes closely, trying to see if her message was sinking in. "I don't feel casual about you at all," she continued. "But I'd like to spend as much time with you as I can before you have to go home. And after you get back."

"I don't have to go into work until ten tomorrow..." he said, one corner of his mouth quirking up.

"Would you like to spend the night? With no expectations?" If he felt the need to pump the brakes on their physicality, she was just going to have to be okay with that.

"Okay." His voice was so quiet it was almost a whisper. "No expectations." He kissed her neck sweetly, making her eyes roll back. *Unf.* Why did that always undo her? Continuing up, he pressed his lips to the shell of her ear, his breath tickling until she shivered.

"You're potentially throwing around some mixed messages here if you don't want me to hump your leg again," she grumped.

He pulled back. "Sorry. I didn't mean to send mixed messages. I wanted to make sure that expectations weren't in the stratosphere."

"Well, you're just going to have to be a lot worse at sex if you want to keep my expectations low." She poked him in the sternum and enjoyed the flush on the crests of his cheeks. It was so easy to make this redhead blush. She loved it.

"I just like pleasuring you," he admitted. "But maybe we should take a nap or something. You did say you were tired."

"Hmm," she said as his lips softly skimmed one of her cheekbones. She loved that he alternated sweetness with a more direct physicality that drove her wild. It reflected both sides of his personality—the thoughtful care, like his gift of the signed graphic novel, that contrasted so deliciously and surprisingly with his confident carnality. "How are you even real?"

He pulled back, his pupil-blown eyes scanning her face. "What do you mean?"

She blinked, trying to assemble her thoughts into something that was even slightly coherent. "How are you a sweet, kind of grumpy guy who actually *fucks*?"

Okay, that wasn't the coherent statement she was looking for. But Simon's eyes slid closed as his lips curved up, and his head bent until his forehead rested against her as he laughed softly. "Thea," he said, his voice barely a whisper. "How are you so perfect?"

Bafflement and a warmth she couldn't name blended in her middle. "Perfect? You're confusing me with some other girl."

His hand skimmed up her side to cup her jaw, angling her mouth up to meet his in a deep, bone-melting kiss. "I'm not confusing anything," he murmured against her mouth. "How are you a confident, almost reckless woman who is so tender?"

"I guess we both contain multitudes," she murmured before lightly biting his earlobe.

"That's it," he said, getting up from the stool and walking her backward into her bedroom until her legs hit the mattress.

Simon watched Thea's eyes closely, ready for a *no* or a *not now*, but her face was shining with laughter and her arms were wound around his neck, pulling his mouth to hers for another long, lush kiss.

He loved sex with this woman, but even just kissing her could possibly end him. There was something decadent about kissing Thea's lush mouth, the way she was a willing coconspirator in their passion.

And he was sure now that they were on the same page and that was everything. They set a slow pace this time, kissing softly and taking their time getting out of their clothes, hands mapping each new uncovered inch of skin. The gradual buildup left them both shaking by the time he slid into her, simultaneously feeling like the world was going to end in the next minute and like he could do this, be this person connected to her forever. They rocked together, her legs wound around his and holding him tight to her, until her eyes slammed shut and her inner muscles contracted around him and he knew she was close.

"What do you need?" he gasped, feeling her grip him again.

"This. Just this. A little more…" She heaved a huge breath, and he pressed tighter to her, never breaking contact, giving her the friction that was making her eyes squeeze shut and her breath come in tiny, frantic pants. She was squeezing him so hard now he had to control his own breathing to keep him from losing control.

Then, without warning, she shuddered and bucked, giving him permission to lose himself in her as her legs loosened their grip. He stroked once, twice, then felt his own release flood through him.

He pressed his lips to her temple. "Thank you, sweetheart," he murmured as she tightened her arms and legs around him one last time in a full-body embrace, his heart so full it felt like it might burst into a confetti of spangles and light.

When he came back to the bedroom after dealing with the condom and slid into bed beside her, she was already asleep.

Twenty-One

Simon slid into slumber as if Thea's sleep could tether his own consciousness, tugging it down and away. When he woke up early the next morning, her side of the bed was already empty and he could hear her moving around her little kitchen. He stretched, appreciating again the way the bookshelves that walled off her bedroom created privacy while the gap between them and the ceiling still made the space feel light and airy.

And, well, full of books, which was always a winner with him.

Sitting up, he looked around the room to try to locate his clothes. There was a simple wingback armchair in the corner he hadn't really noticed before, but now it had a neat stack of his clothes from yesterday.

With a little groan, he pushed to his feet. He was just pulling up the waistband of his boxer briefs when Thea appeared in the doorway, smiling with so much mischief he didn't know whether to feel excited or nervous.

"What's up?" he asked, reaching for his shirt. Thea was fully dressed, in jeans and a T-shirt, more casual than what she'd worn to work or for their date.

"I have an idea," she said, her dark brown eyes positively glittering with excitement.

"Yeah?" A reluctant smile tugged at the corners of his mouth.

"It's about all the prep stuff you love. For the holidays, I mean."

He shrugged into his shirt and started to button it. "Um, okay. Where are you going with this?"

"And I need content," she continued as if he hadn't interrupted. "I need to prove myself in order to keep this job."

He finished buttoning and grabbed his pants, shucking them on before sitting on the chair and tugging his socks on. "And?"

She didn't respond, but just grabbed his hand and tugged him behind her to the kitchen, a whirlwind of energy and good cheer, his sock-clad feet slipping on the hardwood floor as he hurried after her. "Voila," she said, waving a hand at a bowl that appeared to be full of some sort of batter and what looked like a miniature waffle maker.

"What am I looking at?" he asked.

"A *pizzelle* maker!" she said, glee in her voice.

He looked from the device to her grinning face. "I must be missing something. What are we doing with it?"

"Besides making delicious *pizzelle*? Appliance fire safety demonstration," she said. "You should always check appliances, and if you only use them once a year, be extra careful. Those kinds of seasonal things tend to get jammed into the backs of cupboards and stuff and the cord can get damaged. But also, *pizzelle* is yummy and it's a part of my family's holiday preparation, so I thought maybe you'd like to make them with me."

Warmth bloomed in his chest. He felt so intimately *seen* it almost hurt, and something clicked into place. Yes, he loved holiday prep. But nobody had ever volunteered to do it *with* him. It was his domain, but it was also his responsibility. Suddenly, Thea was making it fun in a way he hadn't experienced before. "Sure. What do you need from me?"

She rubbed her hands together, glee practically sparking off her, and something more than warmth spread across his skin. It was like the sparks from her were sent aloft, touching down on him and calling tiny fires alight. "Well, first we do the video. I've got some notes here." She pointed to what he'd thought was a recipe scrawled in her chaotic handwriting. Apparently, it was a shot plan. "Then we make *pizzelle*. Because everything's better with sugary carbs."

Thea wasn't sure why she was so giddy. Maybe it was the aftereffects of mind-blowing sex and a lovely night's sleep. Rediscovering Simon's carnal side was a revelation. She knew she shouldn't assume anything about anybody and the most buttoned-up exteriors could harbor all kinds of surprises when the clothes came off. But Simon's rule-following public persona hid some truly shocking creativity when it came to giving her pleasure and seeking it for himself.

She knew her cheeks were pink from the memory of them in her bed, but she hoped it wouldn't show on camera for the entire world to see. Maybe viewers would just think it was the chilly December weather.

In her home. Right.

She powered through the feeling while Simon filmed her. She demonstrated the best way to store cords if they could be removed from the appliance, talked about keeping an eye on any appliance that heated up, and gave other tips about kitchen fire safety. Holding her phone steady to catch every moment, Simon looked both amused and proud. When she'd run through her script twice and gotten a few close-up shots she intended to use, she finally took back her phone and plugged in the *pizzelle* maker.

"Now, the deliciousness," she said.

"So, it's like a…waffle?" Simon asked.

She goggled at him. "You've never had *pizzelle*?"

He shook his head. "*Pizzelle* virgin here."

She opened the press and scooped a dollop of batter into it, closing it securely and using her phone to time it. When it was done, she popped it out with a spatula and placed it on a cooling rack.

"Pretty," he said, examining the patterned surface of the cookie and reaching for it.

She slapped his hand away. "Patience," she said, proceeding to make a few more thin vanilla-flavored cookies as she explained her family Christmas traditions and how they mostly revolved around food. "Like any good bunch of Italians, if you come to our house during the holidays, you're going to eat and eat well." All her best holiday memories revolved around food, in fact. From savory seafood and pasta to sweet *pizzelle* and panettone, her opinionated, chaotic family was at its most peaceful when eating.

When she had six cookies ready to go, she grabbed a sieve and some powdered sugar and dusted the cookies with it. "Now." She handed him one of the sugary treats. "Now you can eat it. Careful with the sugar."

He took a hesitant bite, seeming to hold his breath. Butterflies swooped and swirled through her stomach as she waited, the tender crunch telling her she'd gotten the texture just right. But what if he didn't like it?

You'll live, she reminded herself as he chewed slowly and swallowed. Then a smile spread across his face. "I like it. Light. Crunchy. Not too sweet."

"Right?" she breathed, wondering why she was so relieved that he appreciated one of her favorite treats. Grabbing one for herself, she took a big bite, but in her breathless haste, she made the worst of all rookie mistakes.

She inhaled powdered sugar. Coughing and wheezing, eyes watering, she saw Simon regarding the front of his shirt, which now looked as if he'd just come through a minor snow squall. "Oh my god. I'm so sorry," she said, unable to fully repress the giggle that rippled out of her.

"It's fine." But his face went a little set, as if he was suppressing something. "I should get going anyway."

She bit her lip. "You don't really have to go if you don't want to."

"I should get changed before I go into work. I've been in the same clothes for hours."

"Well, technically you were naked for a lot of those hours…"

He huffed a short sigh and she nearly cringed. "Okay," she said. "Do you want to take any *pizzelle* home with you?" If he rejected this little peace offering, this tiny bridge between them, she just might cry.

She couldn't tell if his expression softened or if she just wished it did. But he said, "Yeah. Thanks. That'd be nice."

Simon retrieved his coat and his shoes from where he'd left them and returned to the kitchen, feeling like a total tool. It had been a knee-jerk reaction, to close down when she laughed at him, and he couldn't seem to find a way to walk it back.

She handed him a plastic container, not meeting his gaze. "Hey," he said. Her eyes lifted about to the top button of his shirt. "I had a really good time. I just gotta go. Just a couple more days of work before I have to fly out, so I have a lot to do."

She cleared her throat. "Yeah. Okay."

"I mean it." God, the more he talked, the less convincing he sounded. "Can we maybe do something Friday?"

"Christmas Eve? You'd want to spend that with me?"

"Absolutely. Unless you're busy."

This time, her eyes met his. "Not busy. I'd be honored to spend it with you."

He got that warm feeling again, thawing the hardness he'd felt. "I know it's silly that I'm going out for no time at all, but that's the deal I made. And Noah's only going to ask 'why?' every minute of the day for a little while, right? Can't miss that."

The look she shot him held some of the humor that he was so used to, but she didn't reply.

"Right? Please tell me this stage is short-lived," he pleaded.

She lifted a hand, laughing a little. "Yeah. He won't be that way forever. Probably will have outgrown it in six months or less."

"Well, that's a relief. I'd hate for him to go on a job interview and just ask why all the time. He'd be unemployed forever."

"Get out of here," she said, pushing his shoulder a little. "Go to work."

"I'll see you Saturday?" he asked.

"Yeah," she said.

"I have to pack in the morning, but my evening is all yours." Now that she was pushing him to leave, perversely, he wanted to stay.

"It sucks that you have to keep librarian-ing," she said. "You're awful good at this social media stuff."

A pang went through him at her faith in him, but weirdly, he had the urge to argue with her as well. Her support threw a spotlight on aspects of his job he didn't always think about. "It might be harder to be plugged in to everything that goes on if I was social media full-time. When I straddle both worlds, maybe it's more organic. Anyway, the funding just isn't there for it, at least not now. It is what it is." He bent and pressed a brief kiss to her forehead. "I'll see you Saturday. And when I get back from California, we can regroup. Okay?"

"Okay," she said, giving a firm little nod as if to put a seal on their agreement.

He walked out into the cold, wondering if he was ever going to figure out how to successfully be with someone.

Thea made *pizzelle* until she was out of batter, then cleaned up the kitchen, feeling oddly restless. Her little home seemed too large, too empty without Simon in it. She puttered aimlessly, tidying up as much as her somewhat spartan space needed, which wasn't much.

"Ugh." She slapped her hands on her thighs. "Enough of this." She was going to end up running in endless mental circles if she didn't stop it now.

The only solution was to do something. And she had exactly the idea to distract herself. Grabbing her bag and her keys, she shoved her feet into boots and shrugged on her coat as if someone was standing over her with a stopwatch. Then she dashed out to her car and hurled herself in before she could think twice. Thea could see Mrs. M's big showpiece Christmas tree in the bay window as she drove past the front of the house.

For the first time, Thea was going to have *her* very own tree. When she'd split her time between her little house and the fire station and hadn't been home as much, it hadn't seemed to make sense. But now? Especially when she could share it with Simon? It made all the sense in the world.

Trundling down the road to the garden center, she envisioned it in her mind's eye. A small one, smelling of fresh evergreen and twinkling with colored lights. She had a small cache of ornaments that her parents had collected for her since she was born so she'd be able to decorate her own tree when she got one. She'd need to buy those lights though. Compiling a mental list, she whistled "Here Comes Santa Claus" as she pulled into the garden center and parked.

Hopping out, she took a whiff of the wood-fired brazier and the resinous smell of cut fir before she wandered the little lot, examining as many of their smaller offerings that she could find.

"Need help?" A deep voice behind her made her whirl. An East Asian man in overalls and a canvas coat stood slapping his heavy gloves against his thigh with a welcoming grin.

She grinned back at him, fizzing with energy. "I hope so. I need a little guy. I guess you don't get a lot of call for that around here." She thought about the houses in the area: mostly big, when they weren't absolutely huge.

"Not so much, but I do have a couple." The guy waved at an aisle of trees that she hadn't ventured down yet. "I think we can get you set up."

Thea followed in happy anticipation, finally feeling like it was Christmas.

Simon tossed his clothes into the hamper, feeling more than a little bereft. He hated that he'd gone straight to his most defensive, reactionary self—and for nothing more than a brief laugh at his sugar-coated expense. Thea's infectious, somewhat chaotic enthusiasm was appealing, but it was also a little scary. Thea kind of *threw* herself at things. Yeah, she had a basic plan for her video. And she could obviously follow a recipe in order to make delicious waffle cookies.

But there was something manic about all of it that always kept him a little off-kilter.

Calm down. She's a lot like Chloe in that regard, and you roll with her just fine.

Going into the bathroom, he turned on the water, trying to not compare this sterile little apartment building cubicle with the gleaming tiled room with its big shower enclosure. At least the water was hot and plentiful, he consoled himself as steam filled the room and he stepped in to lather up. His body, a little too responsive to mere thoughts of Thea in the past, was now tired and still spent. He got clean with brutal efficiency, then got out of the shower to dry off. His phone rang in the bedroom and nearly groaned. It had to be Ashley. He wasn't going to answer her demands for a video call in a towel though. Another call shrilled while he examined his face and wondered if he could get away with not shaving. Finally, when he had shrugged into his bathrobe, the third demand came. He picked up the phone and tapped to answer. His sister's exasperated face appeared on the screen.

"What, Ash?"

"Where were you?" Ashley snapped, her face pinched, her red-gold curls wilder than usual.

He took a deep breath to regain his composure. "I was in the shower. I'm getting ready for work. Is there some kind of emergency?" All of a sudden, his stomach swooped. Their parents—were they okay?

"No." A dull, red flush was creeping up her neck, visible even on his phone's small screen. "I just can't believe you couldn't come out sooner. Everything's a fucking shambles and I don't know what to do to fix it."

In years past, he might have felt guilty. But this time, he

heard what she didn't say. She didn't miss him. She didn't want her brother. She wanted her holiday drudge to do all the things she didn't want to.

"Well, I can't come any sooner. You know this. I don't have the leave. And even if I was able to fly out today, that would only give me a couple of more days. The horse is out of the barn."

"It's totally unfair that your job won't give you more time to be with your family—"

"*Stop*, Ash. Just stop. It's totally unfair that you and Ray and Noah and Mom and Dad moved all the way to the other side of the goddamn continent and expect me to be able to stop by as if you went one town over. Just stop it. If you wanted a long family holiday together, you all could have come back here."

She gave him a look that said she thought he'd taken leave of his senses. "Do you know how expensive it is to fly five people cross-country?"

He almost laughed at how obtuse she was being. "Yeah. I have some notion. Because it looks like I'm going to be the one who's always going to have to be doing it. I have to upend my life, spend half a day flying in each direction, deal with jet lag, and this time I'm only going to be there just long enough to get over the jet lag before I come home again. Trust me, I get how expensive it is. I get how unfair it is. I just don't think you get how expensive and unfair it is *to me*. I didn't choose any of this and I'm the one who has to accommodate *all* of it. And I'm sick of it."

Ash's face had gone brick red. She glared at him for a long moment, and he steeled himself for another verbal onslaught.

"Well, I'm sorry we're such a burden." His phone beeped softly and the call ended.

Simon tossed his phone on the bed and scrubbed his face with his hands. *"Fuck."*

Twenty-Two

I might have overcompensated. A bit. Thea pulled to a stop in front of her house, the top of her little tree bobbing over her windshield. Her back seat was full of bags from the big-box craft store she'd stopped at after going to the garden center. When Alan, the nice guy on the tree lot, had asked her if she wanted a fresh cut on the trunk so the tree would take up water more easily, she realized she didn't have a stand to put it in. And the tree had been a bit bigger than she'd intended, but it was perfectly symmetrical and, well, just perfect. She'd fallen in love with it on sight and named it Noel.

She felt proud that she'd already remembered she needed lights. But the craft store was a big mistake. In addition to the tree stand, she picked up some glass balls for filler, since her tiny cache of ornaments wasn't going to decorate Noel adequately. And of course she needed a tree skirt. And a topper. And then there were a few more items that looked so wonderful and Christmassy and...

She had a *lot* of bags in the back seat.

"Okay," she said, trying to regain her former buoyant mood. Getting out of the car, she regarded Noel. "Sorry, you're going to have to stay up there for the time being." She opened up the back door and grabbed as many bags as she could, then lugged them inside. Dropping them on the sofa, she moved over to where her desk sat under one of the front windows. She shoved that farther into the corner, making room for Noel in front of the window. She would be able to see the twinkling lights from her car when she pulled up. Rummaging through her shopping bags, she realized the stand must still be in her car. She dashed out again and brought the remaining bags inside, finding the box with the stand and unpacking it.

"Music," she muttered, and turned on the portable speaker in her kitchen so she could stream something suitable from her phone. Once she had that going, she grabbed a pair of scissors and went outside again, cutting the twine Alan had used to tie Noel to her roof rack. She had dragged the tree halfway to her front door when she realized her biggest problem.

She wasn't going to be able to get it set up in the stand without help.

Resting the tree on the wall next to her front door, she let herself back into her house, thinking hard. Was there any way she could rig this up on her own? No. She tapped a fingernail on her front teeth. Mrs. M was too old for either tree wrangling or for getting on the floor to adjust the bolts that would hold the trunk in place. Simon had just left not even a couple of hours ago, and besides, he was probably already at work by now. Her sister would be dealing with her family, and anyway, Thea was still pissed at her, apology or no apology.

Her brain still had the rhythm of her old firehouse schedule as if it had worn grooves into her frontal lobes. Felix and Sean would be off right now. But would they be available? They might have plans with their partners.

Would you dither like this even a few months ago? She knew the answer. She wouldn't.

Sighing, she dug out her phone and opened up their group chat, which had been silent for weeks.

Hey guys. I have a problem.

Their reactions were nearly simultaneous. Sean: **What's wrong?** Felix: **Problem-problem or Thea problem?**

She smiled, but her throat was tight and her eyes itched. She typed rapidly. **Nothing's wrong. Thea problem.** Stepping outside, she snapped a photo of the tree. **His name is Noel and I can't get him in my tree stand by myself.**

This time, the response was simultaneous and identical. **On my way.**

Simon paced around his apartment, furious energy coursing through him, leaving him unable to do anything but move and seethe. He stopped in the kitchen for a glass of water, drinking slowly, trying to calm his racing heart.

His phone rang from the bedroom.

"I swear to god, Ashley, if that's you, I *will* fly out to California just to throttle you with my bare hands," he muttered as he strode to retrieve the device.

But the name on the screen wasn't his sister's. It was his mother's.

Great.

Taking a deep breath, he answered, thanking whatever generational habit made his mother prefer voice-only calls. His face must be as bright red as his sister's had been.

"Hi, Mom."

"Honey, what is going on with you and Ashley? She called me in an absolute tizzy and didn't make any sense."

He pinched the bridge of his nose. "What did she say?"

"Just that you were being unreasonable and wouldn't help with Christmas, and I don't understand. You always help." Her voice sounded bewildered, her enunciation careful.

He took a deep breath and worked his tight jaw. "She seems to think I can drop everything and fly out early because I'm usually the one who does most of the preparation."

"Oh—could you?" His mother sounded delighted at the idea.

He held back the strangled growl he wanted to emit. "No, Mom. I told you. Because I got so much leave at the holidays last year, I can't do that again this year. We have to trade off. That hasn't changed."

"Oh." His mom's voice sounded so tiny and tragic he felt like he wanted to sink into the floor.

He pinched the bridge of his nose and breathed deeply. It would be just like his impulsive family to never think about the consequences of their actions in moving all the way across the country.

"Have you ever thought about moving out here with the rest of us? That way we could always be together at the holi-

days. The libraries out here are really wonderful. I could see
if any are hiring. I think you'd enjoy it."

He shouldn't have been surprised that this was her solution. Somehow though, he was. He tried to make his voice
gentle, but he was so frustrated he wasn't sure if it was working. "No, Mom. I have not thought about it. And before you
start, I'm not going to think about it. I like my life here. I get
why you and Dad moved. It's great for you to be there to see
Noah growing up. But I'm not going to upend my entire life
because you made that choice."

"But what if *you* have children someday?" His mom's voice
was high and tight, like she was trying not to cry. He felt like
his heart was an empty soda can being crushed by a giant fist.
He hated it when his mom got this way. But it was also just
like her to not ask this question *before* she moved to the other
coast. Ashley always came first. She always had. It was easier
to ignore when it was just the background noise of daily life.
But the move had magnified everything, and he couldn't ignore it anymore.

"If that happens, then you're just going to have to come out
here and visit them. I'm not going to arrange my life around
you guys. I'm sorry, but that's just the way it is." *I'm not going
to help you make me into even more of an afterthought.*

"Oh." Now her voice sounded small. There was a rustling,
and then his dad was on the line.

"Simon? What are you doing to make your mother cry?"

Great. Just what this situation needed. "Nothing. I just can't
come out any earlier for the holidays and Ash is having a fit
about it." He didn't repeat his mother's ludicrous suggestion

that he make a cross-country move just to make everyone else's life a little more convenient.

"Oh." That single syllable told him that his father had just about had it with his sister at this point. And maybe his mother too.

That made two of them.

Felix arrived at Thea's first, giving her a hug and looking at her little Christmas tree, leaning forlornly against the side of her house. "This is the critter, huh?"

"Yeah. I mean, I don't exactly need both of you to help, but it's nice of you and Sean to offer."

He scrubbed the top of her head, making her feel simultaneously loved and exasperated.

"It's not just about helping you, silly. It's about getting to see you. You've made yourself pretty scarce lately." He raised a hand when she inhaled to speak. "It's okay. Really. Just as long as you don't stay away forever. I know that change can be hard. We both do. But we also miss you."

"Yeah." The urge to say something, to defend herself for her isolation, drained out of her as fast as it had come. Sean pulled up then, hopping lightly from his truck and looking every bit as healthy as he had the day before that horrible house fire where he'd been so badly injured.

"Hey there, Gracie Lou Freebush," he said as he wrapped her in a strong two-armed hug. The old joking nickname squeezed her heart as hard as his arms did her body.

"Hey there, yourself. Looking good," she said. "How's Eva?"

He stepped back and grinned. "Beautiful, brilliant, amazing, wonderful…" His expression went a little loopy as he trailed off.

"In other words, our human golden retriever is as infatuated as he was the moment he met that woman," Felix said, but his gentle smile was indulgent. They'd all watched Sean tumble ass over teakettle into love with the college professor, and Thea knew Felix was just as glad as she was that it was working out.

Sean clapped his hands and rubbed them together. "So, let's get this little bitty tree set up for you."

Without another word, he strode forward and picked up the tree one-handed. It looked like a toy in his big paw. Felix opened her door and they all went inside, Thea feeling more and more silly about having both of these guys show up for such a small task, but also loving the warm familiarity of them being together. Sean got Noel set up in the stand while Felix lay on the floor, adjusting the bolts until Thea told them it was straight.

"Okay, what now?" Felix asked as he got to his feet. "Want us to string it with lights?"

"No!" Thea said, then clapped her hand over her mouth.

"That was an awfully emphatic 'no,'" Scan said, one eyebrow going up. "Don't you trust us to string some lights?" He was joking, but there seemed to be a little hurt behind it too.

She dropped her hands away from her face. "I do," she said. "The thing is, I have this friend. And he really likes doing holiday prep. And I was thinking maybe he'd like to help me decorate…"

Felix's brows knit together. "Why didn't you ask him to help you set up the tree, then?"

Thea swallowed hard. *Caught.* "Um. He was already here today. And he had to go to work."

"Aha." Felix wagged one finger, his expression lightening as he apparently did the it's-late-morning-now math. "You don't just have a friend, I'm thinking. You have a *naked* friend."

"Well, when he left he was wearing clothes," she said, sticking out her tongue and trying to regain her usual bantering vibe with these two. But it had been a while since they'd seen each other and everything felt a little off.

Sean just chuckled though. "So, that means he wasn't wearing them at some point earlier, I'm guessing. Good for you. Who's the guy?"

Thea sighed. "His name is Simon. He's the librarian who's teaching me about social media." For the first time, she let herself wonder how these two guys—practically brothers to her—would react to Simon. They'd never met any of the guys she'd sporadically dated during her time on the squad. But even though she didn't have brothers in her birth family, she knew they could veer toward protectiveness as a breed.

"Damn. You both went and snagged yourselves some literary types," Felix said. "Should I assign Kevin a reading list to get him up to speed?" His boyfriend was a money manager at a small firm in the District. A lovely, smart guy, but not a huge reader.

"Kevin is perfect, and you're as smitten with him as Sean is with Eva, so don't even start with that," Thea said, pushing her friend's shoulder, the oddness slipping away as they fell into their usual teasing banter. "Don't try to change him. You know you'd hate the results."

Felix grinned. "Yeah, I know. But hey, good for you, my friend. As long as he's sweet to you."

Thea's gaze landed on the comic book he'd bought her. "So far, so good. Very good."

"I really wish you didn't have to come all this way out for such a short trip," Simon's dad said on a sigh. "But you know how your mother and Ashley get when they've got their hearts set on a thing."

Yeah, Simon knew. And he also knew that his father was always going choose his battles, waiting for a conflict he had more of a stake in. When it was just Simon's being buffeted by his sister and his mom, his father would leave him to twist in the emotional hurricane the women could generate without even trying.

But there was no point in trying to play this game any other way than by filling the role he always had in the family. The one who played nice, who didn't make waves. "Okay, Dad. I've got to go get dressed and get to work now. Try not to get caught up in the drama."

His dad sighed again. "Yeah. That's not gonna happen."

No, it wasn't, he reflected as he hung up the phone. He and his sister had always been more different than they were similar, despite their physical resemblance. Where he was stolid, Ash was a whirlwind. Where he planned and appreciated routine, Ash created and seemed to relish chaos. Where he preferred solitude, Ash would always demand that everyone rally around her. It didn't surprise him at all that she was making a mess of the preparations for the holiday. She had no idea what method or planning actually were.

His sister was, frankly, exhausting and his mom was only a hair less so. Not for the first time, he contemplated his upcoming trip with dread. Now that he really thought about it, it *was* pretty wild that flying all the way across the country for two days was less trouble than enduring Ash's tantrums and his mother's tearful disappointment if he just stayed home.

Walking into the kitchen to pack a quick lunch, he spied the container of *pizzelle* that Thea had sent home with him. Popping it open, he took out one of the fragile cookies and looked at the patterns on its golden-brown surface. He didn't have any powdered sugar, but he took a bite, liking it all the better for being slightly less sweet.

At first, he'd thought Thea was the same kind of chaos engine his sister was. But he was starting to learn that wasn't the case. She was more impulsive than he was, for sure. But so was 99 percent of the population. He took another bite, marveling at how it was tender and crunchy at the same time. Yeah. Chaos couldn't make anything like this.

His phone chimed and he stuffed the rest of the cookie into his mouth, then scrubbed his hands over his face before he picked it up to look at the screen. He had zero ability to deal with any more family drama today. But it was from Thea. He smiled as he crunched and opened the text app.

Thea: Are we still on for this weekend?

Simon: Sure, if you want.

Thea: I want. This time, I get to plan, okay?

Simon: Now I'm intrigued. Do I get a hint?

Thea: No hints! Just come to my place as planned.

Simon thought about how he'd have to go to the airport on Saturday morning. He had his plans already set, but Thea was asking, not demanding. And he wanted to spend more time with her before he left. Hell, he wanted to spend more time with her period.

He could pack his bag and leave it in the car. Just in case.

Simon: You're on.

Twenty-Three

"Mmm. Thea, I've missed this deliciousness," Sean said thickly through a bite of *pizzelle*.

"Don't talk with your mouth full." Felix rolled his eyes and then laughed as his friend reached out to swat him on the arm. They were sitting at Thea's kitchen island with coffee and cookies, festive music still burbling from her little speaker. The guys had declared that she'd bought too many strings of lights for a tree of Noel's size, so they took it upon themselves to string the excess over the top of one of her bookcase bedroom walls.

It was really festive, even with poor Noel sitting dark in front of his window. *Sorry, dude. You're going to have to wait a while for your full dress-up.* At least it had a nice stand full of fresh water and was emitting a lovely, soft, piney scent. She couldn't suppress a little wiggle at the thought of Simon's reaction to it.

"So, tell us about your new job," Felix said, picking up his cup and leaning forward to waggle his eyebrows at her. "Or the new coworker, if you prefer."

Sean was sitting between them, otherwise she'd also try to smack him. Instead, she decided to shock them both by being demure and professional.

"He's not my coworker anymore. If he ever was, really. But I learned a lot. I've put together a schedule for posting stuff over the next month or so. I did a menorah safety video with Larry Cohen. I've also tried to get ahead of next winter and talked to some people about making sure I'm putting out more stuff that's useful for people who celebrate Hanukkah, Diwali, Kwanzaa and other holidays." Just enumerating that list made her realize how much she'd accomplished in a few short weeks. Pride overtook the worry about probation for the first time since she'd begun.

Sean nodded. "Eva plans her semesters around students' holidays too. The university doesn't officially recognize them, but she knows it's important so she builds flexibility into the school year."

"I knew I liked her." Thea nodded. "Anyway, I've also made a couple of home safety videos, and I'm going to be going to Station 31 after Christmas to do a video on how they respond in icy or snowy weather conditions..." She waited a beat, looking at her friends with what she hoped was utter innocence.

Sean, who had a cookie raised halfway to his lips, dropped it back to his plate. "You wouldn't."

"Wouldn't what?"

Felix leaned forward to peer around Sean's bulky shoulder. "Have you forgotten us *already*? That stings, man."

Sean, living up to his human golden retriever reputation, gave her actual puppy-dog eyes. "Seriously. Where's the loyalty, Thea?"

"I can't play favorites, guys. You know that. I work for the whole county now." She waited another long beat while they looked at her until she couldn't stand it anymore. She started laughing, then the realization that she'd been messing with them dawning on their faces made her laugh even harder until she could hardly breathe. Her guys were still her guys. She had a new job she genuinely loved *and* she still had her two best friends from the squad. That fear that she might lose Felix and Sean in the process of finding her way in this new gig had come to nothing.

"So you're *not* featuring our biggest charity fundraising rivals before us," Felix said with an expression she couldn't read. It wasn't bad, but he also wasn't laughing. Neither was Sean.

"Did you guys seriously think I would do that?" she asked, her laughter drying up. "I know I haven't been around, but I haven't turned into a different person entirely. I'll probably have to feature all the stations, but I wouldn't put them before you guys."

"So when are you going to come back and do something with the old squad? We've missed you," Sean said.

Thea bit her lip. Okay, the guys had a point. "I'm sorry. I just… I didn't think you'd…" She didn't want to say *be hurt* because that wasn't their vibe. "I'm sorry," she said again.

Sean grasped her arm, squeezed. "It's okay. We're all going to change, you know?"

"Speaking of which," Felix said, grinning now in earnest as they turned to look at him. "Kevin and I are going to get married." He threw his arms in front of his face as Thea yipped and Sean roared. "Enough, guys! We don't have a date set or anything. But yeah. We're going to make it official."

"*Finally,*" Sean and Thea said in unison.

And then, at last, they all laughed together.

"So," Chloe said, draping one arm dramatically over Simon's cubicle wall on Monday morning, striking a pose and affecting a husky voice. "Tell me about your *girlfriend.*"

"Keep it down," Simon said, his eyes darting to see if Mary-Pat was anywhere in the vicinity.

Chloe waved a careless hand. "The Wicked Witch of the East isn't on the schedule until our meeting after lunch. A fact I'm sure Amy is regretting to this moment. Poor dear. It's her one day a week to take the afternoon and evening shift. However will she cope?" Chloe struck another dramatic pose, this time with the back of her hand to her forehead. Collapsing back into her usual posture, she grimaced. "Come on. I've got roaming reference in five minutes. Give me some *details.*"

"How do you know it wasn't a disaster?" Simon asked.

"Because you look too disgustingly pleased with yourself for words," Chloe promptly replied.

That brought him up short. He'd never been accused of having a face that was easy to read. "Seriously?"

Her expression went sincere. "Seriously. I've never seen you look so happy. And I'm happy for you, dude."

"Considering my sister is constantly trying to make my life a misery these days, that comes as something of a surprise," he said, rubbing the bridge of his nose between a thumb and forefinger.

"What the hell did she do now?"

He sighed. "Just her usual out of whack expectations whacking into my life. She seems to think I could have just jetted out whenever and take as much time as I want over the holidays. Then she got my mother wound up and…"

Chloe's eyes went wide. "The audacity."

He gave a little nod. "And with that, your reference patrons await, my friend. I'll be taking over the desk right behind you."

Chloe glanced at her phone with a muttered, "Oh shit," and darted off without another word.

"Peace at last," he muttered as he dropped into his chair and powered on his computer. After checking his email, he reviewed the library's social media accounts. Thea's holiday appliances video was already posted with some sassy copy. He rubbed his jaw as he watched it for the second time.

The library approves of appliance safety. Fire isn't good for books either, he responded from the library's account. That wasn't exactly characteristic of his usual social media work, which tended to be more factual, and he continued rubbing his chin, wondering whether or not he should let it stand or delete it.

Heck with it. He did a quick scan of his email, then checked his scheduled posts for today and was reminded that he and Chloe were doing virtual readers' advisory. Something to look forward to over the lunch hour.

A notification popped up on his screen. The Emergency Services social media account replied: **What about romance novels? Aren't those kind of hot?** Followed by a few flame emojis. Cheeky Thea. He smiled, but decided to leave the decision about whether or not to reply for later. He'd never used the library account to interact with anyone other than patrons in the past, but maybe he should reach out to other library accounts to see if they could do something collaborative. Maybe extend the readers' advisory feature to be a more regional thing, rather than just something they each did with their patron groups.

Wow, that sounded like an idea Thea would have, not him. He was supposed to be teaching her and here she was inspiring him. *Very cool.* He liked the fact that they could both support each other and grow. The equality of it appealed to his rational nature.

Suppressing the smile that thoughts of Thea gave him, he pocketed his phone and headed out to back Chloe up on the reference desk.

What about romance novels? Aren't those kind of hot? Thea stared at her own message as the replies and quotes started to rack up. Eek. She hadn't meant to start anything, just to share a little joke.

Well. People were apparently enjoying the joke, at least according to the early responses.

OMG, so cute. The fire department is flirting with the library!

I spy a social media romance brewing. Is the librarian going to take off her glasses for the hot fireman?

Okay, that was annoying. "Gender essentialist much, @Aubrey245?" she muttered at the screen. She scanned a few more of the messages, mostly people amused or charmed by the two-message exchange. It seemed that only one person found it distasteful. @MaryPat4Books had written, This looks like a misuse of county resources to me.

Well. She seemed fun.

Meanwhile, Simon hadn't responded. *Leave it be*, she told herself sternly. He had a job to do, same as her. Which reminded her that she had some statistics to gather. The thought of what those numbers might mean made her guts freeze, but she opened up a new window and started to pull the analytics from various platforms. Little by little, her shoulders eased from their tense hunch. It was early, but the trends in engagement and follower counts were ticking in the right direction since she'd taken over. *Line goes up and to the right. Good.*

It was only a few weeks, but it was something. She closed out of the spreadsheet and glanced around her tidy little house. Everything was ready for Simon's arrival. Boxes of lights and ornaments were near the little tree. There were ingredients to make fresh pasta in the kitchen. She'd even snagged a bottle of prosecco for them to enjoy while they worked.

Now the evening just had to hurry up and get here.

"Come on," Chloe said to Simon as they closed out their social media readers' advisory hour. "One more meeting and then you can start your minuscule holiday with your family." They trooped into the conference room, and Simon felt a little pang. He'd spent a lot of time with Thea here, but now she was fully launched and wouldn't be back in this room again.

On the other hand, when he did see her, they didn't have to talk about work. He didn't have to mentor her or pretend his feelings were nonexistent in the pursuit of a professional facade. Seating himself at the table, he found Mary-Pat was directly across from him. And she was glaring at him.

Great. What had he supposedly done now?

Amy entered then, closing the door behind her and sitting at the head of the table. "I won't keep you all for long. I just wanted to go over the final year-end numbers for all of our programs before I send them up to the director. I would like to congratulate everyone on doing a really excellent job this year. Engagement is up significantly, due in large part to the social media campaigns that have given our marketing greater reach. So, thank you, Simon, for a job well done."

There was light applause from everyone but Mary-Pat, who continued to glower. When it died down, she took a deep breath and said, "If everyone is just going to ignore how unprofessional he was this morning, I am not."

Simon's face, which was already hot from the recognition, now blazed with embarrassment and confusion.

"What are you referring to?" Amy said, her expression carefully neutral.

Mary-Pat, her lips a tight line, whipped the cover off her iPad and tapped at it, then handed it to Amy, pointing at the screen. "He's been using the library's resources to *flirt*, it appears."

Amy frowned at the screen and tapped it. Then she shot an inscrutable look at Simon. "I don't see anyone flirting here. I see two social media managers having a fun interchange that got a whole bunch of positive responses."

Mary-Pat pointed at the screen, her lips thinning, eyes snapping in annoyance. "Amy, you were the one who talked about making the social media position a *professional* one. This is not professional behavior. Besides, I know they met at her home when he was doing her so-called training." Jesus, had Mary-Pat actually been *spying* on him? His gut froze even as he reminded himself he hadn't done anything wrong. But he knew all too well from dealing with his sister that being innocent didn't mean he wouldn't get pilloried. He swallowed around a lump in his throat.

Sighing as if she had a headache, Amy said tightly, "First of all, Simon's whereabouts are none of your business. Nor is his personal life. Second of all, professional social media doesn't have to be serious all the time. In fact, it shouldn't be, otherwise there would be minimal engagement with it. We try to have fun events that engage the community, and we try to make our social media presence equally fun and engaging. This is a perfectly professional use of our social media accounts, and if you have any other complaints, I encourage you to come privately to me, and not blindside your colleague in public. Now. Let's look at the year-end numbers."

"Breathe," Chloe whispered in Simon's ear as the meeting moved forward and his body tried to catch up to the fact that he wasn't about to be reprimanded or worse. "Amy finally dropped a house on her."

Twenty-Four

Simon still had a headache from his workday when he pulled up in front of Thea's house that evening. She met him at the door, eyes bright with excitement and with a kind of manic energy fizzing off her that made him even more tired.

God, could they maybe just watch a movie and go to bed? To sleep? He wasn't sure he had it in him right now to even make out with her on the couch.

"Come on in," she said, tugging him inside. "I have a surprise for you."

He was about to try to let her down gently from whatever plan she had when he noticed the small evergreen in front of the window. And those were definitely Christmas carols streaming softly from her little wireless speaker in the kitchen area.

"It's time to do your favorite stuff," she said. "I got the tree—his name is Noel, by the way—a couple of days ago, but I wanted to decorate him with you. Then we can make homemade pasta, which is something my family always does in the run-up to Christmas. And anything else you want to do, of course."

Okay, that was…wonderful. Thoughtful. But he was still wrung out while she fizzed with energy. "I love it. Thank you." He winced a little before he went on. The last thing he wanted to do was hurt her, especially when she was obviously doing all she could to make this so special. "But can we just do the tree and see how it goes?" he asked. "I don't want to be a buzzkill, but I've had a kind of shitty day and I'm wiped."

"Sure," she said, her brows coming together in evident concern. "Why was your day so shitty?"

"I have a colleague who's a pain in the ass. You met her that first day, I think," he said, setting his overnight bag down on the floor. "She hates the fact that I run social media, the way I do it, basically everything about me. She tried to get me in trouble with our manager over the interchange you and I had today."

Her hands flew up to cover her mouth. "Holy shit, Simon, that's awful. I'm so sorry. That was all my fault." Crimson stained her cheeks, and he reached out and pulled her to him.

"No. It's not your fault at all. We weren't being out of line at all and my boss didn't think we did anything wrong. And sadly, it's just the most recent in a long line of shitty things this woman has done. I think it was more about the fact that my boss had just praised my work in front of everyone that pissed her off the most and she was lashing out."

"I wish she wasn't able to use something I did to hurt you though," Thea said.

He squeezed her to him, feeling better with his arms

around her. "Nothing hurt me. *You* didn't hurt me. Mary-Pat embarrassed me and made me mad, but didn't hurt me. You'd never hurt me."

"Again," she said.

"What?"

"I'd never hurt you again. I did it in high school."

He rubbed her back, feeling some energy return just from holding her. "Forget about that. It's in the past. We were kids and we did what kids do, which is be insufferable little shits. Now," he said, more energy returning to his body as he contemplated Noel the Christmas tree, "let's get some lights on your baby."

Thea regretted the way her impulsive energy had just kind of splattered all over Simon before she'd even checked in to see how he was. He was carefully stringing the colored lights on Noel, his posture a little more relaxed than what it had been when he had first come in. So that was good.

But she could see how all her plans were overwhelming. They didn't need to make pasta tonight. She grabbed the prosecco from the fridge and poured two juice glasses for them, bringing one over. "Sorry I don't have any champagne flutes, but the wine should taste fine regardless," she said, handing him his and tapping it lightly with her own. "Here's to new traditions."

"Here, here," Simon said, his weary eyes crinkling at the corners. "And here's to lovely little Christmas trees. Noel's a beaut."

"Hey…" Thea said, an idea forming in her mind. "I know you don't usually go on camera yourself, but maybe would you mind helping me by doing a safety video with Noel as your costar? You can say no, it's okay," she added.

He considered her carefully. "What kind of thing did you have in mind?"

Well, that wasn't the outright *no* she'd been expecting.

"Um, as usual I'm shooting from the hip a little bit. But extension cords and Christmas lights have been the bane of firefighters' existence for a very long time now, so just a simple 'Do this, don't do this' kind of thing would be a good start."

He rubbed his chin. "Yeah. Okay. I'd prefer it if you didn't put my face on camera though. Mary-Pat would probably have a field day accusing me of… I don't even know what. But she'd think of something."

"Fair enough," she said. She hadn't gotten a dedicated camera for work yet, so she grabbed her phone and walked him through what she wanted him to demonstrate. She focused on only his hands, trying not to think about how those hands had given her pleasure and how much she enjoyed watching him as he manipulated plugs and showed the new wires that weren't frayed or damaged.

"I'm going to miss you," she said when they were done.

His startled gaze flew to her face. "When?"

"When you're in California."

He huffed a brief laugh and stood from where he'd been crouching next to the tree, stretching out his back. "I'm only going to be gone for a few days. I'll be back before either of us knows it. The only way you'll be able to tell I've been gone is my sleep schedule will be entirely fucked up." He drew her to him and kissed her temple. "But thank you. That's really nice."

★ ★ ★

Thea was giving him such a woeful look, Simon had to smile. "Seriously. You won't have time to miss me."

She shook her head, looking down at her hands, which were twisting together. "It's not just missing you though. It's knowing you're going to be going to so much effort and not getting any credit for it. You deserve better."

He cupped her cheek. "That's sweet of you. And maybe next year I'll be able to do something different."

In the back of his mind, hazy almost-plans were turning over. About spending the holidays with Thea instead of his family. Of having cozy little scenes like this. Just the two of them, decorating, baking, cooking, wrapping presents. He'd barely ever done those things with anyone else before—mostly he hadn't even wanted to. But he wanted more of that feeling he'd been thinking about earlier: the way they complemented each other. She'd already taught him about *pizzelle*, and she could teach him about pasta. He could show her the family sugar cookie recipe. They could make new traditions of their own. That last bit sounded really appealing.

Ashley would have kittens.

Well, maybe it was about time Noah got a pet.

"Lights are done," he said. "You said something about making pasta?"

She shook her head. "You're too wiped. I'll just make some soup and grilled cheese and call it dinner, okay?"

His knees nearly buckled with relief. "That sounds fantastic. I can start putting ornaments on if you like."

"Only if you want to. You're going to have a grueling

few days ahead of you, and you should be able to relax before then."

When was the last time someone had taken care of him like this? He honestly couldn't recall. But paradoxically, her permission for him to stop decorating made him want to go on. When she turned to go into the kitchen and get dinner started, he opened up the boxes of ornaments. Some had never been touched, their commercial seals still intact. But one held mostly handmade decorations, lovingly packed into a sectioned-off box to keep them from knocking into each other. A set of glass icicles were wrapped in tissue. He set about putting them on the tree, his unfamiliarity with the collection making him slow and deliberate. It was nice and almost meditative with the soft Christmas music and Thea moving around the kitchen putting their simple dinner together.

Even though he had only just tried to convince Thea that she wouldn't have time to miss him during his short trip, he knew he was going to miss her.

"Come and eat," she called. She'd set up their dinner at her little dining table, a candle flickering between their places. Something turned over in his chest as he slid into his seat. The soup and grilled cheese smelled delicious and comforting, and he nearly groaned as he dipped a corner of the neatly cut sandwich into the soup.

"Mmm." Crunchy, savory and warm in beautiful contrast to the cold night outside. The only thing that could have improved the scene was if the little house had a fireplace.

Thea's phone chimed and she picked it up, one eyebrow lifting. "Hmm. Apparently there's a not-insignificant chance of a snowstorm overnight."

Simon scoffed. "Snow before Christmas? Never happens in Maryland."

"Well," she said, laying her phone down and picking up her spoon, "we can hope."

Twenty-Five

The wind howled overnight, and Simon wound himself around Thea in a way that made her feel so cherished and happy that she shed a few tears before dropping off. But when she woke up in the morning, the intense brightness from the window made her lift her head in confusion. She stared at the blanket of white that mantled the garden outside her house. Sliding carefully out of the bed to avoid disturbing Simon, she could see that the forecast had been correct. It had actually snowed overnight. A lot. The normally dim predawn was bright with reflected light.

A veritable Christmas miracle.

Bedclothes rustled behind her, and she turned to find Simon squinting. "What time is it?" he asked.

She crawled back into bed and kissed him lightly. "I think it's time for you to check and make sure your flight isn't canceled. Because it actually did snow last night. A lot."

"Really?" He sat up and stared out at the wintry scene.

"Holy shit. I didn't think it would be possible." He grabbed his phone off the nightstand, his hair sticking up adorably in all directions as he looked up the information. "Wow. Yeah. My flight is canceled." He lifted his eyes to hers, his expression wondering and almost dazed. "I don't have to go to California."

She flung her arms around him and crowed with glee. Those words *have to* had gone straight to her heart. He had been so selfless when it came to his family and they didn't seem to appreciate what he was doing one bit.

It was about time he got to do something for himself, have something for himself.

"Are you okay spending Christmas with me?" she asked, pulling back to study his face.

His expression brightened. "Are you kidding? I've wanted nothing more. I was already halfway making plans for next year as a consolation for the fact that I thought I couldn't spend it with you this year."

Oh. This man. His vulnerability slayed her and he didn't even know it. And he was already making plans for next year? Had her eyes *literally* turned into hearts? She grinned. "Well then. You know what this means."

He chuckled. "I have no idea what this means."

"We have to make pasta today."

"Fine. We'll make pasta. And do all the things."

She threw up her hands in glee. "All the things!" Well, maybe not all of them. She was due over at her parents' house today, but if there was still a foot of unplowed snow, that wasn't happening. Too bad, so sad. More time spent in her cozy little home with... She didn't quite dare to call him her *boyfriend*, not even in the privacy of her own mind. Not even with him making plans for next year, somehow.

Simon, a dirty gleam in his eye, reached up and threaded his fingers with hers, bringing her hands down and kissing each one. "I have some idea of what all the things might encompass," he said, his voice low and throaty. A thrill ran up her spine.

"Yeah?" her own voice was less sexy. In fact, it veered up into a squeak.

"Yeah." His eyelids drooped and his gaze fixed on her mouth. Panic spiraled up inside her.

"Morning breath, dude!" she said, pulling back and covering her mouth with her hand.

He just grinned a dirty, delighted smile and leaned forward, pinning her hands to the mattress and gently pushing her to lie on her back. "Okay, fine," he said softly, his gaze roaming over her face. "If I can't kiss you on the mouth, I'll just have to kiss you somewhere else."

Simon crawled backward, down Thea's body, until he could tug at the panties she'd slept in. A hysterical giggle bubbled out of her. "Dude, I was going to suggest brushing our teeth."

He hooked his fingers in the elastic waistband. "I like my idea better." Her head thudded back onto the mattress, and he grinned as he dragged her underwear down and flung them away like they had offended him. Running his hands up her inner thighs, he pushed them apart as she shuddered and groaned, her pussy glistening like a flower in the rain, the scent of her arousal making his already hard cock throb. He shifted, adjusting himself on the mattress, and then lightly bit her inner thigh, appreciating the way her body jerked with surprise.

Then he started to tease her with the lightest touches of his tongue until she was tense and trembling. "God, Simon," she groaned, and he gave her inner thigh another nip, making her yelp.

"I've got you," he told her, pushing her thighs even wider, then sliding one finger into her slick heat as he lashed her clit with his tongue. A second finger pulsing inside her and a more concentrated pressure from his mouth gave him the shaking, wailing, pulsating response he wanted. He pulled his fingers out and crawled back up her body. "Ready to kiss me now?" he asked.

Thea laughed helplessly, one hand flung over her closed eyes. "You evil bastard," she muttered as his mouth descended on hers, encouraging her to open. She groaned and parted her lips, her tongue sliding against his, her hips pulsing against his boxer-clad dick, the friction making him moan into her mouth.

"Condom. Nightstand," she murmured against his lips, and he pulled away long enough to pull off his boxers and rip a packet off the strip. He turned, leaning against the headboard to roll on the condom, smiling as Thea straddled him.

"Now you're getting the idea," he said as she sank onto him, giving her hips a little swivel as she fully seated herself.

"Ngh. No talking. Just fucking," she said, her eyes closed as she rolled her hips and squeezed him with her inner muscles. He gripped her hips and moved with her, gratified when her eyes popped open.

"Did I do a good thing?" he asked, unable to keep a grin from spreading across his face.

She leaned forward and cupped his cheeks in her hands. "Such a good thing. Do it again."

Dear lord, but when Simon tucked his hips up when she rolled just like *that*… She kind of thought the top of her head would fly right off. He was giving her that evil grin that she'd discovered she liked maybe a little too well, and she kept up her steady movements as he threaded his fingers with hers, holding her hands up and steady, giving her a source of leverage.

He grunted, his eyes slamming shut. "Oh. Yeah. That. That's good."

There was silence then, punctuated only by the sound of their increasingly labored, ragged breathing and the creak of Thea's bed frame. Thea's abs and hips began to ache. "Simon? You close?"

He cracked one eye. "Do you need me to be?"

"Not sure how much longer I can keep this position up," she admitted. "But I want you to come at least as hard as I did."

One corner of his mouth curled up, and he released her hands to grab her hips, holding her in place as he drove up into her, his breath stuttering and face tense as he pressed hard one final time, then eased, wrapping his arms around her back and holding her against his chest. She let herself relax there, his pulse against her cheek lulling her.

"I'm so happy your flight got canceled," she murmured, looking at the snowy expanse outside her window. The snow

had eased to light flurries that drifted and fluttered before fi
nally falling.

He sighed. "I am too. But my sister is going to be a nightmare about it."

She lifted her head and looked at him. "Why? How?"

He sighed and lightly slapped her hip. "Up. Condoms don't
work if I stay inside you for too long."

She disengaged, groaning at the loss of contact and rolling onto her side to watch the flex of his ass as he strode off
to the bathroom. When he returned a few minutes later, face
washed and smelling suspiciously of mint, she sat up, outraged.

"You brushed your teeth."

"Oral hygiene is very important," he said with mock seri-
ousness, his eyes twinkling with suppressed humor. How had
she ever thought this guy was rigid and joyless?

"Damn straight, it is," she said and marched into the bathroom to deal with her own fuzzy teeth and morning breath.
When she returned, Simon was sitting up, the covers over his
lap, phone pressed to his ear. He was rolling his eyes.

"I don't know what to tell you, Ash, but I can't magically
erase a foot of snow or make airlines un-cancel their flights."
From a few feet away, Thea could hear the squawk of his sister's voice, which only grew louder as she slid into the bed
next to him. Damn. The woman had lungs and she knew
how to use them. She thought Gia was bad, but her sister had
nothing on this woman.

You okay? she mouthed.

He rolled his eyes again and nodded. "Ashley, I'm not going
to be able to get any more vacation time, my flight is canceled,
I should never have tried to make that ridiculously short trip

work in the first place, and maybe we need to think about what holidays mean to all of us as a family moving forward. I'm going to go now. You need to get back to bed anyway. I can't believe you called me so early." His voice was incredibly gentle, and Thea marveled that he was holding it together against what sounded like a completely unreasonable onslaught. In fact, his sister was still yelling when he gently tapped the screen to end the call. Sighing, he tossed the phone to the coverlet where it bounced once and lay still, the dark screen looking weirdly ominous to Thea.

"What happens now?" she asked, wanting to touch him, to give and receive comfort, but suddenly not certain if he would welcome it.

He scrubbed his hands over his face, blowing out a frustrated breath. "If I know my family, my mom will start blowing up my phone next."

"Why?"

"I'm not sure what the reason will be, but it's going to happen. Trust me."

They'd gotten dressed and were outside to assess the snowfall and bring in the suitcase he'd packed for California when his prediction came true. Thea was happily humming to herself because she'd be able to do an electric snow thrower safety demonstration video that she had planned out, and Simon was basking in her energy and excitement. How had he ever been put off by her energy? She was pure delight.

"Pretty sure we got about a foot!" she crowed as his phone vibrated in his back pocket. Sighing, he let his suitcase crunch into the powdery snow and dug it out. Yup, it was his mom.

"Merry Christmas, Mom," he said, trying to head off the emotional shitstorm he knew was coming.

"Ashley tells me you aren't coming." Well, crap. She was already crying. He could hear it in her voice.

"Yeah. There's a foot of snow on the ground and my flight is canceled," he said as calmly as he could. From the way his mother phrased her statement, he had a bad feeling about what exactly Ash had said. "I'm not sure how she thinks I'm going to get across the country under these conditions."

There was a long pause, then his mother took a deep, shuddering breath. "Is *that* why you aren't coming?"

Rage shot through him like a hot spike. "What, did you think I'd make all those plans and buy a plane ticket on my salary and then just *not come* on some sort of whim?" Ashley had pulled some bullshit in the past, but this was next-level.

"I didn't know what to think," his mother shot back, apparently retreating to a full defensive crouch.

"But you didn't bother to check on what had to look like a really dodgy explanation before you flew off the handle." Any desire to soften things for his mom was now gone. She was willing to take Ash's unreliable word *and* assume the worst of him?

The desire to not spend Christmas with his family had never been stronger.

"Well, it's been clear that you haven't really wanted to come out, so what was I supposed to think?" It was terrifying, sometimes, to consider how much his mother's and his sister's brains worked in tandem. Shifting blame, obscuring facts, anything to make sure that neither of them were ever wrong.

Fighting to keep his voice level, he said, "Mom, my flight's been canceled, I can't even go anywhere local until the roads are plowed, and we're going to have to reevaluate how we do holidays in the future because this just isn't sustainable for me."

There was silence. Enough to make Simon look at his phone's screen to make sure they hadn't been cut off. But then he heard a muffled, "Talk to your son," and his father was on the line.

"What's going on, Simon?" His father sounded both exhausted and exasperated. Simon guessed his mother had a big meltdown before she called him, so that tracked. He explained the situation with as much brevity as he could muster, realizing that Thea had come around the side of the house with a snow shovel in her hand. She wasn't using it though, she just stood there, watching him as if he was doing something that required a spotter.

And maybe he was. It was the emotional equivalent of bench-pressing twice his own weight.

Thea scowled as Simon ended his call, stuffing the phone roughly into his coat pocket and picking up his suitcase.

"Everything okay?" she asked.

He trudged toward her, exhaling roughly. "It will be. I think. The person who's really getting the worst end of the deal here is my dad. He's going to be in the thick of Ashley's and Mom's tantrums, and he's not a guy who loves drama." Well, maybe it was his turn. Simon hadn't realized how much he was the emotional buffer for those two until he'd had some distance. And now that he had Thea, he knew life didn't have to be that way at the holidays or any other time.

Thea leaned the snow shovel against the wall and opened the front door for him.

"Go on in and get that suitcase settled, then come out so I can do a snow thrower safety video. Then we can have Christmas by ourselves. If we get plowed out in time, maybe we can go to my parents' house?"

He paused at the open door, grinning. Her family might have its own drama, but at this distance it looked like nothing. "I'd love that."

Twenty-Six

Thea, bundled up with a lumpy handmade hat on her head, made an adorable picture as Simon filmed her demonstrating how to use an electric snow thrower without severing the cable and possibly either electrocuting the operator or blowing out the power for an entire block. By the time they finished getting all the rough footage, her cheeks and nose were pink from the cold and the path between her house and Mrs. M's was perfectly clear. Mrs. M brought them hot cocoa, her blue eyes twinkling with mischief and delight.

"I guess Simon's set to spend Christmas with you, then?" she asked Thea as the younger woman blew on her cocoa.

"Simon's flight was blown all to heck and he is actually perfectly happy about that," he responded.

"Well then. I hope you can also make it to my Boxing Day party tomorrow evening."

He nodded, a warm glow suffusing him despite the cold. Yeah, he was going to enjoy this reprieve from being the go-to person, the one who was only appreciated for the role he filled. Mrs. M and Thea just wanted him around because they liked him.

It was sad that that felt so unusual.

Thea gulped the last of her cocoa, handing the mug back to a grinning Mrs. M. "Okay, we have pasta to make, then I'll clear your paths. Hopefully the plow will come soon."

Mrs. M waved an airy hand. "They'll come when they come. As long as my guests and caterers can get here tomorrow, that's all I care about. And Katrina, of course. My other kids are spending the holiday with their families."

"Sweet!" Thea said. "Katrina's awesome."

"You two always did hit it off. I just wish she could find someone special the way you two have. Okay—you kids go off and do your holiday stuff. If you need anything from me, you know where I'll be." Mrs. M collected Simon's mug and went back inside her massive home.

"We're stopping by later and bringing her something, right?" Simon murmured as they trudged back to her house.

"Totally." She twinkled up at him, loving how natural and couple-y his question had felt. "We're not monsters."

Thea loved making fresh pasta. There was something about the simplicity of it: four ingredients, a little bit of effort, patience and a surprisingly small amount of skill were all that was needed to create toothsome deliciousness.

"That's it?" he asked as she wrapped the dough to rest.

"That's it," she said, washing her hands before she dug in her cabinets for her pasta machine. "If you're a true purist, I guess you need to use a rolling pin, but frankly I don't know anyone who does that." She cleared the rest of the stuff off her island to make a nice long landing pad for the pasta before she clamped the machine to the top. She attached the handle and gave it a spin. "This bad boy can make *so* much pasta so much quicker though." She'd made a double batch of dough, just in case they were able to get to her parents' place today.

And heck. If they couldn't, she could freeze it. Selfishly, she'd be perfectly happy with spending the day alone with Simon and making enough pasta for them and Mrs. M. Those future plans he talked about had begun to spin out in her head too. Not just special occasions either. Somehow she knew that even the simplest of meals would be more fun, more romantic, more special with Simon.

"While this rests, do you want to set up a video call with your family, maybe?" she asked. "It might help settle your sister and your mom down."

He sighed and scrubbed his face, and she felt like a heel for popping their little bubble. "Yeah. Good idea. I'll go through Dad though. He'll hopefully be able to keep a lid on the fireworks." He dug in his back pocket for his phone and typed out a quick text. Just a few seconds later, his phone chimed and he nodded. He looked up from the device and shot her a crooked grin that made electricity zip down her spine. "Unless you hate the idea, I'm going to introduce you to my family."

She shrugged. "Works for me."

One auburn eyebrow lifted. "As my girlfriend?"

Her stomach fluttered. "That works for me too," she said, her voice going kind of squeaky.

"Good." He tapped his screen and the phone began to warble, then a man's voice boomed out.

"Son. Good to see you. Can't believe you've got yourself a white Christmas."

Simon grinned. "I couldn't believe it either. But we do. Looks like a greeting card out here."

"Where are you? That doesn't look like your apartment."

"It isn't." He reached out and drew Thea to his side, and she could now see a man whose graying hair and beard was threaded with the same auburn Simon had. "This is my girl-friend's home. Dad, this is Thea."

She waved, feeling a little silly, but the man's face broke into a smile almost as handsome as Simon's. "Hi, Mr. Osman. Nice to meet you."

"Same here. Let me get the rest of the gang together." He called out to Simon's family, and then the phone was passed from hand to hand. Greetings were exchanged, Simon's nephew wanted to see her tree and, with a preschooler's knack for not understanding geography, demanded that Uncle Simon come over and play with him *now*.

"Apple doesn't fall far from the tree. He sounds just like Ash," Simon murmured out of the corner of his mouth as Noah disappeared and Simon's brother-in-law took over. "Hey, Ray. How's it going? Merry Christmas."

Ray, a husky man with thinning sandy hair, scrubbed his hand over his face. "Well, we're doing our best here, man."

"I take it that means Ashley's not going to be wishing me any happy holidays?"

Ray sighed. "No, she's here." He angled the phone, and a pretty woman with strawberry blond ringlets came into view on the screen. Her mouth was tight and she gave them a curt wave.

"Hi. Merry Christmas. I didn't catch your name." Her voice was flat and inflectionless.

"This is Thea," Simon said, squeezing her shoulder as he spoke. "And I am sorry I can't see you guys in person, but I'm glad you can at least meet her virtually at this point."

At this point. This was really happening. Her heart was so full it might actually explode.

After the call with his family, Thea deemed the pasta to have rested long enough in its cling-film shroud and un-wrapped it, cutting it up and spreading the first piece into a disc with her hands until it was thin enough to go through her little hand-cranked machine. She spread a layer of flour on both sides and cranked it through, then ratcheted the roll-ers one notch closer together.

"Now you," she said, handing him the lengthened piece of dough.

He took it gingerly, dipping it into the gap and rolling it through. He'd never made pasta before, but he had made sugar cookies, so he was half expecting the dough to stick or the machine to jam, but the thinner piece emerged smoothly. "Magical," he said.

"Yup." Thea cranked the machine down another notch, her breast pressing against his arm. A pulse of heat went through his midsection.

"You're doing that on purpose, aren't you?"

She raised doe eyes to regard him. "Doing what?"

He moved his arm, pressing his biceps against her softness. "Distracting me with your hot bod from the task you set me." He cranked the piece of pasta through as she chuckled and moved off to dampen a kitchen towel and drape it over the other pieces of pasta.

"Momentary lapse of judgment," she said, shooting him a sunny grin.

"Well. Don't let it happen again." He infused his voice with mock sternness that made that grin stretch even wider.

"Flour that before you run it through again."

He looked at the dough and realized he'd settled into the rhythm of the little hand-cranked machine. It was soothing in a way that he'd never have achieved if he'd been with his family, even without the cross-country flight.

Who would ever have thought that being with the human hurricane that was Thea Martinelli would be *soothing*?

She moved around the kitchen as he steadily made the pasta longer and thinner, until she finally called a halt.

"That's great." She spread the length of dough out on the counter and dusted it with flour again, then moved the crank to a different hole. The machine was in some ways basic and in other ways really clever. "Now we cut it. I'm thinking fettuccine. It's my favorite."

"I'm with you all the way," he said, fascinated as he helped her feed the sheet through into another set of rollers, which cut the pasta into long ribbons.

"And that's it," she said. "Now this can hang out and dry a bit and we can make it for lunch."

Simon craned his neck to peer out of the windows. The driveway was still covered in a thick blanket of snow. "Are you thinking we're not going to get plowed out in time to go to your family?"

She shot him a wicked look as she pressed out the second

piece of pasta. "I'm thinking I don't much care. I'm selfishly having far too much fun with you."

He tugged her to him and kissed her gently. "How is it possible that we're so different and yet we are so much on the same page? I was thinking the exact same thing."

"Just lucky I guess," she murmured against his lips. "Now let's roll out the rest of this pasta and really get lucky."

It was a perfect Christmas. They finished making the rest of the pasta, then Thea dragged a very willing Simon into her bed for slow, achingly intimate sex, the winter light painting pale shadows on their bodies. They lounged in her rumpled bedsheets, exchanging quiet confidences until Thea's head lifted off Simon's chest. A dull rumble and scrape outside made her squeeze her eyes together.

"It's the plow," she groaned as Simon quirked an eyebrow at her. "We're getting cleared out. But I don't want to go anywhere. I just want to stay here with you."

He cuddled her head back to his chest. "Well, then we stay here."

"But we're plowed out," she groused. "My parents will expect us to be there."

He chuckled. "How do they know we're plowed out? For that matter, how do we know all the roads between your house and theirs have been plowed?"

She turned her head to place a kiss in the center of his chest. "I really like the way you think, you know that?"

He gave her bare bottom a light slap. "Well, you promised me pasta and made me work up an appetite, so let's get in the kitchen and start cooking and give them a call. That way we have all our family obligations out of the way and can just enjoy the day."

She sat up and kissed him. "Mmm. I *really* like the way you think now."

They got cleaned up and dressed. He set a pot of water on to boil while she thawed a frozen batch of tomato sauce she'd made over the summer. She set her phone up on a little tripod on the kitchen island and called her folks. Her mother appeared on the screen, the family's elderly fake tree in the background. "Hi, Ma. How is it over there?"

Her mother waved, making an extravagant sad face. "Still snowed in here. Missing my girls and my grandbabies today."

"Yeah. Same here. We made pasta though, so traditions will continue. Just not together this year." She gestured behind her at the pot of water that had yet to come to a boil.

"We? Is Mrs. M spending the day with you?"

Thea shook her head, suppressing a smile, and tugged Simon by his sleeve into frame. "Nope. Meet my boyfriend. Simon, this is my mom. Mom, Simon."

"Hello, Mrs. Martinelli," Simon said stiffly.

Her mother gasped with delight as Thea knew she would. "Well, hello, Simon. You call me Anita. Roger!" she bellowed for Thea's father as Thea cracked up and Simon's cheeks reddened. Her parents were utterly predictable. "Come meet Thea's boyfriend!"

A grumbling sound ensued and Thea's dad came into view. "Merry Christmas, sweetie," he said gruffly. Then he appeared to examine Simon as closely as he could under his thick, dark brows. "Young man."

"Yes, sir," Simon said, straightening his spine.

"You love my baby girl?"

"Dad!" Thea exclaimed. "Simon's my *new* boyfriend. Don't put him on the spot like that."

Simon put an arm around her shoulders. "It's okay. Like Thea said, it's early. But I can tell you that I respect her and like her and admire her a whole hell of a lot. She's a really special person and I'm glad you care about her too."

Thea's heart did a full revolution as her dad grinned and said, "Good. Now go make that pasta and have a Merry Christmas, and we'll see you *both* next Sunday for dinner, okay?"

"Okay, Dad. Merry Christmas." She ended the call and they did have pasta, and when Simon produced a little box with an enamel pin of Inferno Girl in it and she dashed over to grab his present from under her tree—an ornament shaped like a library with windows that lit up—Thea's heart was so full she thought it might burst.

Twenty-Seven

"This okay?" Simon asked as Thea pulled a necklace out of a jewelry box on her dresser. She turned, her face softening as she took in his corduroy trousers, open-necked shirt and navy blazer. He tugged at his lapels and rocked his head from side to side, muscles tight. "Not too casual for Mrs. M's Boxing Day party? I didn't pack a tie for my folks' Christmas."

She shook her head, abandoning the necklace to reach up and massage the muscles in his shoulders and neck. "No, it's perfect. Mrs. M may be rich, but her party is kind of eclectic in terms of what people wear."

"Want me to get that for you?" he asked, sighing with relief as the knots dissolved and gesturing at the necklace still on her chest of drawers, a cascade of glittery silver snowflakes.

"Yeah, thanks. I'm pretty garbage at these stupid clasps." She gave him a kiss before she tweaked his muscles one more time, then turned her back to him. He looped the chain around her neck, pressing a kiss behind her ear as he met her eyes in the mirror. She shivered and smiled, and he wrapped his arms around her waist, closing his eyes and letting himself—just for a moment—envision the future spooling out in front of them. At one point he'd only been able to see to the end of her training. Then without even realizing it, he'd seen next Christmas. But now he could see even further than that. A life together.

Because he *could* envision it. And as much as it scared him, he wanted this. Wanted her. Wanted their life to continue together. It felt so incredibly right.

"Ready?" she asked, turning to him, her eyes bright. Maybe a little too bright.

"You okay?" he asked.

"Yeah, why?"

He ran his hands up and down her arms, relishing the moment. "Because you seem kind of emotional."

She sighed. "I have no chill. I'm sorry. I was just thinking that yesterday was so perfect and wonderful, and I guess I feel like it was so great that there's no way to go but down from here."

"Hey." He captured one flailing hand and brought it to his lips. Her obvious nerves made his own zing with anxiety, but it was his turn to be the sure one. "What we have is wonderful. And it's only the beginning, so I happen to think it can get even more wonderful. What do you think about that?"

"You really think that?" Her eyes looked huge, her face pale.

"I do. In case you haven't noticed, I think you're pretty goddamn awesome, and I want to see just how far all this can go."

"How far do you think it can go?" Her face had gone a little shy and like she wasn't quite sure what was happening.

"If we keep talking and supporting each other and doing what we've been doing? All the way."

She smiled, her lips trembling. "You really think so?"

He released her hand to slide his arms around her waist. "Hey. I may be a pretty grumpy perfectionist, but that just means I know a good thing when I see it."

"Well. I think you're a pretty good thing too," she said, lifting a hand to trace one of his cheekbones.

He kissed her again, then pulled back, his gaze solidly on her. "Let's get to this party. I'm ready to show the world my hot girlfriend."

It wasn't the first time Thea had attended Mrs. M's Boxing Day party, but it was the first time she'd ever come with a date.

No, not even a date. A partner. Someone who was committed. The idea sent a thrill of electricity up her spine.

The big house smelled like spiced hot cider, evergreen and expensive perfume. A shifting mass of people moved from room to room, sampling finger food, sipping drinks and chatting. She'd worried a bit that Simon might retreat into a corner, but he was surprisingly adept at small talk with strangers.

They were just getting their champagne glasses refilled by a passing waiter when Thea heard an exuberant, "There you are!" from across the den with its cozy fire and tree. She looked up to see Mrs. M's youngest daughter, Katrina, launching herself across the room to give her a huge hug.

"Hey," Thea said, laughing as Katrina disentangled herself.

"Katrina McAnally, this is Simon Osman. My boyfriend." Another thrill shot through her. Simon had given her so much. A launching pad to her new career, affection, trust…

And, let's face it, great sex.

Katrina's face lit up, and she thrust out a hand for Simon to shake. "Oh my god. I am so happy to meet you!" Her expression went serious, and she leveled a finger at him. "You better be good to my friend."

Simon shook her hand and gave her one of his cautious smiles. "Definitely working on it."

"Good." She gave his hand a little businesslike pump before she released him.

"How have you been?" Thea asked. "I haven't seen you in a while. The job keeping you busy?"

Katrina made a face. "Yes. Kyle has been a total pain lately. The countdown to our CEO retiring is probably going to start any minute, and Kyle thinks he's the only choice to replace the man. I've been putting in the hours to show the board that he's not."

"That stinks," Thea said. She had no real conception of what went into running the McAnally empire, but Kyle's brand of officious shittiness was not a good quality for any kind of leader.

Katrina sighed. "It'll all come down to whether the board thinks someone who heads operations," she said, pointing at herself, "or someone who heads finance has the best qualities to take over the biggest corner office."

"And I'm guessing that your brother is the money guy," Simon said.

"Yeah," Katrina said, flicking an approving glance at him,

then she flapped her hand dismissively. "Anyway, enough about that drama. Put out any good fires lately?" she asked Thea, obviously trying to defuse the current situation and not realizing she'd stepped into an entirely different situation.

Thea straightened her shoulders, summoning all the pride in her new role, knowing Katrina would understand. "Nope. I'm the county's Emergency Services social media manager now."

At least, she was for now. She hoped she still was in the New Year.

Katrina's jaw dropped open. "Shut the front door! That's awesome."

Thea gestured at Simon. "Yeah, it's how I met this guy. Well, reconnected with him. We knew each other in high school." She explained the arrangement the county had struck between the library and ES, and Katrina beamed. "What about you? Anyone new in your life?"

Katrina hooted. "God, no. Too busy to do anything but work. You'd have to knock me out to get me to take my eye off the ball these days. But I *love* your story. The county thought they were getting some synergy, but they were also fostering a love affair." She folded her hands over her heart and tilted her head to the side. Then something caught her attention across the room and she hastily excused herself. "Oops. Mom's calling me over." Her attention briefly refocused on Thea. "We should get coffee in the New Year. Tell me all the things about your new job and everything else." She winked at them and dove into the crowd.

"Wow. She's a lot," Simon said.

"Too much?" Thea asked, worried that her personality was a little too close to Katrina's if he did think that.

He took her hand in his, his expression telling her he had an inkling of what made her nervous. "No. In fact, I think Katrina's apple didn't fall far from the Mrs. M tree, and you know how I feel about your landlady."

She tapped her wineglass against his with a gentle chime. "You're a good egg, Simon Osman."

They left the party before it started to wind down, trudging across the snowy ground to Thea's cozy, quiet little home.

"Do you mind if I stay?" he asked after they'd pulled off their boots.

She turned wide eyes his way. "Yeah. If you want to stay, please do. I love having you here."

He padded over to her, his stocking feet noiseless on the hardwood floor. "And I love being here. But I never want you to feel like you can't kick me out and have alone time if you need it."

She reached up, feathering a hand through his hair, and he nearly purred and leaned into it like a cat. "I don't need so much alone time. But I know you probably do. So, let's just keep using our words like grown-ups and we should be great."

"We are great," he said, grinning and bending to press a fleeting kiss to her lips.

"That we are."

"Let's be great in your bed," he murmured against her lips.

"Good idea." They started to move like a single clumsy being, still kissing, teeth clicking and Thea giggling as they made their slow way toward her bed. But it was perfect. Messy

and raw and tender and perfect. Their clothes came off with
soft touches and murmurs, their mouths parting only long
enough to peel off a shirt or focus on a recalcitrant button.
Then they fell onto her duvet, her breath leaving her in a
whoosh as Simon pressed on top of her. She hooked her leg
over his hip, and they ground against each other, Thea de-
lighting in the familiarity of his touch, the way his tongue
curled into her mouth, his groan and the tightening of his
closed eyes as she rubbed against him just *that* way.

They broke apart just long enough for Simon to get a condom and roll it on. He slid into her, their mouths fusing again,
their bodies writhing and rocking. The constant fullness and
pressure against her clit was intoxicating, and Thea dug her
fingernails into his back and moaned into his mouth. She'd
never gotten so close to coming so fast.

"You like that?" Simon murmured, pushing even harder
into her.

"Yeah." She gasped as bright pleasure flared. She bore down
around him, seeking that final tipping over, that spangled
release, but he slowed, his mouth leaving her to nuzzle her
neck, his hips slowing. "Simon." His name came out as almost a whine.

"Mmm?" Lips and tongue teased the side of her neck, making her shiver, but the imminence of her orgasm was ebbing.

"Simon I was *right there*."

He chuckled. "I know."

She smacked his ass, the noise ringing in the quiet room.
"Bastard." But she was laughing too.

"Trust me," he said, his voice smooth and seductive in the

dimness as his hips began to roll more firmly again and her arousal started to build again, teetering so close…

And another retreat. She groaned and her head thrashed back against the pillow.

"Trust. Me." This time, his voice was commanding and the tone itself was enough to make her body wind up again. He moved softly inside her for a few more moments, and she willed herself to relax, to give up.

To trust.

"Good girl," he said, kissing her again and starting to move in a way that made her pant and writhe, and then suddenly she was flying, soaring into the most intense, shattering orgasm she'd ever experienced. Gasping and shuddering, she barely registered Simon following her over the edge with a shout and a rapid pumping of his hips. When she could move her slack limbs again, she clutched at him as he moved off her.

"No sweetheart, I need to deal with the condom," he said, pressing a kiss to her forehead while she whimpered as visions of IUDs danced in her head.

Merry Christmas to all and to all a good fucking night was her last, loopy thought as Simon returned to the bed and slid in behind her, spooning her close.

Chapter Twenty-Eight

"Déjà vu all over again," Thea muttered to herself a week later as she waited, fidgeting, outside Landseer's office, her laptop in hand, ready to show him the posts and metrics she'd assembled over the last month. Then the door swung open and he was there, kind eyes twinkling behind wire-rimmed glasses.

Were his eyes *too* kind? Was he about to let her down gently?

"Come on in and sit down, Thea."

She did as she was told, sitting at the edge of his guest chair, on edge, nerves zinging.

"Relax," he said, his voice shaded with laughter.

"How can I relax? Probation is stressful!" she blurted.

Landseer's expression softened. "I'm sorry. It shouldn't have been. You've been doing an exemplary job. The metrics you sent prove that. This meeting is merely a formality to offer you the role on a permanent basis."

Incomprehension flowed into elation as Thea absorbed this. "Really?"

Landseer nodded. "Really." Then he reached a hand across the desk. "The job is yours if you want it. And I couldn't be happier with this outcome."

Thea clasped his hand in hers, hardly knowing what to think. "Thank you. That's...that's great. I definitely want the job."

"Excellent. Let's just get your signature on this paperwork, and congratulations."

Thea took the pen he extended to her and, exhilaration flooding her veins, she spun it around her thumb. *I did it!* she exulted internally before signing her name with a flourish.

She'd done it all.

A month ago, she'd faced having no job, an uncertain future and a lot of loneliness. Now she had a new career and a new relationship, all while being able to keep the found family she'd gathered during her firefighting career. When she thought about it, the transition was dizzying. Electrifying.

Perfect.

Thea left the administration building feeling as if she was floating. Simon, waiting outside the front door of the building, stepped in front of her. "Well?" His face held all the confidence she'd learned to expect from him.

"I'm in!" she exclaimed, wrapping her arms around his neck and letting him lift her up and spin her around. "We're officially a social media empire, you and me."

He set her down gently on her feet, pressing his lips to hers. "All hail my social media queen."

"Do I get a tiara?" she asked, giggling against his mouth.

"Anything you want."

"Well, I want you."

"You got me."

"New year, new social media empire," she said. "Let's go celebrate."

★ ★ ★ ★ ★

Acknowledgments

As always, I must first thank my lovely husband, Mr. B. No writer could possibly have a more supportive, loving, wonderful partner in life.

Vanessa North, thank you for answering questions about how being a social media manager works. And any errors that might have made it into the final product are most definitely all mine.

To all of my Italian friends—Thea wouldn't have been possible without being so fortunate as to enjoy a lifetime of your generous hospitality and spirit. Thank you.

My agent, Katie Shea Boutillier. I've benefitted so much by having you in my corner and I look forward to many more books in our future.

John, Stacy, Errin and the rest of the team at Harlequin Afterglow and HarperCollins—I love having you all in my corner. It's a joy and a privilege.

To all my author and reader friends on social media and in

person. I am made both a better author and a better person by your insights and friendship.

You—yes, you! Authors wouldn't write without readers and the fact that you decided to read this book means the world to me. Thank you.